Trapped By A Lie

Book 3 in the "Moms Who Lie" Psychological Thriller Series

Brett Monk, McKenna Langford

Big Why Media

Foreword by Brett Monk

Welcome to *"Trapped By A Lie"!* This is the third book in the 5-book *"Moms Who Lie"* series. What started out as a slow burn is now about to burst into flames as the action and drama escalates to an entirely new level. As in the first two books, McKenna and I are just having a blast working together to bring you this story.

In addition to the five full-length novels in the series, there's also a special FREE bonus novella called *"The Lying Begins"* that's not available on Amazon or anywhere else other than the link below. It tells the story of just what happened twenty years ago, the night of the prom when Maddy and Amelia were in high school together. Once you're thoroughly hooked on this story, you're definitely going to want to read it, too.

https://www.brettmonk.com

When you join my reader's community, you will not only get free books and other content by me and some of my friends, but you will get the inside scoop on discounted products and upcoming releases. Plus, I share some personal thoughts and "behind the scenes" photos and notes about my life, media adventures, and favorite grilling recipes. :-)

Community members also get to vote in polls and make suggestions for upcoming books and projects. You might even want to consider being a "beta reader" or an "advance review reader", both of whom get to read the books before they're available to the public.

But for now, enjoy *"Trapped By A Lie"*.

- Brett

Contents

CHAPTER 1

AUDREY

Lyla's First Day Missing

It's been complete chaos and horror since we discovered my twin sister, Lyla, missing earlier this morning. It seems as if the news had spread like a suffocating wildfire through Toxey about it, too. But how could it not? That's how it is here. Everyone knows everything about everyone, whether you want them to or not.

I have never seen Mom like this. Usually, she is a much put-together, brave, confident woman. The type who refuses to let anyone see her upset or vulnerable. I've always admired her for that ability, as a matter of fact. But she's not being like that now; she's been crying nonstop. Not audibly, however. Tears have constantly been streaming down her face while she tries to go about her business, cooperating with the police and doing whatever she and Dad can to try and get my sister—their daughter—back.

My dad, Gentry—a smart and usually charming man whose long brown hair is already graying even though he's not even forty yet—has taken total control, but only of finding Lyla. It's like Joey—my foster brother—and I don't even exist, not that I blame him for acting that way. I'm glad all his attention is on making sure Mom is okay and that the police are doing everything in their power to find my sister.

The police have been searching from the moment we reported Lyla missing. That was hours ago. It's getting pretty late, and knowledge of that fact terrifies the crap out of me. What is it they say about the first twenty-four hours of a missing persons case?

No, Audrey. You can't think like that. It's not healthy.

Lyla will come back. She has to.

I just hope that wherever she is, she is unharmed.

I can't stop thinking the worst: I can't stop thinking about the masked man. Yes, he's only attacked me so far. But I get the feeling that whoever the man behind the disguise is isn't just out to get *me*. Lyla has been messed with, too. Just in different ways. And so has our friend, Warner. We think it's the same person messing with and tormenting all three of us.

What if the masked man has Lyla?

I swallow and peek out the blinds of the front room again. What I want is for me to open them and see that Lyla is making her way up the driveway back into the house.

It doesn't happen.

Mom is so out of it that she doesn't even care that I'm in her glamorous, all-white front room. Usually, it's off limits to her kids—Lyla, Joey, and me—especially if our dirty shoes are on, like mine are now.

I feel helpless when I look out the window for the millionth time.

"I have a feeling you're not going to see her out there," a timid, nearly faint voice says from by the front door in the foyer area. I look over and find that Joey is creeping on me. His dark eyes are red, and the deeply tanned skin of his face is puffy from crying—just like I've been—and he looks stressed and worried—also like me. His eyebrows are raised so high they're practically hidden behind the bangs of his dark brown bowl cut.

"You never know," I try, offering him a smile. I don't know why, but I feel this need to make sure I keep my head and spirits up in front of him. If Mom and Dad aren't even trying to keep it together in front of him, then I feel like someone has to.

And that someone has to be me. His older sister.

Joey is much younger than Ly and me—only in the sixth grade: he's been living with us for three years. Right now, I don't even want to think about what might happen to him if we don't get Lyla back.

I can't think about the ifs.

"You're not supposed to be in there," Joey reminds me. He's right in front of the plush white rug, looking like he's almost tempted to break the rules with me and come join me on the white sofa in front of the handsome fireplace with the natural wood mantle.

"I think in circumstances like this, Mom won't mind if we break the rules a little."

He looks over his shoulder, then he comes and joins me. Then, just like I had done, he peeks his eyes through the blinds in search of our sister.

"She'll come back," I say.

"How do you know?" He doesn't sound convinced. I don't blame him.

"Because she's my twin. I just do. I can sense these things."

"Yeah, right." He sniffs, then more tears spill from his eyes.

Thinking quickly, I wrap my arms around him and pull him close to me. I rub his back and shush him, and I'm glad his head is tucked under mine so that he can't see that I have started to cry again, too.

I don't know how or when, but eventually, we both fall asleep like that.

When I wake later, with a start that wakes Joey, too, it's because of a loud knock on the front door.

Quickly, Mom goes to answer it, Dad following closely behind her.

I have no idea who it could be or what time it is.

But I hope it's Lyla out there on that doorstep.

"Hello, officers," Mom says in a sad, tired voice.

"Any news?" Dad adds.

"Mind if we come in?" one of the officers asks. I don't recognize his voice, and when Mom and Dad step aside, I don't recognize either of the officers who have entered our home. But I guess I should be glad it's not the detective I would recognize—Craig Fritz.

Dad closes the door behind them, and they all stare at us.

"Maybe we should take this somewhere more private?" the taller, broader one says.

I stand quickly, nearly knocking Joey off of me. "I want to know what's going on."

Dad and Mom exchange looks. Then Dad turns to Joey.

"Go wait in your room, Joey."

"Why can't I know, too?"

"Just listen to your father," Mom says. She still sounds so, so tired.

Dragging his feet, Joey does as he's told and heads up the staircase behind everyone.

Then the officer speaks.

"It appears one of our officers found something we believe might belong to Lyla," the shorter, rounder cop says.

I'm terrified to know what it could be. But I have to know.

"What?" Dad asks.

"Just tell us," Mom demands in a terse whisper.

"We've located a long, blonde wig. Does Lyla own one of those?"

We all exchange looks. I'm confused at first.

"I don't know anything about her owning a wig," Mom says, turning to me. "Do you?"

I shake my head.

But then it dawns on me.

Long. Blonde. Wig.

Lyla cut all her hair off. It's down to barely her shoulders now. It used to be as long as mine. And when it was, it was nearly impossible to tell us apart.

Wherever Lyla disappeared to, she went pretending to be me.

CHAPTER 2

LYLA

Nineteen Hours Earlier

I'm shaking.

I don't know why I decided to do this.

It had seemed like the right thing to do initially. Some monster in a mask had been tormenting my sister. My best friend. My other half. And I wanted it to stop. So, when she got that text while she was in the shower giving an address to where to meet if she wanted to get answers about what really happened to Sydney Hutton the night she died, I wanted to be the one who went. I wanted to stop this terror once and for all. And it felt like it was up to me. Like it was my responsibility. I had felt brave and ready.

But that had been when I first left the house. I went on foot because the address wasn't terribly far away. I'm almost at the location now. According to my phone's map, it looks as if the destination is going to be some trailhead at the edge of the woods. Already, I know this isn't a good sign.

Bad things happen in the woods.

My steps have gotten slower. My heart has started to beat faster. The wig on my head feels itchy and uncomfortable like my body is telling me it's wrong to have it on and that I should remove it. I shouldn't be pretending to be my sister. I should have just told the police to go to this address. But who am I kidding? They probably wouldn't go. And even if they miraculously did somehow, whoever is waiting for Audrey would probably dip into the thick mass of trees and disappear out of sight, then the police wouldn't trust me even more.

There is a small parking lot in front of the trailhead. A couple of cars are in it, which surprises me—and terrifies me—seeing how late it is. Is the masked man in one of them? Is the person who has been messing with not only Audrey but with Warner and me, too, in one of them? And if so, what do they want?

I step off the sidewalk and into the parking lot. Then I look over my shoulder to see if there are any signs of cars coming. Anyone who might be able to see me in case something happens to me. I don't know what it is, but I just have a horrible feeling about this.

I stop walking and stand in the middle of the lot, unsure what to do next. I don't have Audrey's phone, so I can't text the unknown number back and let them know I— "Audrey"—have arrived.

My eyes scan each of the three cars. I don't see any movement in any of them. But I still focus on straining my eyes to see in the backs of the tinted windows, just in case.

I don't even notice it at first when a figure emerges from the trees behind me.

Not until they step on a twig, and it cracks, and I spin around with my heart lurching.

There he is.

The masked man.

I've never seen him before. But he's exactly like what Audrey described.

All black outfit. A cartoonish mask of an average male human face with overly exaggerated facial features.

I look at his right hand.

There, enveloped by a black glove, is a long blade shimmering in the moonlight.

He tried to lead Audrey straight into a death trap when he sent her that text.

"What do you want?!" I call, still many feet away from the predator.

I don't know why I even bothered asking him. It's clear he's not going to answer me. If I know who he is, then his voice might give him away.

But who could it be?

Instead, the man takes a slow step toward me.

"I'm here. I did what you said. I just want answers." I'm trying to sound like my sister. I'm wearing a long-sleeved shirt, so the scar on my bicep from the car accident isn't visible.

He takes another step toward me.

I want to run. Everything in my body is telling me that's what I need to do.

But I came here for answers.

"Just tell me who you are."

Nothing. Just another step. I've had enough of it.

"Stop messing with my sister and Warner. If you want me, come and get me."

I don't know what I was expecting the man to do. Maybe I didn't think he'd listen to me.

But he does.

The masked man is suddenly sprinting towards me.

Adrenaline pulsing through me, I turn around and run. Back toward the street. Back toward where I hope a car drives by and sees what's going on.

I have a bad leg. It prevents me from being able to run as fast as I used to. And when I peer over my shoulder, I see that the man in the mask is much, much faster than me.

I pump my arms harder. I don't know what I was thinking. I made a mistake.

I make it a short way down the sidewalk on the unlit, deserted street. That's when strong arms wrap tightly around me, and a body slams into my back.

I scream at the top of my lungs. But a hand slaps over my mouth harshly while the other keeps a tight clasp on me as I thrash about.

There's a car far in the distance. I can barely see their headlights. I hope they can see the man and me tugging me towards the trees.

I continue to try and break free. To try and kick and scream. But whoever this person is, they're strong. Much stronger than me.

So when the car grows nearer, I'm unable to stop him from plunging us into the darkness behind the trees. My wig snags on a branch and rips right off as we go. It doesn't deter the masked man. He must know now that I'm not Audrey. But he still keeps dragging me back.

Finally, I connect my heel with his shin. In pain, he drops me, and I fall to the ground. I scramble to get up, but he's quick to grab me by the ankles with both hands. I don't know where his knife is. Maybe I made him drop it when he ran to tackle me.

"LET ME GO!" I shriek as I use my arms to try and prevent him from dragging me back. And he does let go, only after one large tug on my legs that brings me close to him. Then he reaches out and is suddenly on top of me, pulling something out of his pocket. I think it has to be the knife. That he's going to take the knife out of his pocket and plunge it into my chest, and that will be that.

This will be how I die.

How long will it take them to find my body?

I'm confused when I see a white cloth instead of the knife. But I don't have much time to think about it before mid-scream; the cloth is over my mouth and nose as he smothers me.

Then I can't think about anything at all.

CHAPTER 3

Maddy

I go back to the hospital to check on my son again. After I exit the elevator and walk to his room, I find his bed empty and no one else inside.

"That's weird..." I trail off, looking around myself, confused. Nobody told me they were moving him. Immediately, I'm worried. Why would they have to move him unless something bad had happened? What if he was in the ICU now?

I turn sharply on my combat boot-clad heel and march up to the nurses' station.

"How can I help you?" a sweet-sounding, overweight woman at the desk asks me when she sees me standing there.

"I'm looking for my son, Warner Carpenter. Did you guys switch his room?"

"One moment." She types some stuff and does some searching—or at least that's what I assume she's doing—and then something in her face falls as she looks back up at me carefully.

"I'm going to have you just wait right here."

"Why?" I ask sharply. "What happened to him? What's going on?"

The lady ignores me and wheels her rolling desk chair back to talk to a coworker. Around me, it seems like doctors and other nurses are apprehensive and moving quickly and talking in whispers quieter than normal. And maybe I'm crazy, but I feel like many of them keep looking at me.

I can't hear what the woman is saying to her coworker.

"Hello?" I ask, my tone showing how impatient I am beginning to get.

The woman she was talking to, a tall woman with different colored scrubs from the first one, stands from her seat and walks around the desk toward me.

"You're Madeline Carpenter?"

"Yes. Look, I just want to know where my son is."

"I'm so sorry to inform you of this, but we cannot locate your son. He seems to have left his room without any of the staff members' knowledge."

"Are you kidding me?" It's not me who said it. It was a man's voice. A familiar one at that.

I turn. There Dean Reeves is the father of my child. Not that Warner knows this. For now.

His chocolate brown hair looks disheveled. The minimal lines on his face—the only giveaways to his aging since high school—look deeper than usual. Full of worry and irritation.

"Dean," I snap, but I can't talk to him right now after what I've just heard, so I turn back to the nurse—or whatever her label is—so I can sort out what the heck she just told me. I don't want Dean listening in, but I don't have time to tell him to go away right now.

"What do you mean he left?" I demand to know.

"We cannot locate him," the woman says, looking apologetic. "I was just about to call you."

"H-how long have you known this?"

"Erm, we found out about twenty minutes ago."

"And you didn't call me?"

"I'm so sorry, ma'am. Like I said, I had been just about to. We're doing all we can to see if he's around here at the hospital somewhere."

"He's not," Dean says. "If he wanted to leave his room without anyone's permission, then I highly doubt he stuck around here."

The woman looks displeased to see him standing there. It's the same as I feel. "I'm sorry," she says to Dean. "But who are you in relation to the patient?"

"I'm his..." Dean trails off and looks at me.

Say "father." I dare you.

"His coach," he finishes.

That's what I thought.

"Have you called the police?" I ask. "Called his cell?"

"Would you like us to?"

I roll my eyes and turn from her. I stomp away from them, but I can feel that Dean is following me closely. I pull out my phone and give Warner a call. What the heck was he thinking, just *leaving* the hospital? Already, I know why. Because of Lyla. He must think he knows where she went or how he can find her.

His phone rings and rings, but he doesn't answer.

I mumble angrily under my breath and hang up.

"No answer?" Dean asks. I spin to him and shoot him a look.

"What are you doing here?"

"I came to check in."

"Why?"

"Maddy, our son was in a—"

"*Don't* call him that."

"It's not like he can hear."

"But other people might!"

"Fine. I just wanted to make sure he was doing okay."

"He was pretty badly injured, actually," I inform him. "Not in any state to be leaving his hospital room."

"How do you think the explosion happened?"

I had been dead asleep. Then I woke to an incredibly loud, booming noise right outside my window. I leaped out of bed, rushed outside onto my front porch, and saw my car engulfed in flames. And beyond the flames, I saw Warner lying in the street.

I say, "I-I don't know." But I do know. It was a handmade car bomb.

A car bomb.

I don't know if it was meant for Warner. It was in *my* car, so I am terrified that it was meant for me. That because someone was out to get me, Warner got his life put in danger.

When I saw him lying in the street, unmoving, with the blood that covered him...

I can't even think about it. It hurts too much. It makes me feel like I am going to collapse to my knees right here in the middle of the hospital hallway.

"Look, I can't do this right now," I say. "I need to find him."

"Okay," Dean replies. "Let me help you, Maddy."

"This isn't any of your responsibility."

I don't know who Dean thinks he is. I don't know why he would even *want* to help me. Where was this "want" when I was still a teenager, just finding out I was pregnant with his child?

Dean stands there and gives me a look. One I don't want from him. Especially right now. He starts to say something, but I cut him off.

"I don't need your help."

And I don't want it, either.

CHAPTER 4

WARNER

I t doesn't take too long for my mother to annoy me enough that I finally answer her insistent phone calls. Then she yells and cries and makes it impossible for me to do anything other than return to the hospital unless I want the police brought out to search for me when they should be spending all of their focus searching for Lyla. That's the only thing that makes me agree to go back.

And fine. I *am* still in a lot of pain from the car explosion.

So, I return to the hospital after seeing Detective Craig Fritz talking to Audrey and Lyla's aunt, Nora. After finding out that Dean Reeves is more than likely my biological father, and my mother may or may not have known about it my entire life. And after Lyla has been missing for much, much too long. The police should have found her by now. Someone should have been able to get ahold of her by now.

And get this.

When I am put back in my hospital bed after being embarrassingly wheel-chaired back from the lobby, I am put into restraints and labeled as a flight risk patient. I can't do anything with my hand tied to the bed and my other one in a brace. I can't get on my phone to check any notifications. I can't grab the remote to put the news on the TV, so I can keep track of the developments in the case of Lyla's disappearance.

"Mom," I complain loudly as just the two of us are in my hospital room. I tug at the restraints aggressively to show how annoyed I am. "Make them take me out of these."

She has tears streaming down her cheeks as she shakes her head no at me. "I'm sorry, Warner. I know you're under a lot of stress right now, and I know you're worried about your... friend. But I am worried about your safety. I can't tell them to let you out."

My voice raises a decibel with every word I throw at her. "Are. You. *Kidding*. ME?!"

She jumps back.

I don't believe it. My own mother. Afraid of me.

I've always had this suspicion in the back of my mind that she thinks I had something to do with Sydney Hutton's death. She's the girl who drowned in Lake Oshwana during the upperclassman camping trip not long ago. The girl who I think might have been the start of me, Lyla, and Audrey getting into this huge mess in the first place.

And sitting here in my stupid hospital bed in my stupid hospital gown, watching my mother jump back as I yell at her, it makes it even clearer to me; she thinks her own son might be capable of murder.

And if I have some sort of gene in me that she thinks makes me capable of murder, then who would I have inherited that gene from? Her? Coach Reeves?

"Warner, please," Mom begs. But I am so mad about everything that has happened in the last twenty-four hours that I don't even want to hear it.

"Get out." My voice is low and sinister.

She takes a step toward me. "I just want you to stay safe and get better. You have to understand, hon—"

"I said *get out*!"

CHAPTER 5

AMELIA

I am a complete mess. I can't do anything. I can't eat. I can't sleep. And I can't think about anything other than the fact that my daughter is missing.

And that she might be dead.

I also think about the unfairness of it all. I already almost lost her once. I didn't know I would have to go through this all over again.

Lyla, please come back to me.

"Amelia."

I snap my head in the direction of my husband. He's talking to me in a stern voice. Apparently, I've done something to set him off because his jaws tense, and I can see the frustration all over his face. It ages him a few years. And since this morning when we discovered Lyla missing—in the short amount of time it's been—I think both of us have aged a few years.

"What?" I ask him in a snippy voice, similar to how his voice had sounded.

"Are you listening to me at all?"

"Honestly, no, I'm not." My voice falls flat and dull. How can I listen to him when my daughter is missing? How can I listen to anything? Focus on anything else but that?

"Doesn't she have any other friends we can reach out to to see if they know anything? Or tell the police to reach out to them?"

"We've gone over this, Gentry; her only other friends were the girls Audrey hangs out with more, Trinity—who is longer with us—and Sydney—who is also no longer with us."

"What about that Warner Carpenter kid?"

"What about him?" My shoulders tense.

I don't like him mentioning Madeline Carpenter's son. Maddy is one of my best friends—my only best friend—and even though I'm having some internal issues with her at the moment, I still don't want her son spoken poorly of by Gentry, who hardly knows him. Heck, I hardly know him.

"He's been hanging around her. And from what I've been hearing around town, many people don't trust him, Mia. They think he's involved in the Sydney Hutton thing."

"Newsflash, hon, but it's been talked about that our daughters have a part of it as well. Remember when we went in for questioning?"

"Well, maybe he coerced them into doing something. Into keeping his secrets. And maybe Lyla said she didn't want to keep his secret anymore, and he did something to her because of it."

"You need to check your facts. Warner has been in the hospital. Since Maddy's car exploded outside her house with him nearby. Remember?"

"I didn't even know that."

I let out a frustrated growl and get off my bed. I've been sitting on my side of it; my legs draped over the edge. He's been lounging on his side of the bed, lying on the comforter, reclined with his head in his hands, propped up against our oak wood headboard. But now, I don't want to be in the same room as Gentry. I don't want to be sitting still.

I catch a glimpse of myself in the mirror hanging on the wall above our dresser. I don't even recognize my appearance. My hair is dull and flat. I haven't bothered to wash or style it or even do a thing as simple as putting some dry shampoo in it. And usually, I'm so put together. My eyes right now are bright red from my continuous crying. I didn't even have it in me to put any makeup on today. It's probably for the best because I've cried so much I would have surely wiped it all off by now or smeared it all around my face.

Gentry gives me an exasperated sigh. "Where are you going?"

"I... I don't know."

"Well, do you think you can stay?"

I pick up my cell phone from the dresser and don't answer him.

He continues. "I think we really need to put our heads together so we can try and figure this out."

Typical me would've agreed with him. Typical me would've sat back down and gone over every possible scenario with him. We would've strategized. But this Amelia, the one I don't even know, doesn't know what she's doing. And she knows it's not Gentry's fault that Lyla has gone missing, but she doesn't want to talk to her husband anyway.

Without saying a word or looking at him, I step out into the hall and close the door behind me.

I've taken three steps when my phone in my hand rings. I don't recognize the number, but I step into our study anyway and close the door to take the call privately. I don't want anyone overhearing in case it's bad news about Lyla.

Especially my kids.

"This is Amelia Bailey," I say, my stomach rolling.

"Mrs. Bailey, how are you? This is Sandra, Joey's case worker from Child Protective Services."

Great.

Why on earth would Joey's foster care case worker be calling me? And why now?

"How can I help you?" My voice is not at all polite.

"I know this probably isn't the best time," Sandra says, apparently able to read my mind. "But that is the reason why we are calling. I've received news about your daughter, Lyla Bailey, going missing?"

"What about it?"

Sandra takes a moment to clear her throat. "I'm just calling to check up on Joey. To see if he's doing okay. This might not be the best environment for him to be in right now. I know he's been in your care for a very long time, but—"

"He's fine. This house is still the best home for him." I can't believe this is happening. "There is no need for you to worry. I appreciate you checking in, but we have this all under control, and Lyla should be coming home any moment now."

"Well, that's good to hear, however—"

"I'm sorry, I really don't have time to discuss this right now. I have... things I need to do. Joey needs help with his homework. You'll have to call me later."

I don't even let Sandra get another word in before I hit the end button. I drop my hand to my side, but it's trembling so hard that I lose my grip, and the phone clatters to the hardwood floor.

CHAPTER 6

WARNER

It's after midnight when I am actually discharged from the hospital. I shouldn't have been released, but my mom decided that since they couldn't keep a good eye on me there, she didn't want me to stay there any longer, and she said I could be treated at home.

The whole drive home, Mom and I are silent, except for the fact that every so often, I can hear Mom sniffling as she drives. The only other noise is the windshield wiper that squeaks against my jeep because they need to be replaced, and it's barely sprinkling out.

I don't get why my mom is crying, but I don't feel like asking her. I don't want to talk to her. She lied to me. My entire life. Sure, I don't outright know for a fact that my mom knows that Dean Reeves is my father. And yes, I guess I don't know for a fact that Dean Reeves is my father. It's just that Detective Craig Fritz gave me some pretty good evidence suggesting so. In my gut, I know it's the truth. And in my gut, I know my mom knows.

And she decided to lie to me about it.

"There are some prescriptions I'll pick up first thing in the morning since all of the pharmacies are closed now," Mom finally says to me as we enter the dirt roads of our neighborhood. We live in a slightly bad part of town, where all the poor people are. My mom and I are poor. She works as a hairdresser. I have a part-time gig as an assistant soccer coach. Our house is small, run-down, and always dirty, and we can barely keep up with the bills. In fact, a lot of my paychecks even go toward paying the bills and not toward saving for college in Florida, where I want to go.

"Okay." It's the only answer I can give her. It's the only thing I feel like saying to her. I don't want to make conversation.

We pull into the driveway, and I look at the remnants of the burn marks on our driveway and the front of our house. It takes me back to that night. The explosion. I have a few second-degree burns, but I was far enough away that the blast sent me flying instead of burning me alive.

I need to know who did this. And why they did it to my mom's car.

"Do you need help out?" Mom asks as she parks the car and hops out herself.

"I got it." I push the door open, unbuckle my seatbelt, and slowly climb out. My entire body is aching. I hadn't felt like this earlier when I had snuck out of the hospital because I had been so worried about Lyla. I still am worried about Lyla. But I'm trapped. That's how it feels, anyway. I can't go looking for her. Mom won't allow it.

She walks around to my side of the car anyway to make sure I get out okay on my own, and to show just how much I don't need her, I storm past her and make it to the house first. But of course, she has my car keys, so she has the key to the house, too. I have to wait for her anyway to unlock the door and let us in.

"Your accident," she says once we're inside with the door closed and locked again. The deadbolt included. "And that thing happening with Sydney Hutton... Warner, do you think they're related? And do you think whatever happened to Lyla could be related to it, too?"

"You know what, Mom?" I ask in a very, very tired voice. "I've kind of had a long day, in case you haven't noticed. I'm not really in the mood to get into any of this."

"I get it," she says quickly, looking at me with sincere eyes. "You should rest for the next few days. I don't want you going to school. No football practice. And call your boss and let him know that you can't work for the time being. I'm sure he'll understand."

I rotate my shoulder slowly, trying to get it to be less stiff. "Mom, I can't just stay home from school."

"Yes, you can."

Stay calm, Warner.

"I can't. There's too much going on. I can't miss schoolwork. And I can't have my absence making people think I'm part of why Lyla is missing—if she isn't found by Monday."

My stomach sinks at the thought of it. Please let them find Lyla before then. Let them have already found her now. Let me just turn on the news and see that she's home safe.

I glance at my phone in my hand and see that I still have no updates from her. From anyone. Which means she's still missing.

"Warner..." Mom trails off in that motherly voice. I can come up with a hundred more excuses if I need to. But I'm not going to tell her the truth about why I really need to go to school. About why I can't stay home.

I need to go to school because I need to get away from her.

CHAPTER 7

Audrey

It's way past Joey's bedtime. But as I hang out with him in his room, the door closed and some of his favorite music playing on his Bluetooth speaker, I don't say anything to him about it. He's clearly scared and worked up. He's never seen Mom like this. Nor have I, for the matter. I just want to keep him company and distract him. Nobody else is going to do it. Not when Mom and Dad are too busy worrying about Lyla. And it also helps that hanging out with Joey is also distracting me. But only slightly.

"It's your turn, goof," I say as we sit on the floor in his room and play the board game Sorry. He draws a card, his face in a permanent frown.

"It's starting to rain outside," he says, nodding his head toward the window. I look out and see drops of rain only in front of where the street light shines because everywhere else is too dark.

"I see that," I say, my voice cracking slightly.

"Do you think Lyla is somewhere warm?"

"I hope she is, kiddo."

"Can you try your twin telepathy thing with her again?"

Lyla and I obviously don't have actual twin telepathy. Or I would've known she was going to do this. And I would've known the reasoning why. And I would've known why she was pretending to be me wherever she went. But still, I am willing to try anything. So I nod my head at Joey. And then I put my fingers to my temples, and I think really hard.

Ly, where did you go?

Silence.

Please just give me any sign that you're at least okay. That you're not harmed. That you're not somewhere horrible where you need to be rescued.

Nothing.

Did someone kidnap you? Did you leave on your own accord?

I concentrate so hard that I'm hurting my head with how much force I use to press my fingers to my temples. And still, I don't feel anything.

The only thing keeping me going is the strange sensation I have within me. I don't know if it's in my heart, stomach, or head. But something is telling me that Lyla is still alive. That if she died, I would just know.

"Anything?" Joey asks.

I shake my head regrettably. He frowns even deeper and takes his turn. I get one of my pegs knocked back into home.

"You always beat me at this," I complain, trying to sound upbeat. But he doesn't even seem pleased with himself that he's in the lead.

"Do you think aunt Nora knows?" he asks.

I take my card. Then I move my small yellow piece to two squares.

"About Lyla?" I ask. "I'm sure she does."

"I heard Aunt Nora left because she and Mom got into a fight."

"Where'd you hear that?" I ask. A fight? Aunt Nora did leave rather abruptly, so I assumed something had to have gone down, but with so much going on in such a short amount of time, I haven't really given it any thought until now.

"Dad."

I shake my head. Dad shouldn't be telling little young Joey about Mom's private information. If Mom wanted Joey to know that she and Aunt Nora got into a fight, she should have told Joey herself.

I hear a gentle tapping noise against the window. I look over again and see that the rain sprinkle has turned into a sudden downpour.

But I also see something else.

Outside, down on the street, I see the shadow of a person. They're looking up into the house.

I jump to my feet, knocking over a couple of my pegs in the process.

"What is it?!" Joey asks loudly, getting to his feet as well. "Is it Lyla?"

I go to the window. But out on the street is an empty sidewalk. But I could've sworn I saw somebody. They were just there. And it looked like they were staring right into Joey's room at me.

"I don't see anything," Joey says in a disappointed voice as he comes to stand next to me.

"M-me neither," I say.

Maybe I'm losing it.

CHAPTER 8

MADDY

A little after Warner goes into his bedroom, I creep down the hallway and slowly crack his bedroom door open to check on him. He's fast asleep in bed, his pain meds having kicked in quickly.

With my phone in hand, I send him a quick text for when he wakes up.

Me: Headed out to meet a friend. I'll be home no later than when the bar closes.

I want him to know in case he wakes up, finds me missing, and begins worrying about me. And it's also good for him to know in case I don't come home when the bars close. Because then he'll have a way of knowing that something has happened to me. Not that I think anything will, but I guess you can't ever be too careful. Especially not in this town. This town, I once considered a safe place. Where I once considered the only bad thing to happen to be when Mia and I killed Carson Price.

But I guess everybody has their secrets. Who knows which ones are buried underneath our soil?

I steal Warner's car—I think it's an unspoken understanding that I'm going to have to use it a lot now—and I drive to The Mix to meet Steven Hall. Steven Hall is a well-groomed, delectable-looking, straight-toothed man I'm currently obsessing over. Not literally, but I do feel super into him whenever we're together, and I think about him a good portion of the day whenever we are apart.

He doesn't fit in at a dive bar like The Mix when I meet him there. He is dressed in a button-down and slacks and looks like he just got off a long day at the office. But he doesn't work at an office. He owns three restaurants, one of them The Viper, where I met him. I had thought he was just some random hot guy coming up to flirt with me. Little had I known he was actually the owner checking in to make sure I was enjoying myself. But still, we hit it off.

When he sees me, his smile nearly kills me. I meet him at his spot at the bar, where he gets up and envelops me in a warm, deep hug.

"How's your son doing?" he asks me immediately. His hair is gelled back, and he has a deep look of concern. It only makes me melt. All I want is to find a man that also cares about my son. And Steven has a son, too. A boy named Wrigley Hall, just a year under Warner. Could it be any more perfect?

"He was released from the hospital today," I tell him with a heavy sigh. Recognizing what I am in desperate need of after my long day, Steven is quick to flag down the bartender like he owns the place. He has this energy about him that makes him seem like the most important man in the room, regardless of where he is.

One of the bartenders, Miguel, comes up, and upon seeing me and the look on my face, he immediately turns back to the fridge, knowing exactly what I want.

An ice-cold beer.

He hands it to me how I prefer it, right in the bottle. Then I take a seat next to Steven.

"You don't seem relieved to be saying that," Steven says about my comment about Warner.

I take a long, deep sip. "Because I'm not so sure if it's a good thing. You heard about that girl who went missing, right?"

"Lyla Bailey?" he asks. "Of course I have. She's my son's classmate. He seems pretty upset about it."

I nod. "Yeah, so is my son. I think... I think he has a thing for her, actually. He... sort of escaped the hospital to go out and try and look for her."

"Are you serious?"

"Well, he won't tell me directly that that's why he escaped. But a mom just knows, you know?"

"And so, these two have a thing for each other, and Warner just happened to be by your car when it exploded, and then his friend went missing shortly after?"

I'm surprised at how quickly Steven catches on. I can tell that he's wondering the same things that I am. If it's all related, somehow.

I want to tell Steven everything, which is rare for me. I'm generally a pretty private person who likes to try to solve issues on my own, but there's something about the way Steven is looking up at me. About the way he just seems to understand me, no matter the situation I'm in.

I take another sip of beer. I think it over for one more minute, then I've made my decision. "Yeah," I say, looking directly into his eyes. "About that..."

I'm about to tell him. It's exactly what I want to do. But as I'm sitting here, I have a perfect view of the entrance to my left. And walking in right this moment is none other than Craig Fritz.

"Oh no," I groan. I meant to do it internally, but I couldn't help that the words escaped me.

Following my gaze, Steven turns around and watches with me as Craig goes to the other end of the bar and flags down Miguel. He's in his full police uniform. His beard is thick and scruffy and not groomed. His hair is getting longer and shaggier by the day, and it looks like he hasn't combed it in quite some time. Still, Detective Fritz, my ex-boyfriend, is one of the better-looking men I've met in my life. Even when he's in this state.

"That police officer?" Steven asks, looking back at me with an eyebrow cocked. "What's he got you reacting that way for?"

As I said, I want to tell Steven everything. But with the way Craig Fritz is currently eying down in a sinister way at the end of the bar, there's no way that I can.

CHAPTER 9

AMELIA

Normally I would've gone to bed hours ago. But how am I supposed to sleep when my daughter is still out there? How am I supposed to stop trying to call her cell phone and send her multiple text messages even though I know her phone is off?

I don't know when Audrey and Joey went to bed, but I checked on them not too long ago and saw Audrey sleeping on the floor in Joey's room. I'm glad that she is comforting her brother. I just can't multitask right now. And so much as looking at Joey sends a revolting feeling through my stomach.

I already have to deal with Lyla missing. I can't deal with the prospect of Joey possibly being taken away from me, too.

The news has been on all day. I have refused to turn off the TV or change the channel to anything else.

I've just finished leaving Lyla another voicemail when the filming of Gentry's and my press release earlier replays on the screen in front of me.

"Lyla is a young girl who has already been through so much," I say into the microphone. It's horrifying to watch myself like this. To see how wrecked I look. How distressed. How worried. Then I wonder if people think it's all an act. Some humans are just like that. Some humans think the worst. That Lyla is being dramatic and ran away for attention, and I know it, and I'm just covering it up. I'm sure people think it. "I don't know where she went, and I don't know why; all I know is that I need her to get home safely. And I need any of you, if you know anything at all, to come forward please and help my husband and me—and the police—get her back home to us where she belongs."

Standing beside me, Gentry has his arm around me and rubs my shoulder. His voice is hoarse when he speaks next. And he has trouble looking at any of the cameras directly.

"Lyla, if you were somehow able to watch this. If you're out there somewhere, just know that we love you, miss you, and want you to come home. You're one of the best things that has ever happened to us, and all we want is for you to have the world. If you can get yourself home, please do it. Your mother and I—" He pauses while his voice cracks. "Your mother and I will do anything."

Then Gentry turns away from the microphones and goes inside our house. I stand there, left alone to answer some terrifying questions from reporters and townspeople.

Then the video finally ends.

"Was that the press release?"

I jump, my heart nearly flying out of my throat. I turn around and see Gentry standing behind the couch. I had been so engrossed in watching the press release rerun that I didn't even realize he had walked into the room.

"Why were you watching that?" he continues to ask, not even seeming fazed about how he just scared the crap out of me.

"I-I didn't mean to watch it. I was just watching the news, and it... it came on."

"Oh." He pauses. "The police are still out there searching. And I think they're getting ready to start getting some search parties involved, too."

But I'm barely hearing anything he's saying. I'm just thinking about the press release. And about how it hadn't mattered. Because it has to have been twenty-four hours—or at least close to it—since my daughter went missing, I don't know if I'm ever going to get her back.

The realization of this brings me to my feet, and suddenly I'm running away from Gentry through the arch into the hall toward our bedroom.

"Amelia!" Gentry calls after me. I go into the bedroom and try to make it onto the bed but don't. I simply sink to my knees on the floor in front of it. Sobs rack my whole body.

In seconds, Gentry walks in behind me and closes the door. He races to my side silently and sinks to the ground behind me. He wraps his arms around me, and I fall back into his arms. He falls back into the dresser with a thud because of the weight of me crashing against him, but he doesn't say a word about it. I continue to sob. I don't want my children hearing me upstairs, but there's nothing I can do. I can't stop.

Behind me, I feel Gentry's body begin to shake, and it almost seems as if he could be laughing at me. But then I hear the snot-filled sniffle. He's crying harder than I've ever seen him.

What happened to our daughter?

CHAPTER 10

LYLA

I wake up groggy and confused. For a long while, as I sit there and try to familiarize myself with my surroundings, I think I've had the strangest dream.

But then I realize that the floor underneath me is hard. Made of wood. Old, rotting wood. And it smells damp in here. Damp and moldy.

It's pitch black, and for a while, I think it's just taking my eyes a bit to adjust to the darkness. But it stays pitch black.

My head is pounding. My body feels achy. I get myself to a seated position and feel the ground around my legs. I'm not tied to anything. I'm not gagged or bound. So I think maybe, maybe, I haven't really been kidnapped by the man in the mask. Maybe he had realized I was Audrey when my wig snagged and simply let me go.

Or even better, maybe I had imagined the whole thing in the first place. And I had simply fallen asleep because I was out in the darkness so late, and I sleep-walked myself to here, wherever here is. I wouldn't put it past me—after all, I have sleep-walked before. The last time was when I ended up in the woods behind Trinity's house. And when I made it out, Trinity's parents were on the porch in their backyard, and they totally caught me.

I shiver and climb to my feet. I am dizzy, and everything feels foggy. I have no way to describe the feeling. Maybe this is what being drunk feels like. Not that I would know. I only know what I've seen in movies and on TV. And the way I feel seems a lot like how I've seen actors behave while pretending to be intoxicated in front of the camera.

But I know I didn't drink anything.

I stumble around with my hands out in front of me. I run into a couple of things, but I have no idea what they are. They clink and thud together. Then I finally feel a wall, also made of wood. I feel around desperately, getting splinters in my hands and not even caring.

Finally, my hand finds a handle. A thin, vertical one made of metal. I give it a tug. Nothing happens.

I give it a push. Same thing.

"Hello?" I call out.

But then I feel stupid. What do I expect somebody to do, say hello back and let me out of here?

The first memory finally awakens in my tired brain. The masked man with the cloth. The one he held over my mouth seconds before I became unconscious.

He drugged me, trapped me in here, and now there's no way for me to escape.

CHAPTER 11

AMELIA

Lyla's Second Day Missing

I wake up with a start. I'm staring at the ceiling of my bedroom. Sometime last night, I must have somehow miraculously dozed off. It must have been from pure exhaustion. It was a dreamless, deep sleep.

I shake Gentry. "Wake up."

He wakes up suddenly, too, taking it a step further and bolting up in the bed. "What's going on?" he asks quickly.

"It's Sunday." I don't know why I say it. Maybe it's because of the fact that it's officially been over twenty-four hours that our daughter has been missing. That we haven't heard a peep out of her.

I force myself out of bed even though everything in my body protests against it. It wants me to stay still. It wants me to rest and recuperate. But I can't. Lyla is still missing.

Gentry gets out of bed, too. The time on my phone says it's early. Barely six o'clock. I've only slept for a few hours.

"I haven't heard anything," Gentry says as he stares at his phone over on his side of the bed. He's gripping it tightly. He seems instantly angered.

"Neither have I," I say. I do have several texts from people checking in. Most of them are from nosy neighbors. One of them is from Maddy, but it was sent after three a.m. last night.

Maddy: I am so sorry about all of this, babe. If you need me to come over, let me know, and I will. I'll be there in a heartbeat. Who cares what Gentry has to say about it? Who cares what our kids have to say? I want to be there for you in your time of need.

Seeing what time it was sent, I get the feeling that Maddy had been drinking last night. This is also because I haven't seen her get this sentimental with me since we resumed our friendship years and years ago.

"What is it?" Gentry asks; see me reread Maddy's message.

"It's nothing. It's just from Maddy." There's no use in lying about it. Gentry found out about our friendship after he walked in on me having some hors d'oeuvres and a drink with Maddy in my kitchen while I thought he was supposed to be out golfing.

"Does she know anything?" Gentry asks.

"We've been over this," I say.

"Well, have you told her to talk to her son?"

"Gentry, stop."

"No, you know what, Amelia? You stop!"

I'm completely taken aback by the fact that he's suddenly shouting at me.

"Excuse me?" I ask in a quiet, trembling voice.

He keeps at it. "I'm sick of this, Mia! I want to find where our daughter is! That boy might have something to do with it! And you don't even seem to want to try and find out! How could you even be willing to take that bet? I'll go over there myself if I have to. I mean it, Mia, I will!"

"How dare you?" I ask, my voice low. But as I continue, it gets louder by the word. "Who do you think you are, attacking me like this? I know our daughter is missing, Gentry! You don't think I'm not worried sick about her?! You don't think I want to do everything in my power to get her back?! How could you even?! Seriously, how could you?!" Tears are already streaming down my cheeks again. It's going to be yet another day where I don't bother showering or doing my make-up. I'm not going to bother doing anything until I get my daughter back.

"I don't want him anywhere near our family again! And Maddy, too, for the matter! Not until we get her back here and we get everything all figured out! I want to know everything! And you need to stop keeping secrets!"

"I'm not keeping any secrets!"

"Are you kidding me? All you do is keep secrets! All you do is lie! You know what I think?"

"What?"

"I think your lies and secrets are why we probably got into this mess in the first place! It's probably what led up to our daughter going missing!"

I'm racking my brain for something to say back. For something that'll get him to take it back. Because he has to take it back, he can't have meant it.

A knock on the door interrupts both of us. Then it cracks open, and sleepy-eyed Joey walks into the bedroom.

"Guys?" he asks. "Why are you fighting?"

Gentry takes a deep breath before he answers for us. "We were just... having a discussion. We're just worried about your sister, that's all."

"They still haven't found her?"

I go over to him and give him a hug. He looks up at me with his big, watery brown eyes, and I have to break his heart and shake my head no.

They still haven't found her.

CHAPTER 12

AUDREY

I wake up to the muffled sound of my parents shouting in their bedroom below. My back hurts as I sit up and stretch. I fell asleep on the floor in Joey's room. I meant to only stay until he fell asleep, but I guess I didn't realize how exhausted I was, too.

The first thing I do is notice that Joey is already out of bed.

The second thing I do is check my cell phone. I am desperate to see a message from Lyla. A missed call with a voicemail of her explaining that she is making her way home. That the craziest thing had happened, and she can't wait to explain it to me.

There's nothing except a few notifications from the news app updating me on how they have yet to find my sister.

I feel hopelessness creeping into my brain. I feel the tears forming at the corners of my eyes. But I get myself to my feet. There's no time for crying. Besides, crying would be pointless because I know Lyla is alive, and we're going to get her back.

I take a deep breath and then see what it was my parents are fighting about.

Downstairs, Mom, Dad, and Joey are now in the kitchen, and Mom is sitting at the table staring blankly at nothing while Dad moves around the kitchen, presumably to make us all something for breakfast. Nobody even says a word to me when I enter the room.

"So... what's going on?" I ask in a slow, careful voice.

"Lyla is still gone," Joey says, wiping his eyes. I'm about to go over and give him a hug when there's a knock on our front door. Since I'm closest, I run over to answer it. There's nothing my parents can do to stop me.

I throw open the door, desperate for it to be Lyla standing out there.

It's only the police. Detective Fritz and Officer Wilde, who had been in the room with Principal Mathers the day I had been questioned about Sydney Hutton at school.

"Have you found my sister?" I ask immediately.

"Goodness," Officer Wilde says, putting a hand to his heart. "I keep forgetting that Lyla has a twin. You scared the crap out of me, Miss Bailey."

"May we come in?" Detective Fritz asks. He gives me a warm smile, but I know well enough that it's fake. That he hates me. And I hate him.

My dad is suddenly behind me. He gently moves me aside and opens the door wider to let the men in. "Come on in," he says in a tired voice. "I assume you're here to update us about Lyla?"

"No new news," Officer Wilde says. "Except we are getting the volunteer groups ready for the search party later today. And that we still have everyone we can out there looking for her. Hounds included." He looks deeply apologetic. Fritz looks as if he's here for other reasons.

"Oh," my dad says in a flat voice. Now Mom is standing beside him, but she has her arms crossed, and she's remaining silent. It's still scary to see her this way, without make-up and still in her pajamas. Her hair is greasy and thrown back in a messy bun. She's so not herself, and it hurts to look at her. "Then what can we do for you?"

"We are wondering if we could ask you some more questions."

Dad motions for them to go into the front room.

"Great. I'll start with the parents first; then, if it's all right with you, I'd also like to speak with Miss Audrey Bailey here."

My parents look at me; then they look at each other, then they look back at Fritz and Wilde and nod their heads.

"Lyl—Audrey," Dad says, shaking his head as he corrects himself for calling me the wrong name. "Go keep your brother busy until it's your turn, all right?"

As much as I want to eavesdrop on every little bit of their conversation, I go and do as I'm told. Clearly, Mom and Dad already woke up on the wrong side of the bed this morning; I don't need to be making matters worse.

Joey never got around to doing his homework on Friday, so I pull it out of his backpack and start to help him do it now. We went to bed so late, and it's so early now that I feel like we could go back to sleep, but obviously, neither of us wants to. And homework is a good distraction—despite how much we both hate it.

Before I know it, it's my turn to go in for questioning. My mom and dad stay in the room and summon me to join them. I sit on the sofa in the middle of them while Detective Fritz and Officer Wilde sit in the leather chairs across the live-edge coffee table.

"Audrey, do you have an idea why your sister would have left the house in the middle of the night?" Officer Wilde starts by asking.

"And do you know where she might've gone?" Detective Fritz adds.

"Of course, I don't know," I snap. Then I look at the nicer officer, whom I'd much rather answer questions for. "I don't know why she would've left."

But that's not entirely true. I have a feeling I do know why she would have left: to get answers. To figure out who is tormenting Warner, Lyla, and me. But I don't say that to the police. I don't know why I don't.

"Have you been in contact with her at all?" Fritz asks.

"No," I say. "I would've let somebody know immediately if she had gotten in contact with me."

"Have any unknown numbers called you or texted you?" Officer Wilde asks. Have you checked your emails? There might be a chance she could've tried to reach out with a different number or email."

"I've been checking my phone religiously since we figured out she was missing," I reply. "I haven't heard anything."

Detective Fritz nods and writes something on his small notepad. For some reason, the gesture irks me. Then he leans forward and put his elbows on his knees. He smiles like this is just another happy Sunday to him.

"Audrey, I'm wondering... Officer Wilde and I would really appreciate it if you wouldn't mind handing over your phone for us to look through. You might have some hints on there that you're not even considering that could lead us to find your sister."

Give them my phone?

"I—I..."

But my dad answers for me. "Absolutely not," he says quickly. "You do not need to look through my daughter's phone. She's answering your questions truthfully. She has no idea where Lyla is, just like Amelia, and I have no idea where she is. That's why we're counting on you guys to help bring her home."

Go, Dad.

"I understand," Fritz says. "But we're just looking for any clues we can find, and—"

"Well, you're not going to find any in my daughter's phone. I won't have it."

"Very well," Officer Wilde says, shooting Fritz a look. Then he slowly gets to his feet. "I think that's all the questions we have for now. We will keep you updated on our findings during the search party tonight. And please come if you can. But try and have someone stay behind in case she makes her way home."

"Thank you," Dad says sternly.

"Please just get her back to me," my mom says in the softest of voices. It makes my heart ache to hear her sound so broken and desolate.

"I assure you," Craig Fritz says, nothing about his expression seeming like he wants to be assuring, "we're doing everything we can, Mia."

CHAPTER 13

AMELIA

After the cops leave, I stand behind the closed door and nibble on an index finger for a while as I ponder it. Then at the very last second, as my family is retreating into the family room, I swing the front door back open and run barefoot out onto the street.

"Wait!" I call. The officers were both getting into the same police cruiser. But luckily, Officer Wilde sees me, and he gets back out of the car. Fritz follows suit.

"I have something I think you guys might want to see."

They look at each other and then look back at me.

"Well, what is it, then?" Fritz asks.

"Wait right here."

I dash back inside and go into my study. I go into one of the desk drawers and pull out the photo of Megan Young—this girl who looks eerily similar to the Sydney Hutton that died in Lake Oshwana during the upperclassman camping trip. Dean Reeves discovered this missing person flyer and showed it to me. We both have reason to believe that Sydney Hutton isn't who she said she was. And why she would lie about it, I have no idea. But it could tie into why my daughter is missing and why Warner Carpenter and Audrey got hurt. So I think the police need to see it.

I run outside, Gentry calling, "What are you doing?!" after me but not following me. Good. He doesn't know about this Megan Young thing. And I don't want him to know about it. There's not even a logical explanation for my reasoning as to why. I just don't want to tell him stuff.

Officer Wilde meets me halfway, and I hand the flyer to him.

"What is this exactly?" he asks, arching a thick eyebrow and stroking his cop mustache with his free hand. He stares at the image, squinting as if he needs to put his readers on.

"This girl, her name is Megan Young. However, she looks an awful lot like Sydney Hutton, who drowned in Lake Oshwana during the upperclassman chip. I think Sydney Hutton was faking her identity. I think there's a reason she came to Blackfell High in the first place. And maybe it ties in with all of this. Somehow."

"How would it?" Fritz asks, joining Wilde and me in my driveway.

"I don't know. That's what I'm hoping you guys can figure out." My tone is a bit defensive. A bit irritated. But ever since I found out Detective Craig Fritz only wanted to be nice to me to get information about Carson Price and to blame my girls for Sydney Hutton's death, I haven't wanted to be nice to him. Not even a little bit.

"I just don't see why Sydney Hutton would have a reason to be using a fake identity." Fritz looks doubtful.

"Neither do I. But look at this photo. Does it or does it not look like her? And don't you think she looked a little old to be in high school anyway?"

"It was one of my first thoughts when I saw the picture of her at her shrine," Wilde says, looking at Fritz like this could be a real possibility.

But Fritz isn't having it. "We'll take this flyer with us. But I highly doubt this Megan Young person has anything to do with any of this."

"Promise me you at least look into it," I demand. I look at Wilde because I feel he's more trustworthy than Fritz.

"We'll look into it," Wilde says to me.

Suddenly, Fritz points his finger at me. "Look here, Mia."

"What?"

"You think that maybe Lyla just... ran away?"

"Excuse me?" I ask, thinking of how Gentry and I talked to her about sending her to a wellness spa for her mental health.

"You heard me. Let's be logical about this. Everyone at her high school recently found out that she was responsible for Trinity Cruz's death. She was probably getting bullied. She was probably getting a lot of heat. She was probably afraid to show her face back at school. Maybe, ashamed of what she had done, she fled."

I open and close my mouth repeatedly. I'm so shocked that he would even think that, that it's rendering me unable to speak. "I..."

"Just think about it. Her disappearance may not even be related to anything that had to do with the explosion outside of the Carpenter house."

"We're still doing everything we can to find her, Mrs. Bailey." Wilde puts a reassuring hand on my shoulder. I'm grateful he's here. If it were just Fritz, I probably would've gone off on him.

I nod because it's all I can do. Then the officers return to their car, and I watch them drive away.

CHAPTER 14

MADDY

I wake up and immediately shudder. I am in my bed and alone, but I'm already replaying the scenes of Craig, Steven, and me at the bar last night in my head. My head that's, by the way, pounding.

After I saw Craig at the bar, and Steven spotted me seeing Craig at the bar, Craig, who had been eyeing me down intensely, grabbed his beer, the same cold, bottled one as mine because we used to drink them together all the time back when we were dating, decided to take it upon himself and sauntered his way over to Steven and me.

My ex-boyfriend interrupted my date.

"Madeline Carpenter," Craig had said. "It's good to see you."

"I wish I could say the feeling was mutual," I had said in a feisty tone. I didn't care if it alerted Steven right away that there was bad blood between Craig and me. In fact, I wanted him to know it. I would explain it all to him later.

"Now, there's no need to be like that," Craig said. "You know I always just try to do my job. To do the right thing." Then he looked at Steven and held out his hand. "I am Detective Craig Fritz with the Toxey Police Department."

"Steven," Steven said simply, reaching out his hand and giving Craig a firm shake. I hated everything I was seeing. I wanted Craig to leave us alone. Immediately.

"Pleased to meet you," he said to Steven. Then he looked back at me. "Hey, any chance you've heard anything strange from your son lately?"

"What are you talking about?" I had snapped. "Warner's been in the hospital because of a horrible accident, and I know you know this."

"I do, I do. I also know that he left the hospital for a little bit yesterday."

"So?"

"So, it's just that... well, with that girl missing and all..."

"Aren't you off duty?" Steven asked, subtly interrupting. "I don't think Maddy, here, feels much like being questioned right now. We're just trying to enjoy ourselves after the long day we've had." He looked Craig up and down, and it made me nervous that there was about to be some massive apprehension between them. "Just like I'm sure you're trying to, too."

Instead, Craig held up his beer in surrender. Then he downed the rest of it in three major gulps. Quickly, he signaled to the bartender for another. Then he turned back to us. "You're right, you're right," he said, shaking his head. "My apologies. It's just a strange town we're living in these days. Who would've thought?"

Then he just stood there and stared at me. And Steven looked back and forth between the two of us. He looked confused. And a little heated. Especially because I stared at Craig right back, I tried to be confident and piercing with my expression. I wasn't afraid of him. But my hands were gripping my beer bottle and the underneath of my stool tightly so that neither of them could find out that they were starting to get clammy and shaky. In all reality, Craig does scare me. He scares me because of how he behaves and what he can do.

"Well, anyway," Craig finally said. He grabbed his next beer from the bartender and tilted it toward us. "You two enjoy your night. Nice to meet you, Steven." Then with one last look at me, he turned and strolled away.

I looked at Steven, mortified.

"I am so tempted to ask you what that was all about," Steven said, taking a sip of his cocktail. "But I have a feeling maybe this is just something we should get into during another date."

"I'm amazed you even want to have another date with me after that," I said. Luckily, he laughed it off and even kissed me on the cheek.

And I hoped Craig Fritz saw it.

CHAPTER 15

WARNER

I find out through social media and on a Facebook invitation that there is going to be a candlelit vigil held at the park by the high school in the early evening before the volunteer search parties begin.

I know I'm still in pain from my accident, and I know I should be resting, and I know I'm on pain medication, but nothing is going to stop me from going to it. I even take my jeep and drive with one hand since my other arm is in a brace. And I don't check with Mom to see if she needs my car to go anywhere before I do it. Nor do I ask her if she wants to come to the vigil. Nor do I ask her if she's going to be joining the search parties later tonight. I don't want to ask her anything.

Except if she knows about Dean Reeves being my father.

I am anxious that I'm going to run into my football coach and old English teacher—and supposed father—when I arrive at the park, a yellowing plot of land that consists of an ancient playground with a metal slide, a green belt, and a large shaded cement gazebo with a few picnic tables underneath it.

The sun is nearly fully set as I make my way into the gazebo, where it seems everybody is getting their candles and crowding around. More people are lingering in the green belt around the gazebo, talking with their cliques in whispers and low voices, looks of pure sadness on their faces about Lyla's disappearance. About yet another tragedy befalling their school.

First Trinity.

Then Sydney.

Now Lyla.

The first person that comes up to me before I even make it to the gazebo is Jessica Vaccari. She is a long, curly-haired brunette in my grade who always seems eager to talk to me.

"Warner, how are you doing?" she asks with a concerned expression. "Isn't this just horrible?"

"I've been better," I admit. It's hard to talk to anyone. It's hard knowing that we're all standing around chatting with each other when Lyla is out there somewhere, possibly in danger.

Scratch the "possibly" part.

She's definitely in danger—I just know it.

"I know I don't really know the girl, but I feel so bad," Jessica says. "I think I've seen you with her a few times. Are you two close?"

"I... I don't know. Kind of. She's Jackson's ex."

But that's not all she is. Especially not after the things she said to me when she visited me in the hospital after my accident.

I wish you had been the one to send that text to Jackson.

"Right." Jessica nods. "And Jackson's your best friend. Or... was?"

"That's... kind of up in the air at the moment." I like Jessica. She's a nice girl. But I really don't feel like having this conversation.

"Oh yeah, because you guys got in a fight. Anyway. I'm not trying to interrogate you. I guess I just never know how to act in these situations. I'm really sorry about your accident."

"Thanks, Jessica," I say. "One thing I know for sure—is that it was no accident." She looks like she's about to say something else to me, so I pat her on the shoulder with my uninjured hand. "I'm gonna go to get myself a candle."

She nods, gives me another pitying expression, and then I feel her eyes on me as I walk away from her.

As I go, I feel eyes on me everywhere. I feel like all the whispering and talking the cliques are doing with each other has suddenly shifted to be about me. About Lyla and me. And I think I even hear Sydney's name being mentioned.

What if they're all starting to realize it? What if everyone's beginning to have the same questions I have? What if my accident, Audrey's accident with the masked man, and Lyla's disappearance are all tied together? And what does Sydney Hutton's drowning have to do with it? How could it all be tied together?

By the time I get a candle and join people on the green belt, I stand alone, not sure who to talk to. I'm thinking about going to join some guys from the football team when a hand grabs my shoulder somewhat harshly, and I whirl around, startled. For a split second, I think it's going to be Coach Reeves behind me. But it's not. It's just Jackson.

"A little jumpy?" he asks. But there's something off about his voice. And when I take a closer look at him, I see that his brown eyes are bloodshot. I think he's been crying.

"Just thought you were someone else for a second," I say, shaking my head quickly. "Dude, are you okay?"

"I should be asking you that."

I shake my head. "I'm alive. And I'm here. That's more than Lyla can say."

He hangs his head for a moment before he speaks again. "It's messed up," he says so quietly that I barely hear him.

"I know."

"No. You don't get it." He looks at me again. "I feel sick to my stomach, Warner. I should've been there. I should've stopped it from happening. I... Do you know what people are saying?"

My stomach sinks. I don't want to know. "What?" I ask anyway.

"I'm not an idiot. And people tell me things. Word spreads fast around Toxey, you know?"

"Jackson, what's going on?"

"People are talking about me. They're saying that I might've done something to Lyla. Can you believe that?"

"You?"

He tightens his jaw and looks ready to punch something. "It's not true, dude. You know me. Everyone in school knows me. I loved Lyla. I love Lyla. I would never do anything to her. Just because I used to be her boyfriend, people think they have a reason to accuse me. When all I want is for her to come back."

"I'm... I'm sorry, Jackson." I don't know what else to say to him. Of course, people are going to think he had something to do with it.

Besides, Jackson was pretty heartbroken with the breakup. He and Lyla had been together since freshman year.

The longer I stare at him, the more I begin to wonder it myself.

Could Jackson have done something to Lyla?

CHAPTER 16

LYLA

"PLEASE! SOMEBODY HELP ME!"

I've been at this for what feels like hours. But I have no way to track the time. I pound on the door. I continue screaming. I've been switching from sobbing uncontrollably to feeling nothing but complete anger inside of me.

"LET ME OUT OF HERE!"

I'm exhausted. I need food. Water. I have to go to the bathroom. But there's nothing in here that will help me. I'm just in an old shed. There's a rusty folding table with an old plastic organizer with three drawers. One of them has old nails in it. One of them has rubber bands in it. And another one has zip ties. There's an old pair of rubber gloves on the table next to it. Then underneath the table are some dusty and damp cardboard boxes. Then there's a mostly uninflated pool floaty covered in dust in one of the corners. And next to that is an old bag of gardening soil.

I can see better now because it's still daylight outside I suppose that's the only way I will be able to track what day it is.

I just hope I'm not in here for multiple days.

I hope it doesn't come to that. I have to be let out of here.

"SOMEBODY!" I try. I hit the door again. "CAN ANYBODY HEAR ME?!"

It feels useless. And I'm just so, so tired.

I sink to the floor. Then I end up curling into the fetal position. I'm not cold; I'm just scared. I just want to be found and rescued.

"Help," I say in the most pathetic voice. No one's going to be able to hear it. But still, continuing to mutter, I drift off into my first sleep.

I sit up quickly, remembering the second I'm awake that I have been locked in a shed. That I've been kidnapped. Held against my will. I look around myself. I'm still here.

Perfect.

I try the door again, just in case this is all been some horrible prank and I've been let go. Still, it's locked. I turn about the room and reassess my situation, trying to figure out if it's the next day or if it's still the same one.

It's getting darker in here. I think the sun has set, but it's still twilight out.

My heart stops when I see new items on the rusty folding table. There are bottled waters. Bottled sports drinks. Mini bags of chips. A bag of trail mix. And a box of protein bars.

Then on the ground, slightly tucked underneath the table, there's a bright red bucket.

Whoever put me in here has no intentions of letting me out today.

In fact, I am beginning to think they don't plan on letting me out ever.

CHAPTER 17

AMELIA

Gentry keeps a close eye on Audrey during the vigil. He doesn't want her out of his sight because he doesn't want her going to talk to Warner. We have a clear view of Warner a little bit ahead of us in the crowd, more toward where the speakers are going up to say something nice about our daughter. Then, as soon as nobody's paying me any attention, I sneak out of the crowd. It's because I have a text from Maddy asking me to meet her in the parking lot behind a big black truck.

When I see her, she gives me a huge hug.

"Hey," she says.

"Hey, how's Warner?" I ask immediately. Mainly so she doesn't ask me how I'm doing. I've gotten sick of hearing that question.

She looks visibly upset. Worried. "I don't really know if I'm being completely honest with you."

"Is he here?"

"He's around here somewhere. Probably with Audrey."

I bite the inside of my cheek. "I don't know about that."

"What do you mean?"

"Gentry—now, first, let me just say that I do not agree with this—but Gentry sort of thinks that Warner should keep his distance from Audrey." I try my best to look apologetic. "He's kind of worried that Warner... has something to do with... Lyla."

"Are you serious?" she asks, visibly offended. "They're friends. Why would Warner have done anything to her? And... besides, it wouldn't even be possible. He's been in the hospital, Mia. And he's worried sick about her. I can see it all over his face. They... I think they might have a thing for each other."

"Lyla and Warner? But isn't Warner Jackson's best friend?"

"Yeah. And you know they broke up, right?"

"Yes."

"Have you talked to Jackson at all?"

"I haven't really talked to anybody," I explain. "This is... this is my first time leaving the house except when I stepped out front to do the press release. And when I went to the police station for questioning."

"Oh. I mean—Jackson is a good kid. I... I doubt he would've had anything to do with it. Right?"

A hand flies to my heart. "God, are people saying that they think he might've done something to her?"

"I don't know. I just think people like to look into the boyfriend. In more cases than not, it's usually them who did something. And maybe their breakup wasn't smooth. Maybe Jackson's really hurting over it."

I can't believe with all of the other possibilities that I hadn't even thought about this. "Oh my God."

She bites her bottom lip and looks at the ground for a moment before she continues. "But I've also been considering something else. That's why I wanted to meet up."

"Okay...?"

"I... I'm sort of thinking that with Audrey getting attacked by that man in your house, and with my car exploding outside of mine right in front of Warner, and with Lyla going missing... I sort of think that maybe it's all tied together. What are you...? What do you think?"

"I... yeah. I've been thinking the exact same thing."

"I think we should figure this out, Mia. Don't you? I think our kids are involved in something dangerous, and they're keeping secrets from us."

Our kids have been keeping secrets from us. Just like Maddy has been keeping secrets from me. And I've been keeping secrets from her. I know because Nora told me Maddy and Nora stayed in touch all those years after the Carson thing. But what Maddy told me was that she hadn't talked to her since then. Why she's lying to me about it, I have no idea. But I am not innocent either. There are things I haven't told her, too. And right now, what's going on with our kids is far more important than our friendship. I need to put the suspicious feelings I'm having about Maddy aside so we can team up and get to the bottom of this.

I smile sarcastically. "They're just like us, aren't they?"

"What are you talking about?"

"The secrets. The lies. Everything they're not telling us. It seems just like..."

"Like us?"

"Exactly."

She nods her head and agreement. "Well, in any case. We need to figure this out. Will you help me?"

"Of course, Maddy," I say. I need to start by telling her about Megan Young. But maybe I'll just leave out the part where Dean Reeves is the one who helped me get the information about her. She doesn't need to know that the two of us have been seeing each other in secret. "I'd do anything to get her back."

She tilts her head at me in sympathy. "You're an amazing mother, Mia. I know you would."

We make plans to give each other a call later on when we have time; then, I head back to my husband. The vigil has just ended, and everybody is beginning to scatter. All of the candles around us are still lit, creating the perfect glow and making me want to cry. But a vigil is not going to bring Lyla back. That's why I didn't mind sneaking out of it for a moment to talk to Maddy. At least she and I are trying to do something about it.

"Ready to go back?" Gentry asks Audrey. Then he looks at me. "Where were you?"

"What do you mean?" I ask. "I've been here the whole time."

He stares at me. Long and hard. But then he decides not to push it further. I know he doesn't believe me.

"I want to say," Audrey says. "Let me join the search party. Other kids are being a part of it."

"Absolutely not," I say. "Not a chance."

"Come on," Gentry says, steering her along back to the car. The last thing we need is Audrey going out there. With everything going on, I'm not so certain that she won't be the next one to go missing. And I can't take that risk.

CHAPTER 18

WARNER

It was hard to be sad about Lyla during the vigil. Mainly because I thought it was stupid. But also because it was being televised, and I could still feel eyes on me all around as people got up and said something about Lyla. I was too distracted to really pay attention to any of it. And I couldn't help it thinking that we should get on with starting the search party.

After it's over, everyone starts getting handed their vests and flashlights to prepare for the search. We're being divided into groups to search different parts of Toxey. I go where I'm told by the adults and stand by myself, not knowing anybody well enough in my search party group to talk to someone. I don't feel like talking anyway.

When I see Coach Reeves walking in my direction, there's no way for me to avoid it. I'm not allowed to leave my group. And I've already met his eye, so if I turn and try to walk away, I get the feeling he's only going to try harder to talk to me.

When he reaches me, I give him a hard look.

"Warner, what are you doing here?" he asks, sounding disapproving.

"I'm looking for Lyla," I say condescendingly.

"Does your mom know you're here?"

"I don't care if she does."

He stares back at me for a moment. "Are you okay?"

"What do you think?"

"I think that you're not. Maybe you shouldn't—"

"Don't try to tell me what I should or shouldn't do, Coach. I'm here to look for Lyla. And that's what I'm going to do."

No wonder we've had such a good relationship since he became my teacher. No wonder I've always felt like he favored me over the other guys. No wonder he's always trying to give me advice and steer me in the right direction. He has to know that he's my father. He has to know, and he's been lying to me my whole life about it, just like Mom has.

"Look, I know you must be worried about her," Coach continues. But all I want is for him to go away. He better not be a part of my search group.

I stay silent. So he continues.

"Do you need to talk about it? Is there anything I can do?"

"No," I snap. I'm being cold as ice with him. I know he can sense it. But yet, he is still trying with me. And I wish he would stop. "You've done more than enough."

I take my phone out and go to compose a new text to Lyla. Before I do, I glance back up at him.

"Do you mind? I have to talk to somebody."

"Okay, Warner." His voice is flat. He stands there for one extra second before he turns and leaves me.

I resume my text to Lyla.

Me: *Please just reply.*

Me: *I'm looking for you, Lyla. I promise. I won't stop looking for you until you're found.*

So maybe I've been doing this since I found out she disappeared. Maybe I've been texting her nonstop. Maybe I keep hoping I'll eventually get a response.

It makes me wonder who else is doing it. Is Audrey texting her nonstop? Where is she anyway? And is Jackson texting her? Is there a chance that Jackson could have any idea where she is? Is there a chance that he could have been so angry about the breakup that he would have done something to her?

No. There's no way. Jackson has been my best friend for years. I know him. I know he would never do something like that. He's basically the king of the school. Everyone idolizes him. His parents. His teachers. Our peers.

But still. As I look around the different groups of search parties, I try to find Jackson but don't see him anywhere. Did he leave? Did he come for the vigil but not for the search party? Maybe this is all just too hard for him.

Or maybe, just maybe, there's more to it.

Maybe whatever happened to Lyla isn't tied to anything going on with Audrey and me at all.

CHAPTER 19

MADDY

After the vigil, I'm standing around wondering if I want to be a part of the search party tonight or not. I feel like maybe I need to stay home with Warner to make sure I keep him safe. But then I realize that Warner is probably going to be out here with everybody else, looking for Lyla Bailey. There's no way I'm going to be able to drag him home.

I start looking around the different groups we're splitting up into to see if I can find my son, but while I am searching, somebody else—one who looks suspiciously like him—comes into view instead.

Dean Reeves approaches me. He looks good. And I hate it. He's the kind of teacher I would've drooled over in high school. He's the kind of guy I normally would've drooled over now, too. But he's a coward. And a liar. And I hate the fact that he exists sometimes.

He puts his hands in his pockets and, in a casual voice, says, "Hey, Mads."

"What do you want, Dean?" I hiss. I'm in no mood to talk to him. I never am. Especially now that I know he and my best friend had a secret fling while they were in college that neither of them ever told me about. I had to learn via a photo sent to me in the mail by an anonymous sender. The photo was of the two of them kissing on a beach somewhere. Neither of them knows that I know.

"I just want to know how Warner's holding up," Dean explains. "He okay?"

I scoff at him. "You know, it's crazy to me that you keep thinking it's any of your business."

"Can you please stop being this way? We've gone over this a million times. I want to help. What more do you want for me? He's going to be eighteen soon, so there's no point in going to court over it. But I'll give you money. I'll do whatever you want, Maddy. I want to be in Warner's life."

"You've already inserted yourself there when you don't even belong. I know you visited him at the hospital. You don't have any right, Dean." My arms are crossed. I want him to know how much he screwed me over. How much he hurt me way back then when he abandoned Warner and me.

"I think you and I both know that's not true," he says.

"God, give it up, will you?"

"Look, I'm just worried about him. I just tried speaking to him and—"

"What do you mean you just tried speaking to him?" I ask, my tone of voice rising. "Can't you get it through your head? Stay away from my son!"

He steps toward me. "Maddy, lower your voice."

"You're relentless!"

"And I'll continue to be. But as I was saying, if you'll just listen to me for five seconds—"

"Why don't you go find Mia? I'm sure she'll listen to you."

He tilts his head back. "What's that supposed to mean?"

"Oh, like you really don't know." Maybe I'm being passive-aggressive. Maybe I sort of want him to know that I figured it out.

"I don't, actually," he says, looking genuinely confused and slightly guilty. But maybe I'm just seeing what I want to see. "Mia? Why are you bringing her up all of a sudden?"

"Never mind."

He narrows his eyes at me for a moment, and he shakes his head quickly. "Just listen to me, okay? I'm worried about Warner. Not just because of his accident. He's in a seriously bad mood. I think something's going on with him that he's not talking to us about."

"Like what?"

"Like... I don't know. Something to do with everything that's been happening? Something to do with Sydney Hutton?"

"What are you saying?" I'm actually shocked. Shocked by what he is insinuating.

"I'm just saying that I'm worried. That's all."

"I don't believe you, Dean," I say; my voice is low and dangerous. "If you have something to say about what you think my son may or may not have done, then say it."

"Maddy..."

I decide to hold up my hand to put a stop to it. "You know what? No. I'm not doing this right now." I can't do this right now. There's no way. So I turn sharply and start walking away from him. If I have to leave the search party to get my escape, so be it.

"Can you just wait a minute?!" he calls after me. But I don't turn back around.

CHAPTER 20

Audrey

I'm furious that I can't go to the search party.

"I just don't get why I can't help!" I complain to Mom and Dad at home. "I'll stay where you can see me. I won't leave your side. I just want to help find my sister."

"It's just not safe, okay?" Dad says. He and Mom are lingering in the mud room, ready to get back out there so they can look for Lyla. It's not fair.

"Besides, Officer Wilde and Detective Fritz want someone to stay here in case Lyla comes back home," Mom reminds me. "We don't want her coming home to an empty house."

I roll my eyes and let out a little growl. "She's not going to come back. Let me just help!"

"Audrey." Mom is using her stern voice. It's the most like herself. I've heard her sound since Lyla first disappeared. "End of discussion."

Standing in the middle of the kitchen, I cross my arms and look away from them, glare on my face. This is ridiculous. My twin sister is out there, and I'm not allowed to look for her?

Dad sighs. "Make sure Joey is okay and that he gets to bed at a decent time tonight."

"Whatever." I'm still not looking at them.

"I'm sorry, Audrey," he says. Mom says nothing.

"Kay."

They glance at each other, looking like they hate being the bad guys, then go into the garage.

I go upstairs and see what Joey is doing. He is watching YouTube videos in bed. He wasn't allowed to come to the vigil because Mom and Dad didn't think he needed to be in such a sad atmosphere. He's been pouting ever since.

I explain to him that I just came to check on him and that I'm going to be gone for just a little bit longer; then I grab my car keys and go into the garage as well. I wait until I know my parents are a safe enough distance away, then I back out of the garage and drive back to the park where the search party is starting. Instead of staying in my parents' eyesight, I'm going to have to try my hardest not to be spotted by them, but they made it this way. It could've been so much easier. And safer. But so be it. Nothing will stop me from looking for my sister.

I get to the park, quickly jump out of the car, and jog to grab a vest and a flashlight and join a group. Already I can see some of the groups starting to walk off in different directions, the search officially beginning. As I'm putting my vest on, I hear somebody yelling.

"There she is!"

It's Danielle's voice—one of three of my "supposedly" best friends.

"Audrey!" Sophia calls. I'm mostly mad at her. Rumors went around the school that I was hanging out with her crush, Bryson Anthony. It was all lies, of course, but she chose to believe the rumors. And Danielle and Olive stayed by her side. Then Sophia had to take it one step further and went after the guy I had a major crush on, the hottest senior in the school Ryan Copeland.

"We've been so worried about you," Olive says as the three finally reach me together. As usual, they look all glammed up for the occasion of searching for my lost sister. It seems inappropriate.

Sophia is the first to throw her arms around me in a tight embrace. Then Olive and Danielle follow suit, and suddenly, we're in a large group hug. When they pull away, they all have different looks of worry and sadness.

"Poor Lyla!" Danielle says. She's always been the more overly emotional and empathetic one with people, and she genuinely wears her heart on her sleeve. She's usually one of the nicest people in our school, and it leads some people to believe that she's fake. Only because she's so popular.

Beside her, Sophia tosses her blonde and brown hair over her shoulder dramatically, like she thinks people are watching her and is trying to look her hottest. "I can't believe this is happening," she says.

"Do you have any idea where she went?" Olive asks, her short auburn hair in the same ponytail as Danielle's. She stands there, nearly a foot shorter than Sophia, and stares at me with her questioning hazel eyes. Standing on either side of Sophia, Olive and Danielle look like her matching little minions. "Do you know if she ran away?"

"You can tell us," Sophia says. "We won't tell a soul. We are besties."

"And I was mad at her about the Trinity thing," Danielle adds, "but now I don't care. I'm over all of that. It was just an accident, and I just want her back."

I can't even believe what I'm hearing.

No, actually. That's not true.

I can believe it. In fact, I'm surprised I didn't expect it. Of course, they would act like this.

I have to stand up for myself. I'm sick of them. I'm more than sick of them. I'm over them.

"Did you guys forget everything that happened between us?" I ask, crossing my arms and raising an eyebrow, trying my best to look bratty.

"What are you talking about?" Olive asks.

"Are you talking about that thing with Ryan?" Sophia joins in. "Look. I'm over it. And I don't even care about you hanging out with Bryson. If that was even true. I'm over all of it. I just wanna be there for you through all of this. I feel horrible." She reaches her arm out like she wants to take my hand or touch my shoulder comfortingly, but I back away.

"No. You know what I think?" I ask.

"Audrey, come on," Danielle says. It's clear she doesn't want us to fight like this right now.

But I stare at each of them in turn as I speak. "I think you're all horrible friends."

"What? Why?" Sophia asks. She looks completely shocked. It makes me roll my eyes.

"What do you mean why? Are you kidding me? You guys don't trust me. You guys are always looking for an excuse to be mad at me. I always feel like I'm seconds away from being dropped by you guys, and then I did get dropped by you. But now that this exciting thing has happened and Lyla is missing, you're all over me again! You're all a bunch of fakes. Phonies. You just want in on the gossip. That's all it's ever been about. You're not there for me because you genuinely want to be."

"That's really not true," Danielle tries.

"Yeah. I can't believe you would even say that," Sophia adds. Of course, she would try and turn herself into the victim in this.

"Whatever." I'm so completely, totally done with them. "I gotta go."

CHAPTER 21

WARNER

Audrey, quickly tugging on her vest and checking to see if her flashlight works, jogs over toward the group I'm in.

"Audrey!" I call out to her. She makes her way over to me.

"Hey, Warner."

A person blows their whistle and says it's time to start the search. Our group begins walking together, heading north. There's an east, south, and west group as well.

"Hey, wanna search together?" I ask her casually.

"Sure."

"You okay?" I immediately want to hit myself after I say it. So I try and correct it. "I mean—of course, you're not. How... how are you doing?"

She doesn't look at me as we walk. But why would she? We are looking for her sister.

Lyla, where are you?

"I don't know," she says. "I'm not supposed to be here."

"What do you mean?"

"Mom and Dad didn't want me to come. I had to sneak out. So I can't be seen by them."

"Oh. Gotcha."

We enter a patch of woods. It's pitch black, but I can see a lot with everyone stretched out in a line with their flashlights out. Everyone is calling out, "Lyla!" at different times. There are a lot of trees and thick shrubbery in these woods, but I try to stay close to Audrey. I don't want to lose sight of her. If her parents didn't want her out searching for Lyla, there's probably a good reason. So I feel extra responsible for making sure she stays safe.

"Do you think we'll find her?" Audrey asks after a bit of silence.

"Of course I do," I say. "We have to."

"Yeah."

Then we're silent some more as we listen to some people continue to call Lyla's name out.

We keep walking.

"I know she's not dead," Audrey eventually continues. She shines her flashlight around, staring hard into where it shines.

"You do? Have you talked to her?" A bit of hope rushes through me. Maybe Audrey's been keeping it from me because she hasn't had a chance to tell me about it yet. Maybe she and Lyla have been in contact this whole time.

"No," she answers, making my heart fall. "But I would just know if she was. It's a twin thing. It's hard to explain."

I nod my head and continue searching. "I just wish I knew where she was," I say. "Or If she was okay. If she was kidnapped, or if she ran away."

"You and me both."

I think back to my conversation with my former best friend. Audrey should hear about it. "I, uh, had a weird conversation with Jackson earlier."

"Oh yeah?"

"Yeah... He said everyone's talking and that they think he has something to do with her going missing. He seemed really beat up about it. But I don't know. What do you think?"

She shrugs, not looking too surprised. "I guess from what I've seen in movies; it's usually the boyfriend behind it." Then she stops walking suddenly. "Wait a minute."

Looking back at her, I stumble over a tree root and nearly fall to my knees, but luckily I catch myself.

"I just remembered something," she says. "I saw Jackson outside my house when Lyla first went missing. When there were all the news vans outside and the neighbors gathering around. He was in a car. He was driving a car."

"What kind of car?" I ask, my eyebrows crinkling.

"Like an old gray Mustang. I think."

"But... that doesn't make any sense. I don't even think he has his license. And I live right next door to him, and I haven't seen an old gray Mustang outside of his house."

She continues walking, so I continue as well. "Yeah," she says quickly. "The day was a blur. Maybe I didn't actually see it at all. But it looked like him. And wouldn't it be kind of strange for him to just be slowly driving by? I don't know."

"It is kind of weird."

We continue searching, the both of us falling silent. But then I think of something.

"Hey. Speaking of weird things. I saw something crazy the other night. I don't even know what to make of it. I—"

"Hold it right there, Audrey Nicole Bailey."

Audrey and I jump and turn around at the same time. Shining a flashlight on us is Audrey's mother, Amelia.

So much for staying hidden.

"Crap," Audrey groans under her breath. Then she gives Amelia a fake grin. "Uh, hi, Mom."

CHAPTER 22

MADDY

I end up joining the search party after all. I just stay in a separate group from Dean Reeves. I need to keep him as far away from me as possible. And if it weren't for the fact that Amelia and I need to put our heads together to figure out what is going on with our children, I would probably want to stay far away from her, too. How could she have a thing with Dean and never tell me about it? I didn't even know they ever felt anything for each other. Amelia was always telling me when we were little that she would never go for Dean because she knew her sister had such a big crush on him. She didn't want to break her sister's heart like that. So she decides to do it anyway, while her sister is in a mental institution, for goodness sake?

I just don't get her.

I walk with a group through the woods even though I desperately didn't want to go this way. I wanted to go in the direction of the cornfields or through the neighborhoods. The woods just spook me. Ever since the Carson thing, I've found that I hate being in them. It was hard enough being in the same woods as where Carson died during the upperclassmen camping trip.

Still, I want to find Lyla.

As I shine my flashlight about and call Lyla's name, I think about Warner still. But when am I not thinking about my son? When am I not trying to make sure that he's okay? When am I not trying to think of how I can make things better between us? It's just that with his accident, with Audrey's accident, with Lyla disappearing—all of this bad stuff started happening after Sydney Hutton died. Maybe there's more to her death that I don't know. Maybe there's stuff the police are withholding. Maybe all of this is related to what happened with Sydney. Maybe it's all related to what Jackson told me. Back in the hospital after Warner had been in his accident. He had expressed to me that Warner explicitly told him during the upperclassman trip that he wished Sydney was dead. And he got his wish.

But at what cost?

I'm so distracted thinking about it all that when I look up again, I realize I'm nowhere near the rest of the group. I've gone off the beaten path, and I am alone. I can still hear the faded voices of people calling out Lyla's name. They sound so far away.

How did I get this far out here without even noticing? It's like I lost a whole chunk of time. I don't have any memory of separating myself from them.

I stop walking. A twig cracks behind me, and I spin around, my heart catching in my throat. I shine my flashlight through the trees, terrified of what I'm going to see, but I find nothing.

I try to turn back around and follow the sound of the other volunteers' voices. When I hear another sound of a branch cracking behind me, I turn back around with my flashlight. Still, I see nothing. But I feel even more afraid. I feel like somebody is following me.

How absurd is that?

Even though I'm just walking—at a slightly quicker pace than usual—my heart is pounding, and I feel out of breath. The corners of my vision are blurring. I think I feel a panic attack coming on. I hate being out here like this. I hate the feeling like I'm being followed.

When I find a hollow log slightly covered in moss, I sit down on it and jiggle my legs anxiously, thinking and trying to catch my breath for a moment. For some reason, being out here in the woods takes me back to the night Mia and I killed Carson. How we saw his dead body, not moving when we pulled him out of the pool. And how Nora found it. Yet, his body was never found. But how could that be? Three people are absolutely positive that Carson Price died.

I shiver violently and get back to my feet, not liking the sudden thought I'm having inside my head.

Because it would be just completely crazy if Carson were still out there somewhere. Right?

CHAPTER 23

Audrey

"What if something had happened to you?" Mom asks when we get home.

"And what if something had happened to Joey?" Dad adds. "You left him here alone. After somebody recently broke in here and attacked you?"

"How could you be so irresponsible?" Mom looks on the verge of losing it.

"You guys can't tell me I can't look for my sister," I fire back. I'm not taking this. I don't regret going out there and trying to look for her. I won't ever regret it.

"I know you want to find Lyla, Audrey," Dad says. "We all do. But there are so many people out there looking for her. We're going to find her. But we don't want to have to be worrying about you, too. Okay?"

"Whatever. I'm tired. I'm going to bed."

"That's probably a good idea," Mom says shortly.

I give them a dirty look and then stomp up the staircase. I go straight to my room, shut the door, and lock it, but I don't go to bed. Instead, I call Jackson. I have to talk to him about what he told Warner tonight. I want to hear his side of things. I also want to hear him say he wasn't outside my house during the press release, and I want him to say that he doesn't have anything to do with Lyla's disappearance. I want to hear it with my own ears so I can gauge if I believe him or not.

But of course, Jackson doesn't answer. I know he can't be asleep. I know he's still at the search party or at home, either feeling sad about what happened to his ex-girlfriend or working on covering up the fact that he's done something terrible.

I don't want to think that, of course. Jackson, responsible for all this? After he was with Lyla for so long? After he made our family like him and after we let him into our home? After I told Lyla, I didn't think it was a good idea for her to break up with him because I thought they were good together. I cringe, thinking back to it now. If it's true, if Jackson is behind all of this, and I was sitting there telling Lyla to stay with Jackson when she was in a secretly terrifying, abusive relationship, I would hate myself.

I hope he calls me back. Or sends me a text message. I want to know exactly what people are saying and if the police have even talked to him.

I need to know everything.

CHAPTER 24

WARNER

Lyla's Third Day Missing

I get to school in a foul mood because I hate that life continues spinning on when Lyla hasn't been found. I hate that last night we were unsuccessful in our search for her. And I hate that I feel so confused and scared.

Not to mention I'm still in a butt load of pain from my accident. But anything beats being at home. I have to keep my mind moving.

After Mom embarrassingly drops me off in the back of the student parking lot since she needs my car to get to work, I head towards the front entrance and notice how miserable everyone seems. We're all upset that Lyla hasn't been found. That we've all returned to school without her.

First Trinity.

Then Sydney.

Now Lyla.

I get to the bottom of the steps when Wrigley Hall, a boy in Lyla's grade who's always throwing parties, who I don't know too well, stops me from getting to the door. I give him a weird look and almost tell him to get out of my way since I'm not in the mood.

"Hey." Wrigley is wearing all black, and his long curly hair looks larger than it normally is in the breeze we have today.

"Uh... what's up?" I ask.

"Have you seen Audrey?"

"Audrey? No, why?"

"I've just been looking for her and can't find her anywhere. And you guys are friends, right?"

"Yeah. We are." I think it's weird that we're even having this conversation because Wrigley and I don't really talk. And I don't know what it is about him. I don't like him.

"Well, thanks anyway." Wrigley turns to leave.

"Why are you looking for Audrey?" I ask.

He turns back around. "I just wanted to talk to her about something."

"About Lyla?" I've seen Wrigley and Lyla together. Lyla has never told me they're friends, but I get the feeling that Wrigley might have some sort of feelings for her.

"Um, yeah." He hangs his head slightly and looks seriously bummed out.

"What exactly is going on between you and her?" I ask. I make sure to talk in the present tense because if I used the past tense, it would make it feel like Lyla was no longer here with us. But she has to be.

"What do you mean?" he asks, suddenly talking quicker. "She's... my friend. Anyway. I gotta run."

He turns and walks away.

Instead of heading inside like I had been planning on before he interrupted me, I stand there with an uncomfortable feeling in my stomach.

The next thing I know, Wrigley pushes the door back open and walks back over to me.

What does he want now?

"Hey, did you know our parents are dating?" he quickly asks.

"What?" I can't have heard him correctly.

"Yeah. Uh, I guess you didn't. My dad and your mom have been seeing each other. Anyway. See you around."

As he walks away again, I stand there speechless, my mouth going completely dry.

This can't be happening.

CHAPTER 25

Lyla

I know I've been groggy and in and out of uncomfortable sleep, but I am getting the sense of whether it's day or night based on the tiny crack in one of the wooden slats of the walls of my prison. From what I think—although I don't know for certain—I'm on the third day. So, I've carved three tallies on the wall with an old nail. I don't want to lose track of how much time I've spent in here. I don't want all the days to start blending. I want to know exactly how long I've been gone and exactly what might be at stake.

Three days is far too long.

I need to get out of here. Today.

No more screaming and crying for help. It's clear that nobody is going to come to rescue me. I have to get out of here myself. I just can't think of a very good idea of how to do so.

But thinking about what happened to me, it makes me mad. It fills me with a wild rage. It sets my bones on fire. If anything, I want to get out even more so I can figure out where I am and who put me here. So, I can finally put an end to all of this and go to the police.

I can do this. I have to do this.

I need to save myself.

I take a look at the door of this entrapment. Then, without even giving it a second thought, I fling my body at it. I use all my force and muscle. It's painful when I slam against it and recoil ungracefully onto the floor. My shoulder is immediately throbbing, and my kneecap stings. I look down and see that I've scuffed it.

But I don't let it stop me.

I get up, brush myself off, and do it again.

And again.

And again.

Until I am a beaten, bloody mess on the floor, I try breaking myself through that door.

But it's impossible. It must be reinforced from the outside somehow.

I'm never going to get out of here.

I wonder if this is my karma. If this is what I get for killing Trinity. For killing Sydney. I know I didn't outright do it, but I might as well have. I feel responsible. I am responsible. I could've stopped both deaths from happening.

I should have gone to Sydney when she asked me to. During the upperclassmen camping trip.

I should've never been texting Wrigley while driving. Heck, I should've never been texting him at all. It wasn't like I was cheating on Jackson with him or anything, but he had just weirdly become a good, sort of secret friend of mine. It was refreshing and new, and it made me distracted. It made me stupid.

I think back to when he first started texting me.

Unknown: Hey, Lyla.
Me: Who is this?
Unknown: *Wrigley from bio.*
Me: *Oh. Random. How did you get my number?*
Wrigley: *Austin Booth.*
Me: *Oh. What's up?*
Wrigley: *You always seem to be killing it in bio. I was wondering if I could get some help with tonight's homework. I don't want to cheat or anything. I was just hoping to ask you some questions about stuff I'm confused about. Lol.*
Me: *Sure!*

Then he really did just that—he asked me for help with his biology homework. But it was after he got all the help he needed that I was surprised.

Wrigley: *So, what are you doing with the rest of your night?*
Me: *Scrolling aimlessly through TikTok, probably. Why?*
Wrigley: *That sounds pretty pitiful.*

Lyla: *High school is exhausting. Sometimes this is all I have the energy to do when I get home.*

Wrigley: *Really? I'm surprised. You make being popular look so easy.*

Me: *I'm not popular.*

Wrigley: *I beg to differ.*

Me: *That's my sister. Everyone just ties me in with her. I know you don't know either of us that well, but we're not that similar.*

Wrigley: *I never thought you were.*

It had been that last text that intrigued me. Somebody who didn't think I was like my sister? Could it be true? As far as I knew, Jackson was the only other person who ever differentiated us. So, interested in talking to Wrigley more, I continued to reply to him. And he continued to reply to me. And then, eventually, he added me on Snapchat. And our texting conversation moved over to there, where we sent random selfies and pictures of parts of our bedroom while writing messages about anything and everything. Before I knew it, Wrigley had become a friend of mine.

And then, recently, he maybe became somewhat more than that.

But now I wonder if I'll ever see him again.

CHAPTER 26

AMELIA

I am leaving my house this morning. As much as I don't want to... as much as I want to be home in case my daughter shows back up miraculously—I'm doing it so I can get away from Gentry.

I didn't get ready again today, so I know the ladies at the office are going to be shocked to see me. But then again, maybe they won't be. How do they expect me to be? How would they act if their daughter had gone missing?

Missing for three days.

Think positive, Mia.

Deep breaths, Mia.

They're going to find her, Mia.

I keep telling myself things as I drive, and when I get to my office, I wave hi to Ivy, my intern, and receptionist. The other ladies are in their separate office spaces working, and I call hi to them but hurry into my office where they can't see me. Then I plop down at my desk and stare at my computer screen, which is already opened to my emails from the last time I was in here.

I take a deep breath and compose the email I should've composed days ago. It's one I'm sending out to all of my clients:

Good Morning,

I don't know if you have heard, but recently, my 17-year-old daughter, Lyla Bailey, has disappeared. There are still great efforts being performed in searching for her, and I am taking a great part in it and doing everything I can to get her back. As you can probably imagine, this is taking up most of my time, and therefore I will need to be pausing all current contracts and correspondence. And unfortunately, this is until further notice.

If any clients are really that frustrated at my need to take a break, then I'm sure I can have one of the other office girls take over for me. But I have a pretty good repertoire with my clients, and they will all understand.

Hopefully.

After the messages send, I rearrange the papers around my desk and try to make myself look busy. I just want to do things to try to keep moving—so that I'm not checking my phone every ten seconds to see if there's an update from the police yet, who are out there still searching. More search parties are gathering today as well, and I will probably be joining in later.

As I'm giving up trying to be productive for the day, my business phone rings.

"Amelia Bailey Designs," I say when I answer. My tone is flat. Devoid of any life.

"Amelia, this is Rebecca Barton."

"Oh, hi, Rebecca." Rebecca is one of my clients. A brand new one whom, until Lyla went missing, I was very eager to work with. Now I could care less.

"I just saw your message, and I've been meaning to call you anyway. I know it's bad timing, but listen, there's been a change of plans."

My heart skips a beat.

"What do you mean?" I ask.

"Don't take this the wrong way, Amelia, but Bryan and I will no longer be needing your services."

"I—I don't understand," I say. "I will be back to work soon; I just need to take a little pause. If it's really an inconvenience, I can pass your work to one of my junior designers—"

"It's not that," she says quickly. Then she clears her throat as if she's uncomfortable. "It's that we've heard about the reason why Trinity Cruz died in that car crash. That it wasn't necessarily the drunk driver's fault, but that it was because your daughter was texting and driving."

"Oh, I..." I don't even know what to say. I can't believe this is happening. I can't believe something my daughter did is a reason why my clients no longer want to work with me.

"I'm sorry, it's just that we really just don't want to be associated with that right now. We have kids of our own, and... it just doesn't look good. I hope you can understand."

"Sure," I say, my voice hoarse. "I understand."

CHAPTER 27

WARNER

During lunch, Jessica Vaccari, a girl in my grade, comes up to me at the back of the line. When I turn around and see her, her dark brown eyes are huge.

"Oh, hi, Jessica," I say, somewhat startled at seeing her there all of a sudden.

"Hey, Warner," she says with a sad voice. "How are you doing?"

"I'm fine," I say. The line slowly moves. "Have you been?"

At the beginning of the school year, I remember Jackson telling me that Jessica Vaccari was into me. We don't talk all that much, but I do catch her looking at me a lot, and I get the feeling that it's true.

"Who cares about me?" she asks, stepping closer to me. "You've been going through a lot lately. First your fight with Jackson, then your accident, and then I heard that Lyla was a friend of yours... or something."

"Yeah. It's... it's rough."

"Hey, if you need somebody to talk to, I'm always here. You follow me on Insta, right? You should message me sometime."

It's now my turn to order. "Yeah," I say to her, just wanting to be polite. But then I think about how I just wanted to be polite to Sydney.

Look where that got me.

Still, I get the feeling that Jessica is harmless.

"Yeah, I will," I say.

She gives me one last long smile, flips her curly brown hair over her shoulder, and then I turn around and place my order.

I wave at her when I walk away, but upon walking away, I run right into Jackson, nearly spilling my tray of lunch on him.

"Dude," he says, slapping me on the back. "I totally saw that. You and Jessica."

"Oh. She was just checking in."

"Let's sit together."

I didn't know we were back to that part of our friendship where we were sitting at the same table. And I notice as I look around that people are definitely staring at us. Have Jackson and I really resolved all of our issues?

I follow him to our table anyway and sit across from him.

"So, you should go for her," Jackson says about Jessica, just like he did at the beginning of the year.

"I don't know," I say. I want to tell him there's no way because I'm crazy about his ex-girlfriend, but I know that that would just add to our problems. Especially when I had already told him nothing would ever happen between her and me.

"Why don't you know?" Jackson asks. "She's hot. And she's totally into you."

"I just don't know if I am really looking to date anyone right now. I have a lot going on."

"Fine."

I go to eat some of my food. But then he speaks again.

"What about Audrey, though?"

"What about her?" I ask, my pulse quickening.

"I feel like I've been seeing you two together more lately. Would you ever go for her?"

"I..." I trail off, trying to think about this carefully. If I don't seem interested in anybody, it might lead to more suspicion about who I really am interested in. "I don't know."

He smirks at me and then dives into his burrito.

I finish my lunch early and make some excuse about how I have to finish homework that was late for economics—the last class I had where Jessica, who sat behind me, was looking in my direction every time I turned around to grab something out of my backpack.

But as I'm in the empty hallway, I round the corner and see Detective Craig Fritz heading towards the exit doors of the school.

"Hey, wait up a minute!" I call without pausing to consider why I'm wanting to talk to him. He's the one who told me that Dean Reeves is my father. Without him, it would've stayed a secret. I don't really know how I feel about it. Typically, I detest him.

Craig slowly turns around and gets a sinister smile when he realizes it's me approaching him.

"What can I do for you, Mr. Carpenter? Or is that not the last name you want to use any more?"

"I would never take any other name," I say boldly. Sure, I may not like my mother that much right now, but I won't let Detective Fritz have the satisfaction.

"Fair enough. It's your own decision."

"What are you doing here?" I say coldly.

He takes a swig from the water bottle in his hand and then replaces the plastic cap on it. "Just taking care of business."

Something seems off about him. But I don't have time to care about that right now. I need to get answers.

"The other night, I saw you talking to Nora Flynn," I say. "What were you doing meeting with her in the middle of nowhere like that?"

"You've been following me, I see."

"Just answer the question."

It takes him a moment. "It just so happens that I ran into her there. And I've been meaning to ask her some questions, but she hasn't been willing to talk to me. So I finally got to ask her some."

"Right. You just 'ran into her' at an abandoned train station. What do you want with her?"

"Warner, I hate to tell you this, but it's better that you mind your own business right now, especially because there's some bad news coming your way, so you should probably focus more on that."

I shoot him a glare. "What are you talking about?" This is just one of his stupid tactics. Some baloney he's making up to try to scare me or get a rise out of me.

He looks me dead in the eye when he speaks. "Just keep your ears open. Because what you are about to find out... it doesn't look good for you."

AUDREY

Everybody went back to school today. Everybody except for me. I stayed home, rifled through the snack pantry, and curled up in a ball on the sectional. It's only my first day staying home from school, and I already went stir-crazy earlier and wandered into the backyard just to get a little sunshine before the clouds rolled in. It started getting windy—it had only been around seven in the morning.

When there's a knock on my door sometime in the afternoon, my ears perk up, and my heart immediately begins pounding in my chest. I feel like the only people who would be knocking are the police or my sister.

Being the only one home, I run over to the door in my socks and skid along the tile the last few steps until I'm at the door. I throw it open without even checking the peephole first.

I'm more than a little surprised to see who is standing on my doorstep.

It's Wrigley Hall.

"Um, can I help you?" I ask. I've gotten the vibe that he and Lyla have some sort of friendship. Maybe more. Definitely more, considering the fact that everyone's saying she had been texting him when she got in her car accident that killed Trinity. But she hasn't told me anything about him. So, as far as I know, he's a stranger to me. We don't have any classes together. I go to his parties, but I never get a direct invite. It's always from somebody else.

Wrigley is classified as the school bad boy, which is weird because I've never actually seen him get into trouble. He just throws his parties, dresses in his moody clothing, and keeps to himself.

"Hey, Audrey," he says in a light tone. Like it's just any other day that he'd be coming over here. Like he does it all the time. "Do you think maybe I could come in?"

I think about how I'm the only one home again. Joey is at school because even though Mom and Dad want me to stay home, they think school will be a safer environment for Joey. I don't know Wrigley at all. And I don't know what kind of relationship he had with Lyla.

So that means I can't trust him.

"Sorry, but no. My parents won't let me have anyone over without them home."

Should I have said that? Should I have let him know that nobody is home?

"They'll be back soon, though," I say to try to correct myself.

"Oh. I just wanted to talk to you about Lyla for a second. It won't take long."

"What do you want to know about my sister?" I ask cautiously.

He sticks his hand in his pockets. "Look. I'll be blunt about it. I sort of have feelings for Lyla. I have for a while. So the fact that she's suddenly disappeared has me going kind of crazy. Crazy enough where I'm standing on your doorstep admitting this to you right now."

I wonder why Lyla never told me. Or maybe she doesn't know.

"I didn't know," I say.

"That's okay. It's not like I ever told her or anything. I just... I'm feeling horrible right now. Everyone is saying that it's her fault that Trinity died. But I feel like it's all my fault."

I would not have expected this type of sensitivity to come from Wrigley Hall. I would have expected him to be the type to say he didn't care what people thought. But he does look pretty upset. It surprises me.

"It was a drunk driver who hit her car, ultimately. Nobody knows exactly what really went down at night. Try not to blame yourself."

He nods his head grimly. "It's just that now she's gone, and I just don't understand it. After my party, when somebody played that recording of a girl screaming... somebody was definitely messing with her. And I know somebody was messing with you. You were attacked in your own house. Do you have any idea who did it?"

So, he's caught on.

"No. I wish I did."

"I'm sorry. You don't think she ran away, right? Do you think whoever is messing with you guys did this to her?"

"I don't think she ran away." I can't bring myself to say she was kidnapped by a vile man.

If my sister had been texting Wrigley during the accident, who knows how long they had been texting. Why they had been texting? Yes, Lyla had been dating Jackson during the time of her accident, but what if she and Wrigley had had a secret fling?

What if all this time, the reason Lyla has wanted to break up with Jackson wasn't for the fact that she feels too different now? Or the fact that she likes Warner. Maybe all this time, she's always been into Wrigley.

"Well, you know she and Jackson broke up, right?" I ask, thinking about how Jackson never returned my last call.

"Yeah," he says.

"I... I'll tell you this: I'm worried he is somehow involved in it all."

"You do?" he asks. Then his jaw tenses. "Whatever is going on, I want to help. I want to get her back."

CHAPTER 29

Amelia

When I head out to the police station to check on their efforts since I haven't received an adequate amount of updates, I walk outside my office and see Dean Reeves getting out of his vehicle.

I am stunned to see him standing before me. As far as I knew, Dean and I were no longer speaking to each other. Our last interaction had been an uncomfortable one. I had sort of put myself out there, telling him I enjoyed spending time with him. And then he got angry, telling me he knew I was flirting with him.

You know how I feel about you.

He had told me he didn't think we should be meeting up anymore.

And yet, somehow, here he is.

He takes one look at me, and I simply melt. I race to his arms and fall into them. He holds me tightly, and tears instantly begin streaming down my cheeks.

"I just want her back," I say.

"Mia, I'm so sorry," he breathes into my hair. It feels so good to be held like this. Held by somebody who genuinely, truly cares for me.

I don't even care if my receptionist can see us out here through the window.

I don't know how long we stay like that before I finally back away from him. I wipe my eyes, feeling slightly self-conscious about how un-together I look in front of him.

"I'm sorry for how everything went down in our last conversation. I didn't mean for that to happen." Dean looks deeply worried for me. I've known him for over thirty years, and I've never seen him give me a look like this.

"Don't even worry about it," I say, shaking my head.

"But I am. Look, with Lyla. I want to do anything I can to help you get her back. And I mean it. I want to help you in any way I can."

"Are you sure?" I ask. I don't want to put him in any position that will make him uncomfortable. Truth be told, I did know that he was in love with me. But I only found out recently. Back when Nora gave me a letter, he wrote her while she was staying in a mental institution, where he confessed his love for me to her. But that had been back when we were kids. So when he told me the other day that I shouldn't be flirting with him when I know he has feelings for me, it came as a total shock.

Fine. I've seen the way he looks at me.

Maybe it wasn't a total shock.

But still, I never expected him to admit it.

"Of course, I'm sure," he says. "Just tell me what I can do."

"Well, to start, I should probably fill you in on everything that has happened since we last talked."

"Please do."

So filling him in is exactly what I end up doing.

CHAPTER 30

MADDY

You know those days in history where you'll never forget where you were when it went down? Days like when the twin towers collapsed?

I am currently having one of those days.

At exactly 2:33 p.m. I ask my coworker, Mariah, to turn up the volume on the TV in the waiting area of the hair salon where I work. The news is on, and the image on the screen is of Sydney Hutton. The headline?

Cause of Death of Teen Girl Found in Lake Determined During Autopsy.

"You okay?" Mariah asks me.

"Shh!" I hiss, wanting to hear the news anchor on the screen.

The woman on TV is wearing a black and navy blue pantsuit as she speaks with a very straight expression. "It was initially determined that the cause of death of Sydney Hutton, the seventeen-year-old high school student at Blackfell High here in Toxey, was accidental drowning in Lake Oshwana during their upperclassmen camping trip. However, new test results report that that information had been incorrect. As of today, it's been officially released that Sydney Hutton's actual cause of death was blunt force trauma. This means that her death was in no way an accident at all, but more than likely, a case of murder."

I don't hear anything else after that because the news anchor suddenly sounds far away, and the lights in the salon overhead are suddenly way too bright. Then it begins feeling like my heart is pounding too hard. So hard that it's going to explode right out of my chest. I can't breathe. My lungs are constricting. I'm getting no airflow.

I hear the muffled sound of somebody calling my name, but I'm already sinking to the floor. Around me, I can sense that people are beginning to crowd me, but there's nothing I can do to tell them to go away. I can't breathe, let alone speak.

I'm having a panic attack.

Rochelle, my other coworker, seems to be the only one who realizes, and she picks me up, scoops her arm under me, and drags me outside into the fresh air. Then she hands me the fast-food bag she had her lunch from and tells me to breathe into it. I do so, although I've never done this tactic before. Does it really work?

At first, when I stick my face into the bag, I make the mistake of inhaling deeply. I almost throw up from the smell of grease and onions. But I try again and eventually I develop a rhythm of breathing in and out. After about ten minutes, I realize that it really does work. My breathing has slowly returned to normal.

"Feeling better?" Rochelle asks me. I like Rochelle. She's one of my favorite coworkers. But I have a hard time trusting other people. So I don't want to explain to her exactly what's going through my head right now.

"I need to go home," I say.

She nods her head sympathetically. "I understand. You go. I'll cover for you."

I hug her, and she tells me to wait here while she gets my stuff for me from inside.

When I get into my car, I go to Warner's name in my phone and give him a call.

I'm thinking about what Jackson told me when I ran into him at the hospital while he was visiting Warner.

He told me that he wished Sydney was dead.

I think my son might've gone to the lengths to make sure his wish came true.

CHAPTER 31

WARNER

Because of my injuries, I have to sit out during football practice. It's a bummer, and I keep thinking that any day now, my position as football captain is going to be stripped from me. I have too much going on. I'm not focused enough. I'm especially not focused now that Lyla is missing. Even though I just told my "coach" that I promise to pay more attention and be more involved. But that had also been before I figured out he was my father.

I can't stop staring at Dean Reeves as the practice goes on. He side-glances at me a lot, and it makes me wonder if he can tell what I'm thinking. If he has any idea that I might know the truth. In fact, the more I watch him, the more I'm certain that he does know the truth. It makes sense. Why else would he have taken such an interest in me ever since I sat in his classroom last year? I'm not an idiot.

I am so distracted by trying to figure out the hidden meanings behind every look Coach gives me that I don't even realize it when everyone begins staring me down during their water break. And I continue not to realize it as they resume their practice. Not until Jackson fumbles in a bad way, and I snap my head to him, surprised to see him playing poorly.

"What was that?" I ask. But even Coach Reeves is on the sidelines, checking his phone and not paying attention to his team.

"I'm just a bit distracted. Don't kill me over it," Jackson says, putting his hands up in surrender. Then I hear some low murmurs as if people don't approve of his comment. I look around, and that's when I realize I'm getting strange looks. More than I usually get.

All I can think is, What now?

"All right, let's call it quits for today," Coach Reeves says, blowing his whistle to signal the end of practice. I carefully get up from my seat on the bench, staring everybody down in a challenging way that says I know that they heard something about me, and I want them to be brave enough to tell me to my face what it was. Instead, they all walk away and shoot me looks over their shoulder as they head back toward the locker room.

It's Coach who comes up to me with a grim expression on his face.

"What?" I snap, not wanting to talk to him. I'd talk to anyone over him.

"Warner, I don't know if you've checked your phone, but I got a news alert online. And I think some of the guys on the team got news alerts on theirs, too, during the water break."

"Shouldn't their phones be in their locker?" I ask, annoyed. Do I have to do his job for him?

"Warner. Listen to me."

For some reason, his voice makes my stomach sink. I wait for whatever it is he has to say.

"Look. Some new information has been released about Sydney Hutton's death."

"Oh," I say, almost in surprise.

"She didn't die from drowning."

I swallow. My mouth feels dry. "H-how did she die then?"

"Let's just say they're considering her case now a homicide."

Sydney Hutton.

Murdered.

That's why everybody had been staring at me.

They all think I'm the one who did it.

CHAPTER 32

LYLA

I wake up from a deep sleep to the sound of footsteps on crunching leaves outside. I don't know how long I was out, but I can tell by the crack in the wall that it's daylight out.

I sit up quickly. My heart is already beating faster because I know somebody is out there, just on the other side of that shack door.

I'm afraid to say or do anything. I'm almost paralyzed and rooted to the spot.

But then I hear the door rattle.

I think it's him. The masked man. He's here to torture me. Or to kill me.

"Lyla?" a voice asks.

But it doesn't sound like the voice of anyone trying to hurt me.

"I'm going to get you out of there."

I crawl closer to the door. The voice sounds a lot like...

"Warner?" I ask.

There's a loud squealing noise, like metal against metal, then something bursts. I scramble away from the door just in time as Warner kicks it open. The sun shines behind him and makes him look like a glorious angel.

"I can't believe you found me!" I immediately cry as he helps me to my feet. I'm so relieved to see him standing there. I instantly burst into tears. He wraps his arms around me tightly and holds me there for a long time.

I always want to remember this feeling.

"I didn't sleep, Lyla," Warner says when he pulls away slightly, his arm still around me. "I couldn't eat. I couldn't think about anything other than finding you."

"Warner..."

The next thing I know, Warner is pressing his lips against mine.

But then my eyes open for real.

A dream. It was all a dream. I'm still in the shack. Nobody's here to save me. I don't hear any noises of crunching leaves on the other side of the door.

I lay there on the ground, tears streaming down my cheeks. I think I started crying with happiness during the dream, but now these tears have turned into ones of misery. I miss my family. I just want this to be over.

And I just don't understand it.

Why is my kidnapper even keeping me alive?

CHAPTER 33

AMELIA

Knowing Dean is on my side fills me with the slightest bit of hope. I know it's been three days that my daughter has been missing, but something about knowing Dean wants to do whatever he can to help me get her back... it's soothing. More soothing than anything Gentry says to try to reassure me. I am not entirely sure why that is.

I stand there talking with Dean for so long that we end up sitting inside his car and talking for even longer. When I finally take a look at the clock on his dash, it's nearly five in the evening.

I've been talking to Dean for about three hours.

"I really should go," I say with a heavy sigh. Especially since our topic of conversation had shifted long ago from Lyla to other things that were getting my mind off of the horror of all of this.

"Okay," Dean says. "I'm going to head to the public library, dig into the archives, and see what information I can get. Hopefully, something on Megan Young." Then he quickly gets out of his car, walks to my side, and opens the car door for me. I get out and smile at him. "Thank you again. So much."

"No need to thank me, Mia," he says. "You know I would do anything for you. Without question."

My stomach swarms with butterflies. "I'll talk to you later, okay?"

I hug him goodbye, but I'm reserved in it. I don't try to be flirtatious about it. I don't want him to get upset with me again. Dean and I are friends. And maybe we went a few years without speaking, but in a way, it feels like we never stopped.

I wave at him as he gets back in his driver's seat and backs out of his parking spot. Then when he's far away from me, his taillights glowing in the distance, I finally unlock my black Range Rover and get in the driver's seat. It's not until I close the door and put my seatbelt on, my finger hovering over the Press to Start button, that I notice something on my windshield outside, tucked into one of the windshield wipers.

That's strange.

Did Dean leave me a note before I started talking to him?

I get out of the car. What looks like a yellow Post-it note is waiting there for me to read it. I pluck it from under my wiper and unfold it.

I reread the sentence over and over again. This definitely can't have been from Dean.

In fact, I know exactly who it's from.

The person who took Lyla for me. They were here. Right here, steps away from me. And I hadn't even seen them.

A single teardrop drops onto the yellow paper.

She's gone because of you.

CHAPTER 34

AUDREY

After finding out about Sydney's actual cause of death from my social media, I ask Warner to meet me at Delilah's at six o'clock. I get there first because of how anxious I feel, and I wait for him patiently in a faded, sparkly red booth facing the door.

When he walks in, his hair is slightly damp from the rain that has started outside. But he smiles when he sees me, despite this terrible situation. Despite this horrible news.

He shakes some of his hair out, takes his backpack off, and slides into the booth across from me.

"You still have your backpack?" I ask. Has he not gone home at all?

"I had football practice. Then my soccer coaching gig. Until it got rained out, anyway. Crappy way to spend my last day with those little guys."

I tilt my head. "What do you mean?"

"I quit."

"You quit your job?" I'm mildly surprised. I know he has a lot going on, but I also know that his mom doesn't make a whole lot of money at her hair salon and that he mainly has a job to pay his way through college and help his mom pay for some of the bills.

Warner shrugs. "It was time. Besides. I know parents aren't going to want a suspect of murder to be around their little kids."

"You're not a suspect," I say immediately. Then a waitress comes over to take our dessert order. I get a vanilla milkshake, feeling bored. Warner orders a hot fudge sundae with extra hot fudge. When the waitress walks away, he gives me a slight smirk.

"You always got to have extra hot fudge on your sundae when you're having one of those days, you know?"

"It's going to be okay." I know that Freaky Fritz is interested in Warner, Lyla, and me when it comes to what happened to Sydney. I have no idea what's going to happen now that her cause of death wasn't an accidental drowning. Now that it's considered a homicide.

"We don't really know that, though, do we?" he asks me, and that's when I see the first signs of bitterness on his face. He's worried. I am worried, too. But I don't want him to know it. I have to keep myself together. I have to be strong. There's no time for letting my emotions get the best of me.

"We know we didn't do anything to Sydney, Warner," I say. "So regardless of what anyone thinks, nothing is going to happen to us. Nothing is going to happen to you."

He clenches his jaw and scratches at the old table surface that's flaking away. He says nothing.

I try to think of something else I can say to comfort him. To make him feel like he has nothing to worry about. Usually, I can be pretty good at this kind of stuff.

"Oh, hey," he says suddenly, looking back at me with an alert expression. "Back to what I was trying to tell you during the search for Lyla. It's about good ole Detective Fritz."

"Oh no, what?"

"It could be something," he says, looking like this is a good thing. "I went somewhere—a place where I like to go to be alone. To think. And I didn't know anybody else went there. Until I saw Fritz there."

"What was he doing there?"

"He was talking to someone. And that someone is Nora Flynn."

My eyes bulge out of my head. "Aunt Nora?"

We stop talking for a moment as the waitress brings over our orders, gives us a funny look, and then walks away again. Then we resume our discussion.

Warner nods and dives into his sundae. "Weird, right?" he says with a mouth full of ice cream. "And I saw Fritz at school, so I tried to confront him about it, and he told me he's been trying to ask her questions about everything going on for some time now, and he just 'happened' to run into her. Makes no sense, right?"

"I..." I don't even know how to reply. It's like my brain is having trouble processing it all. Then eventually, I agree. "It makes no sense." I sip my milkshake, but it doesn't sound very good to me anymore.

"I think he's using Nora," he continues. "I think he's trying to get her to dig up dirt on your mom. And on you and Lyla. Fritz is not even interested in finding out what happened to Lyla; I don't think. I think he's all focused on the Sydney thing. Nothing else matters to him."

"He probably thinks Lyla ran away out of guilt," I say with an eye roll. I don't get why Fritz hates the Baileys, Flynns, and Carpenters so much. What is his deal with all of us?

"None of us are guilty," Warner says. "And we need to make sure Fritz knows that. Audrey, do you think you could talk to your aunt for me?"

"I... I could try, I guess, but she's not really the biggest fan of mine."

"It's kind of important. I appreciate you trying."

"There are just no guarantees," I inform him.

"Any bit of information is useful. We need to take all the help we can get."

I push my milkshake away, feeling completely repulsed by it now since my stomach is swarming violently. Warner is right.

We do need help.

CHAPTER 35

MADDY

When Warner walks into the house from the darkness, he's dripping wet from the storm outside.

"Why didn't you have me come get you?" I ask straight away as thunder rumbles outside. I'm currently sitting in the living room watching some trashy reality TV to try and keep my mind off things. "Where have you been? Didn't soccer practice end at seven? And did it not get rained out?"

It's eight now. A whole extra hour that Warner could've been up to who knows what.

Warner drops his backpack to the ground, looking exhausted. I do feel bad that he didn't call me for a ride. He doesn't need to be walking around Toxey with his injuries.

"I didn't need a ride," he says flatly. "I wanted to walk."

"Okay, that answers the first question," I say, getting up from the couch. "Where were you?"

"With Audrey."

"Warner," I say, my voice stern. "Are you sure that's a good idea?"

"What are you talking about?"

"Have you... haven't you seen the news? Or heard about it? Sydney Hutton's death?"

"I know." He walks into the kitchen, trailing mud on the carpet but not seeming to care. I'm too worried about what is happening to even comment on it. I stare at him apprehensively as he gets himself a glass of water and chugs it while staring at me over the counter.

"What do you think about it?" I manage to ask.

"About her being murdered? It sucks. It's terrible. What do you want me to think about it?"

I swallow. "Why do you seem so upset with me? I don't understand what it is I've been doing. Why I am making you so angry."

"Well, I can tell you one bit of interesting news I learned today that's setting me off a little bit."

"What?" I ask, my stomach dipping.

"I found out that you're dating Wrigley Hall's father."

Shoot.

"Oh. Yeah, I am. But I wasn't planning on telling you about it because I know you don't like to hear about the men I'm seeing. Are you upset about it?"

"Wrigley's dad? Are you kidding me? What are you even doing with him? Isn't he, like, never home?"

"What do you know about him?"

"I've... I just know that he works a lot. Can you just try being alone for a change?"

"Are you kidding me?" I ask. "Haven't I been alone the majority of your existence?"

"You were just dating Detective Fritz, and look how that turned out!"

"Don't raise your voice at me!"

"It's just a bad idea," he tells me. "I don't know why you're doing this."

"Do you have something against Wrigley?"

"Maybe I do." He walks out of the kitchen and lingers in the entrance to the hall. "I got homework," he says before he turns and disappears down it.

I flop back down on the couch, feeling exhausted, even though we barely talked. Then I get on my smartphone and start googling about how to talk to moody teenage boys. About what could be causing them to get into these moods. About what I can do to make things better between us. But as I research, I'm still thinking about his reaction to me dating Steven. It's clear he doesn't like it. It's clear that he doesn't like Wrigley. I wonder if Steven knows this. Because when he told me that Wrigley was his son and that Wrigley knew who Warner was, he never mentioned to me that Wrigley wasn't a fan of him.

And if this thing with Steven is going to turn long-term, our boys not getting along isn't an ideal situation. So I suppose I need to talk to Steven and figure out if he knows anything about why.

CHAPTER 36

Audrey

The very second I walk through the garage door into the mud room of my home, my phone vibrates with a new message. It's from an unknown number.

Unknown: *If you want to get your sister back, you'll come to this location. Tell anyone, and you'll never see her again. 10 O'clock.*

Then another message comes in with the location. I immediately plug it into my maps and see that, of course, it's in the middle of nowhere. In the woods. During a storm.

But this is my sister we're talking about. And finally, I have gotten confirmation about what has happened to her.

She has been kidnapped.

More than likely by the person messing with all of us.

So basically, my worst fear is the truth. She didn't run away. She didn't get lost. She's been taken.

"How was Delilah's?" Mom asks me from the dining table. She's having what looks like some coffee while staring at her phone screen. She looks tired.

"Good."

"Who did you go with?"

"Just the girls from school." I know Mom and Dad want me to stay away from Warner right now. So I'm not going to tell them the truth.

"Fun. Thank you for being home at a reasonable time. I waited up for you, but I think I need to go to bed."

"Wait," I say, stepping closer to her. "Have you heard anything from the police today? Any updates?"

"There's another search party happening right now, and your dad is at it. I just don't have the energy tonight. But they don't have any updates. No sign of her. No traces of her. Nobody calling in a hint. Nothing."

My shoulders sag. I want to tell her about the message I just received. But it specifically said not to tell anybody. I don't know what I'm going to have to do to get her back, but I'm willing to try anything.

"It'll be okay," I tell her.

She gets up from the table and walks over to hug me. She kisses the top of my head before pulling away. "I love you, Audrey."

"I love you too, Mom."

Then with a sad smile, she retreats into her bedroom.

After I think everyone in my house has fallen asleep, I slowly open my bedroom door and creep out of it.

I make it to the stairway when a shadow nearly makes me scream out loud and out myself to everyone about how I am trying to sneak out.

Standing in the doorway of his bedroom is Joey with sleepy eyes. "Audrey?" he asks in a whisper.

I quickly tiptoe back over to him. "Hey, what are you doing awake?"

"Where are you going?"

"I... I just have to go somewhere really quick."

"Wait, you mean you're leaving the house?"

"Um... yes. But it's just going to be super-fast. Please don't tell Mom and Dad."

"Audrey, don't go," he says, shaking his head rapidly, looking afraid. "You can't leave this late at night. You shouldn't leave at all. Especially without telling anybody where you're going. It's too dangerous!"

"Joey, please be quiet!" I whisper urgently.

"You can't go."

"You don't understand," I say. "I have to. But I will be back."

He crosses his arms. "Please," he begs in a voice so pitiful it nearly breaks my heart.

"Just go back to sleep, buddy. I'll be back before you know it."

I ruffle the top of his head quickly, and before he can make me change my mind, I speed walk back over to the staircase and leave.

My family is broken.

But I am going to be the one who puts us back together.

CHAPTER 37

LYLA

When I hear leaves crunching outside the shed this time, I know they're real. I know that I'm no longer dreaming.

Somebody is here.

I get to my feet and lean my back against the far wall. The fact that nobody is calling my name as the sound of their footsteps on the leaves grows closer makes me feel like this isn't anybody trying to free me. It makes me feel like it's the very someone who put me here.

I become even more certain of this when I hear a key slide into a lock.

I hear that lock jiggle.

I hear the clicking noise of the success of its unlocking.

He's here.

And there's nowhere I can go. Nowhere I can run.

Slowly, the door opens. Standing in the doorway, nothing but blackness behind him, is the tormentor. He's wearing that horrifying cartoonish mask. The all-black outfit.

And he has the shiny knife in his right hand.

He's not going to attack me. I won't let it happen.

Screaming, not thinking, I run right at him. I knock into him so hard that he staggers out of the way, and I am free.

I am out of the shed.

I fall to the ground after a collision, but I'm quick to get to my feet.

"HELP ME!" I scream at the top of my lungs. Somebody has to be out here. We can't be the only ones.

I keep running. And when I look over my shoulder, I see he's after me.

You can do this, Lyla. You have to get away from him.

You have to get back to your family. You have to get back to Warner. To Wrigley. To all of the people who care about you. It doesn't matter the mistakes you've made in your past. It doesn't make you not worthy of living.

I want to live.

So, I push harder. I pump my arms and legs faster. But every time I look over my shoulder, I see that he's gaining on me. He's quicker. Stronger.

No, he's not, Lyla.

"HELP!"

I keep going.

And then I trip.

Over a tree root. And as I go down, a branch scrapes the side of my face, and I feel a sharp, stinging pain.

I slam to the ground. I hit my chin on the floor and bite my tongue. I immediately taste copper in my mouth.

"No!" I grumble, trying to get back to my feet.

But he's gotten too close.

His hand is around my ankle.

"Get away from me!" I shout. I yank my leg as hard as possible, wanting it out of his grasp.

But then he starts dragging me. I dig into the mud. I dig into tree roots. I try to hold onto anything I can grab, ripping off some of my own fingernails in the process. But I hardly feel it.

Finally, I get a hold of a tree branch and clutch it as tightly as possible. It holds me for a while, but as he keeps dragging me back, splinters slide into my hands as they slide down the branch, and eventually, I lose my grip on it.

He's too strong.

I try to kick him with my free foot. He's holding me just right that I can't quite get to him.

"SOMEBODY, PLEASE!"

Since the man in the mask is dragging me backward, he's not looking behind him. So he, too, trips over something and lands on his elbows with a grunt.

A manly grunt.

But his hands are off my ankle.

I let out a racking sob and get back to my feet.

I have to keep going.

So I do.

I picture my family waiting for me.

I have to run to them.

As I go this time, I no longer see him behind me. But I can't see anything. I'm in pitch-black darkness.

I don't even know which direction I'm going. Not until I enter a clearing and see the front of an old A-frame house in front of me. I run to it and knock on the door. I know we're in the middle of nowhere, but somebody has to be home. Somebody has to be in here, able to help me.

"Please, let me in!" I beg to the door, hitting it some more. My hands are bleeding. My tongue is bleeding—I can still taste it—and something wet is dripping down the side of my face. It's undoubtedly more blood.

I keep pounding on the door even though it's taking forever for anyone to answer it.

Is nobody going to come?

I look over my shoulder. It doesn't seem like anyone has followed me. Should I keep trying to make my way out of the woods? Should I try to find another house?

Finally, I hear the door unlock.

A great sense of relief washes over me. I'm being saved.

The door swings open.

It's the man in the mask.

"No," I gasp.

How can this be?

I went in a circle.

This is his house.

There's just no escaping him.

CHAPTER 38

AUDREY

I go to the edge of the woods in softly sprinkling rain. It was pouring during my walk over here, but it's lightened up now.

Looking over my shoulder, I enter through the trees. It doesn't seem like anybody has followed me. And nobody is calling my phone telling me I need to come home, which I think means Joey didn't tell on me after all.

It's just me out here.

For now.

I'm not quite at the spot marked on the map yet; I have to walk a little way to get there.

So I walk. I use the flashlight app on my phone to help me see, but I almost wonder if I should keep it off. I don't want to draw attention to myself, and since I can only see what's blindingly bright in front of me, I can't see anything in my surroundings.

I jump every time I hear a slight noise that sounds like more than just rain hitting the leaves on the trees, and I wave my flashlight all around me. But I just see darkness in the distance. Tree branches. Nothingness.

Shudders ripple down my spine. But I keep walking.

"Lyla?" I call. Maybe whoever texted me just dropped her off out here somewhere. Maybe she's tied up to a tree. But she has to be alive. She has to be.

I hear another snapping twig noise. This one sounds so close it makes me gasp, my breath catching in my throat as I whirl around. Again, I don't see anything.

"Lyla?" I call again, but now I can't ignore it—the sense that someone is watching me. The feeling of eyes on the back of my head.

I go with my first instinct to turn my flashlight off. Then I stand still, letting my eyes adjust to the darkness before I continue on my trek.

Upon another faint, light-crunching noise, I turn my head slowly—ever so slowly—to the left.

There in the trees, I see it.

A shadowy figure.

I quicken my pace. I'm almost at the location.

But I think it's better if I stay silent now.

Looking to my left again, I chance a peek and see that the figure is real. It wasn't just a figment of my imagination. It wasn't just my eyes playing tricks on me as they adjusted to the darkness. It's still right to my left. Walking through the woods at the same pace I am. Just feet away.

Who could it be? Who's followed me here?

Or who's been waiting for me?

I begin running.

When I look again, they're running, too.

And then suddenly, they cut through the trees and are heading right over to me.

"Go away!" I scream.

I glance down at my phone, and it says I'm on the location on the map.

But nothing is here.

I've been tricked.

Again.

I quickly turn the other way and run back the way I came.

But they're right on my tail.

With my eyes more adjusted to the darkness now, I can tell who it is. I can see the cartoonish mask.

It's him.

I whimper in terror and keep going. I try jumping over a fallen log, but my foot catches, and I fly forward. I turn around so I'm on my butt, and look behind me. I expect the monster to be right on my tail. To be jumping over the log after me with his knife out, tip first.

Instead, I lift my head slightly and peer over the log; I see them in the distance. They're just... standing there. They're not running at

me. They're not trying to come any closer. They just seem to be...
staring at me.

"Wh-who are you?" I manage to get out. I realize I don't want to
run. I came here to get my sister back. And this person led me here
for a reason. Maybe they just wanted to scare me again, but if I just
run away, I'll never know what the reason was for certain.

They don't say anything. They just keep staring.

"Where is Lyla?" I ask. "What did you do to her?"

Still, I get nothing. It makes me mad. Heat creeps through my
veins even though it's cold and wet outside, and my butt is drenched
in mud.

"SAY SOMETHING!" I feel wetness on my cheek and realize it's
more than just the rain coming down through the trees. I'm crying.
I don't want tonight to end without me getting answers.

Where is my sister?

The person in the mask doesn't say anything, and they don't come
any closer. They don't answer me.

Instead, they turn around.

Then they disappear into the trees.

CHAPTER 39

WARNER

Lyla's Fourth Day Missing

I wake up suddenly before my alarm to the sound of my mother's voice.

"What are you doing?" she's asking someone. "You can't just come in here!"

I have no idea what time it is or who my mom could be talking to, but all I know is I'm suddenly on high alert. I bolt out of bed and grab a sweater to throw it on with my sweat shorts as I throw my door open and go down the hall.

"Stop!" my mom shouts, making me think someone's hurting her. Making me think it's the person who has been messing with us. The person who took Lyla. What if they're here? Here for me?

I can't let anything happen to my mom.

I turn the corner and see who has barged their way in. It's police officers. Two, I don't know. One has a bald head; the other has long red hair pulled back in a bun. They're both men.

My mom calls to me, reaching out her arms like she wants me to go to her.

Instead, I stare at the men. "What are you doing here?" I demand. They can't just come into our house like this, can they?

"Warner Carpenter?" the ginger dude asks me. He's big, scary, and looks like somebody I don't want to mess with.

"Yes?"

"We have a warrant. We're going to be searching your room and taking your phone and laptop."

"A warrant?" I look at the other officer who's holding up a piece of paper. Then I look at my mom, who looks simply horrorstruck.

"A warrant?" My mom repeats. "For what? What is the reasoning?"

"This is in regards to the case of Sidney Hutton's homicide."

"But I didn't do anything to her," I try.

"Where is your room?" the bald one asks.

"No. This isn't fair. I didn't do anything to her." I guard the hallway. Mom shakes her head and looks at the ground. "Warner, you have to let them go back there."

"Mom, I didn't do anything! How can they be doing this?!"

She just continues shaking her head. The officers force their way past me, bumping into my shoulder. Taking a good first guess, they push my bedroom door open and let themselves inside. I just stand there in the hallway staring at them numbly, watching them violate everything personal to me.

"So, what?" I ask as I hear them talking to each other and rifling through the stuff in my room. "Are you saying I'm... a person of interest, then?"

"As a matter of fact, yes," one of them calls.

"A person of interest in the murder of Sydney Hutton as well as the disappearance of Lyla Bailey," the other one calls.

They think I have something to do with what happened to Lyla?

This is probably the only thing they could've said to render me completely and utterly speechless.

This. Is. Not. Good.

CHAPTER 40

AMELIA

Even though I knew it was early, I just felt so tired last night, which is why I tried to lie down instead of going to the search party. I knew I wouldn't be any use if I went. Not when I feel like this. And I didn't like the thought of leaving Joey home alone since Audrey was at Delilah's with her friends from school.

But as soon as I lay down last night, I stared at the ceiling. I watched the fan move in its fast circle, thinking about how Lyla was still out there somewhere. And how while she was out there, I was lying in a warm, comfortable bed, being useless.

So I ended up getting out of bed and going to join the search party. I didn't even tell Audrey or Joey that I was leaving—they were both in their bedrooms for bed anyway.

But it had been another useless night. I walked through a cornfield with some people and found absolutely nothing. I got home around one in the morning and cried until around four when I think I finally managed to fall asleep. But I woke again just two and a half hours later, and now here I am. I'm exhausted from the late night. From crying. From how hopeless I feel. When I force myself to get out of bed, I feel dead on my feet. It's hard to move. It's hard to breathe. It's hard to think about anything other than the fact that I don't think we're ever going to get Lyla back. And I know I should remain positive, but I just can't. Not when it feels like the entire town of Toxey and all the towns bordering it have been searched from head to toe. People keep trying to tell me it might be good news that we haven't been able to locate her. They tell me that at least we haven't found and dug up her body.

It doesn't make me feel any better.

"Did you want to hop in the shower first, or do you want me to?" Gentry asks in a tired voice from over in the bathroom. He has a towel in his arms like he was already planning on getting in the shower.

"What?" I ask. I feel annoyed that he's assuming I want to shower. It's like he knows I haven't been taking care of myself and is passively trying to push me to do it.

"We have the meeting with Joey's foster care case worker this morning."

Oh yeah.

I sigh. "Um, you go ahead."

He nods curtly and then goes to shower.

I walk into the kitchen and see Audrey scrolling through her phone with the news playing on the TV. I decide to go and take a seat next to her.

"Are you okay?" Audrey asks immediately, clicking her phone off and turning her body toward me.

"Um, sweetie, I wanted to talk to you about something."

"Is it about Lyla?" she asks. "Did something happen last night? Have they found her? I haven't heard anything on the news."

"No, honey. I'm afraid nobody found her. She is... she's still... out there somewhere. But I didn't want to ask you about her."

"What then?" She looks disappointed to hear my news about them not finding Lyla. I don't blame her. I'm disappointed, too.

"I was wondering if you can tell me anything about the man who attacked you in here that night." It's a horrible memory to think back on. How Gentry and I saw our front door wide open. Then how I turned down the hall leading to my bedroom and saw Gentry cradling her unmoving, bleeding body on the floor. I still haven't put up all the pictures that got knocked off the walls during the attack.

"Oh, th-that guy?" Audrey asks, suddenly looking terrified. "What is there to know?"

"Just...what can you tell me about him? I know we talked about it before, but are you sure there's nothing you can tell me about it? Nothing you know?"

"He was wearing this freaky human-cartoon-like mask. He was wearing all black. He, um—he had a knife."

"And you don't remember him saying anything to you? No reasoning as to why he wanted to chase you? He had a knife, but he didn't physically hurt you. So he just wanted to scare you. And you don't know why?"

"I don't know why," she agrees. "But... there is something I haven't told you."

"It's okay," I say, putting my hand on her knee. "You can tell me."

She nods and looks at my hand. She doesn't want to meet my gaze. It makes me afraid of what she's about to say.

"It's not the first time that it's happened."

My heart constricts. "What?"

Then suddenly, I'm getting an earful from her. She tells me how a man in a mask chased her through school. About how she feels like she's being messed with, and she doesn't know by who.

I'm terrified. When she finishes, I have to ask. "Do you think it's the same man who chased you that took Lyla? Do you think it's the same person messing with the both of you?"

"I do," she says, nodding her head.

I get even more worried because Audrey seems so put together. This is a horrifying, terrible, scary thing that she's telling me, and she seems fine. Matter-of-fact-like. I think she'd make a good detective.

I lean back on the couch and rest my head on a pillow as more tears stream down my cheeks.

"I wish I knew who it was," Audrey says. "But I'm going to find out."

I feel guilt, too. Guilt because Audrey is acting so certain. So sure of herself. And I'm the opposite. I can barely even get myself in the shower. I can't get myself to say reassuring things. Not even to her or Joey. I can't speak matter-of-factly about Lyla's disappearance without bursting into tears. I'm a mess.

I feel like I'm failing as a parent.

CHAPTER 41

LYLA

I'm back in the shed. It's been cleaned for me. I have fresh food and water supplies. I even have a sleeping bag now. I guess it's my kidnapper's way of telling me to get comfortable. Of letting me know there's no way he's going to chance my near escape happening ever again.

I can't believe I was so stupid. I can't believe I didn't realize I was running in a complete circle. I can't believe I didn't recognize the house from the front and didn't take a moment to consider the fact that it was probably the only house around me for miles and miles. If there were any other houses out here, surely one of them would've heard me screaming.

I had been so close to getting back to my family.

Now I feel as if I'm more close to joining Sydney instead. To joining Trinity.

"I'm never going to get to go home."

A tear trails down my cheek and stings my fresh cut from last night. But I like that I'm injured. I like that I am sitting here trying to pull all the splinters out of my hand with my bloody fingernails. It reminds me that I did try to fight. That I did what I could. I did my part; now I need others to do theirs and get me the heck out of here.

My entire body is sore. Not only from trying to flee from my kidnapper but from when I constantly threw myself against the door to try to break out. And I feel stiff from being cramped in such a small room for a long time.

I go through it in my head again. The list of potential people who could've done this to me. It takes me back to the day everyone found out I was the reason Trinity died. It makes me wonder if the person who did this was angry at me. Angry about her death.

School had been miserable that day. After I found out in chemistry that everyone knew, it seemed like it was all anybody could talk about. And I was mortified.

I wanted to go home. But I couldn't. I couldn't let my parents figure out what I had done. I didn't want to face them. I didn't want them to tell me something ridiculous about how I needed to talk to Trinity's parents and tell them what I did immediately.

So I suffered.

Wrigley tried texting me, asking me if we could talk, but I ignored him.

But when I got to algebra fifth period, there was no way for me to avoid him any longer. And before the bell rang, Wrigley walked right up to me before I could even sit at my desk. Wrigley didn't seem to care that Jackson had this class with us, too, and that everybody seemed to be staring at us.

"Lyla, are you okay?" Wrigley had asked, his eyes full of concern.

I never told him. I never told him why I had stopped texting him before. About how I had been texting him when I got into the accident that killed Trinity. He found out some other way. From all the people spreading the gossip. The gossip that I have no idea how they got their hands on. My therapist knew. Sydney knew. But my therapist is supposed to keep that information to herself, and Sydney Hutton, as far as I knew, was dead.

"Can we not do this right now?" I asked Wrigley, avoiding his gaze.

"Just talk to me, Ly," he tried anyway. "Is it true? I mean, I'm not mad, Lyla. I know it was an accident. Forget what all these other people are saying."

"Why are you talking to that murderer?" a girl in our class asked loudly to Wrigley.

"Why were you ever talking to her at all in the first place?" Jackson asked from over at his desk.

I snap back to the reality I'm in, not wanting to remember any more of that day. About how people treated me horribly. About how mad Jackson was that Wrigley and I had been texting, and he hadn't even known about it.

It had seemed like the entire school hated me that day.

I wonder what they think of me now.

CHAPTER 42

WARNER

After the cops leave with my stuff, I quickly get ready for school and walk into the kitchen, where my mom is sipping coffee, shaking hands holding her mug. She's leaning against the counter, and her brows furrow together when she sees me. "What are you doing?" she asks.

I open up the pantry cupboard and take out a Pop-Tart. "I need to get to school. I'm late."

"Warner," she says, running a hand over her tired face. "Don't you think staying home today may be a good idea?"

"What?" I ask, instantly irritated. "No, I don't, actually."

"Warner, I'm scared."

It makes me pause in my step. I'm scared, too. But I don't need her knowing that.

"I didn't kill her, Mom." I hate that I have to say this over and over again. I hate that I feel like she doesn't believe me. But maybe that's her own issue—she doesn't trust me because she knows she's not very good at telling the truth herself.

"But the police think you did," she says. "And... I've heard some things."

"What things? So, you're telling me you don't believe me?"

"I just..."

"Do you or do you not?" I ask, my voice getting louder.

"Why don't you ever tell me things?!" she suddenly snaps. She slams her coffee mug on the counter so hard that coffee spills out of the side of it. "Why do I feel like I never know where you are or what you're doing?! Why do you always seem so mad at me?! Why do you always seem so secretive?! Why are you constantly hiding things from me?! Why can't you just tell me the truth and be honest and open with me?! Then maybe I wouldn't have these reservations about it all! I am fed up, Warner!"

"You're such a hypocrite!"

"How?!"

I'm about ready to belt it out. Belt out that I know about my father. But I know now is not the time. I don't even want to deal with that yet. And besides, I want her to tell me the truth. Without me telling her, I already know about it first.

I turn to leave. "Just... forget it!" But then I stop and turn back around. "Actually, you know what? I wanna know something."

"What?" she hisses, her chest rising and falling rapidly.

"Nora Flynn. I know you were friends with Amelia Bailey... once. Were you ever friends with her sister?"

"What? Why are you asking me about that right now?"

"Answer the dang question, Ma."

"Yes. She was my friend."

"Was?"

"That's right. Was."

"Did you stop being friends with her after Carson Price went missing?"

"I... it's complicated."

"Well, it's a good thing you don't talk to her anymore. If she reaches out to you, you need to stay away from her."

"Why?"

"Because I think Detective Fritz is trying to get her to dig up information on you and Amelia Bailey. You need to be careful."

I don't even know why I'm protecting her. Not when I'm so angry with her.

"Warner, wait," she says as I go to walk away again.

"No, Mom," I say. "I'm going to school. You're not stopping me." I'll walk. I don't care if she needs the jeep. I'm not going to let that excuse stop me from going.

"Can't you just do one thing, I ask?" she calls to me.

I turn and point a finger at her. "You know what, Mom? You should take a good, hard look in the mirror. You tell me I keep secrets from you?" I let out a sarcastic laugh. Then I shake my head and turn from her. "I can't wait to go to Florida."

"What did you just say?" she asks behind me. I turn around and give her a look full of disdain. "I said I can't wait to get out of here and go to Florida," I say louder this time. "Away from here and away from you."

There's a lump in my throat, and my eyes are suddenly stinging, but I hold it together and grab my bag and walk out the front door.

CHAPTER 43

Audrey

I know it's still early, so I can't help but wonder if I am just freaking myself out a little bit because Warner isn't answering my calls or texts. But if he went to school today, then he should be awake. He should be receiving my messages, right? So why isn't he replying?

What if he didn't go to school?

I have to find out. But I am not talking to any of my so-called "friends" right now. And I'm mad at Ryan for hanging out with Sophia, and things are weird between us right now. So I'll need to ask someone else.

I text Cody, a senior who is a friend of Warner's.

Me: *Hey, do you know if Warner showed up to school today?*
Cody: *He's not here. Everything good?*
Cody: *BTW, sorry about your sister. I hope they find her soon.*

I don't bother texting back. His message was sweet, but I don't know Cody all that well, and I don't have a want to be engaging in conversation with random boys at the moment.

Warner isn't at school. So what does that mean?

I try calling him again. And again, I get no answer.

I walk out of my bedroom and pace the hall in front of the loft and the staircase. I'm worried about him. Worried about what could have happened to him. We've already established that the same person is messing with all three of us and that that person is probably who took Lyla. I don't want to think it, but what if they took Warner, too?

"Audrey?" Dad calls from downstairs. I race down the steps, glad to have something to momentarily distract myself from the things

I am thinking right now. Mom and Dad are in the kitchen, and he looks like he's getting his keys and wallet so the two of them can leave.

"Where are you guys going?" I ask.

"We have to go..." Mom trails off, and I get the feeling that, for whatever reason, she doesn't want to tell me the truth. It makes my stomach sink.

"Uh, to an appointment," Dad finishes for her.

"What kind of an appointment?" I decide to ask, pressing my luck. What if it's an appointment that has something to do with my sister? Or with what happened to Warner? What if they just don't want to tell me because they don't want to scare me?

Well, I'm already scared. And I don't want to be left out of the loop.

"It's just with Gentle Hands," Mom says with a heavy sigh, like it was a huge burden to relay that information to me. "They just want to do a check-in. It's nothing serious. No need to have that terrified, stressed-out look on your face, hon."

Whatever look I have on my face, I change to one of surprise. Surprise because Mom seems so irritated and done with having to talk to me.

"We really need to get going, Gentry," she says, standing in the arch of the mudroom leading to the garage. Dad nods, walks over, and gives me a quick side hug, and then the two leave me alone in the house again.

I get a text not even a minute after they leave. My heart leaps because I think it's Warner.

It's not.

Dad: Make sure all the doors and windows are locked, and don't go anywhere without letting us know first.

I roll my eyes. And yet, I find myself going around the house and doing as I was told anyway. Then I sit on the sectional in the family room and nibble on my fingernail. Now I am back to worrying about Warner.

I'm not the kind of girl who sits around wondering and not doing anything about it. Not anymore. I have to look for him.

I stand myself up, go to my room to grab my car keys, and then when I make it back down to the last step of the staircase, the doorbell rings, and I stumble and fall on my knees to the tile. I pick myself up quickly, and with a hammering heart, I look through the peephole.

It's Warner.

Relief floods me like a dam breaking; I fling the door open. "Warner!" I cry, both glad to see that he's okay and worried because why would he be showing up here like this unannounced?

"Hey, Audrey," he says, his voice wavering and cracking. And then, as he stands before me on our welcome mat, his shoulders sag, and his face crumples. He takes one small step forward and knowing exactly what he needs, I quickly put my arms around him and pull him tightly into me. He's crying, and I have no idea why.

"Come on," I say after holding him for a minute. Then I take his hand and pull him inside the house, close the door, and relock it again.

"I'm sorry to just show up here like this," he says, wiping his eyes and pulling himself together as I lead him to the sectional, and we both sit down.

"What happened?" I ask uneasily. "I've been trying to call and text you. Like—an embarrassing amount of times."

He nods. "I—uh..." Then he starts crying some more, looking down at his lap with his elbows on his knees. I don't know what I can say or do to help him, so I just put my head on his shoulder until he's ready to talk to me again.

Then he tells me what went down at his house before he came over here. About how he's a person of interest in not only Sydney's murder but also in the disappearance of my sister. And about how his mother doesn't believe that he's innocent.

"That's horrible, Warner," I say to him when he's finished filling me in. He looks at me with puffy, bloodshot eyes. "I'm so sorry."

He shrugs in a helpless way. "I don't know what to do anymore."

"You didn't do anything to either of them," I remind him.

"Yeah, but there was even a point where you and Lyla didn't believe that," he deadpans.

I chew on my bottom lip. "Okay. Let's just... let's think about this, okay? We have to get to the bottom of all of this. We have to figure out what happened to Lyla. We have to figure out who is really responsible for all of this. And we need to do it fast."

"What if...?" Warner looks away from me.

"What?"

"What if I go to jail, Audrey?"

I grab his hand and hold it tightly. "You won't." He doesn't look like he believes me. "I promise you won't. I'll do anything and everything I can to make sure of it."

Instead of saying anything, he just leans into me and hugs me again. We stay like that for a long, long time.

CHAPTER 44

AMELIA

Thanks to Gentry and no thanks to me; I think we did a decent enough job when talking with the people at the foster care agency. Gentry has always been very charismatic, and he is often too smart for his own good; he always seems to have a way of dealing with all kinds of different people. Anytime I have a billing discrepancy or need to get something done to my car at the mechanics, I have him handle it because he is the only one who can resolve things—while remaining calm, collected, and nice even. It doesn't take much for me to lose my patience.

I should feel a sense of relief knowing that no one has followed us home to come to collect Joey. But I don't feel any better. I still feel like the home we have given him is in jeopardy. That we're going to constantly be checked on until this whole thing is resolved.

"You okay?" Gentry asks in a flat voice as we pull into the garage.

I don't even bother answering him. His tone of voice lets me know that he doesn't—in fact—care and that he just asked me the question because he felt obligated to.

Instead, I get out of the car and storm inside the house. I am sick of being around Gentry. Completely sick of it.

I don't know how much longer I can keep this up.

Things only get more irritating when I get inside the house.

"Hi, Mom!" Audrey says in a bright, cheery tone as she leaps from the sofa to greet us. Gentry walks in behind me moments later. "Hi, Dad!"

I'm about to ask her why her tone is so suspicious, but another figure gets up from the sofa, and I see who has decided to pay our home a visit.

"Uh, Mom?" I ask. My mother, Susan Flynn, is walking around the couch and heading toward me in the kitchen, her skinny little arms outstretched for a hug. My mother has blonde hair that she's been perming for as long as I can remember, and she has piercing green eyes, the same as Nora's. I got my eyes from my father.

She wraps her arms around me and squeezes me tightly. It's weird because not only do we not see each other often, we hardly even talk on the phone, either. I suppose there was a time once when we used to be close, but that was back before Nora was sent away to an institution, and all of the hard work I had done to save money for my dream school went to paying those bills instead. It's the same situation with my father, too. They're still married, but I hear from my dad, David, even less than my mom.

"Sweetie, how are you holding up?" she asks as she steps away from me. Then she goes over to Gentry and hugs him, too. "This is just such devastating news."

"Mom," I say, thinking vaguely about how maybe I should try not to sound so rude. "What are you doing here?"

It doesn't work.

"Hey, Susan," Gentry says with a soft voice as my mother pulls away from his hug.

Mom looks at me with an offended expression. "I came to check up on you!"

"Okay... but you could have at least called. That way, you could have come at a time when I was already home."

She waves a hand dismissively. "Nonsense, I've been having a wonderful time hanging out with Audrey."

Audrey is still standing in the living room, looking like she has no clue what to do with herself. She hasn't spent too much time with her grandmother in her life.

"You still should have called," I argue.

"Mia, it's fine," Gentry says to me. "Susan, we're glad you're here."

I roll my eyes. "Things are just a little crazy right now, and I haven't been up for visitors..."

"Well, honey, look at you—I can see that," Mom says.

I grimace at her.

"Look, truth be told, I do need to talk to you. In private."

I look at my husband and daughter, who are both looking between my mother and me. "Um, okay, then. Let's go talk... in the upstairs loft."

Mom follows me up the stairs, and then we both take a seat in the two cozy armchairs in the small nook.

"So, what's up?" I ask, avoiding her eye contact.

"Sweetie, I was wondering if you've heard from Nora."

This is a surprise to me. "Nora?" I ask. "Why do you want to know about her?"

"I know she isn't staying with you any longer. What is the reasoning for that?"

"She wanted to leave," I say.

"You mean you two got into a fight."

I grumble. "Mom, if you already knew the answer, why did you ask me?"

"I just... wanted to hear what you had to say about it. You know how Nora can be."

I think about the last time my sister and I spoke. About how she had known for all these years that Dean, the boy she had been in love with since she was four, was in love with me instead. And how she had never mentioned anything to me about it.

"Yeah," I agree. "I do."

Since Nora left, and since Lyla went missing, Nora's checked in with me. But only to know if Lyla has been found yet, and to let me know that she's been going to every single one of the search parties. Otherwise, we haven't spoken.

"What was the fight about?" Mom asks.

"What did Nora say it was about?"

"She didn't want to talk about it. All she said was that you two got into it, and then she left." There's a strange expression on her face. Mom seems... worried. And I have no idea why. So Nora and I got into a fight—was it really that big of a deal?

"Mom, what's going on?" I ask, deciding there must be something she isn't telling me.

"Honey, I already said—"

"I know what you said. But I want the truth."

She sighs. "The truth is that this is a really hard time for you and your family. And I want to be here to help in any way I can."

"Okay, and I appreciate that," I tell her. "But if Nora didn't want to talk to you about what our fight was about, then I don't really want to talk about it either."

"But is everything okay?"

"Between us?"

She nods.

"I... I don t know. Probably."

"But the fight wasn't about anything super serious?"

"Mom, please."

She holds up her hands in surrender. "Fine, fine, I'll stop." Then we sit there in silence for a few minutes while I try and figure out what her real reason for being here is. "Tell me what you have planned for today. And tell me how I can help."

"Um..." I trail off, wondering exactly how long it will be that my mother stays here.

"I know!" she says loudly, perking up in her seat. "Why don't we start with getting you in a nice, warm shower, and then I can help you with your makeup?"

What is it with people insisting I get ready and make myself presentable? I am going through a crisis.

CHAPTER 45

WARNER

I'm almost glad my phone got taken away from me. At least now, my mom has no way of contacting me or knowing where I am. No way of letting me know she thinks I'm a murderer and telling me that I need to get my butt back home so that she can lock me in my bedroom for the rest of eternity.

After I calm down and talk to Audrey—which I am incredibly embarrassed about, by the way—I eventually leave and wander around Toxey aimlessly. I go to my spot even for a little while, but it's hard to get much thinking done there when all I can picture is how strange it had been seeing Detective Craig Fritz and Nora Flynn there together. So, I continue my random trot through this awful town until school ends. Then I decide to skip football practice entirely and head to the library at Blackwell to get some homework done since I don't have my laptop to do it at home. Who knows when I'll get it back?

I find a vacant computer in a cubicle and sit myself down. There are not many people here today, and the ones that are don't even seem to notice me—a fact that I'm glad about.

After a while of doing a surprisingly good job at getting my work done, I get up to get a drink from the drinking fountain over by the entrance to the library. It's over there where, outside the doors, I begin to hear a strange noise. A familiar noise. But the fact that it's so familiar makes it so... strange.

Leaving my backpack and all of my stuff at the cubicle, I leave the library and enter the school's hallway. It's pretty deserted in here, except for the sound of someone. Someone in trouble.

"HELP!" the voice says.

It sounds like Lyla.

"LET GO OF ME!" it continues. "Get off of me!"

My pulse quickens, and I start speed-walking down the hallway. Then my speed walk turns into a jog. Then I find myself sprinting toward her voice.

"Lyla?!" I yell, her screaming getting louder and louder. I don't know what's happening. I don't know how she got here. And I don't know who's hurting her. But I have to save her.

"SOMEBODY HELP ME!" she shrieks.

It's tearing little pieces of my heart off to hear her sounding like this. And I can't run fast enough.

Finally, I turn a corner and realize I'm in the hall where my locker is. I don't see anybody in this hallway. But yet, this is where her voice is the loudest.

"HELP!"

I pause for a minute, but then I keep running. I run all the way to my locker. The screaming... the sounds of struggling... it's coming from inside of it.

But right now, I'm almost too afraid to even open it up. Because right there on my locker door, written in bright red paint, is the word, MURDERER, sloppily thrown across it.

I look around over my shoulders. Who could've done this?

"Hello?" I call over the noise of Lyla screaming. Somebody has to be here. Somebody had to have known I was in the library. They set this up.

With shaking hands, I open my locker. There I find the recording device. I quickly turn it off and drop it to the ground. Lyla was never here. But whoever left this device in my locker has her. And those noises she was making were very, very real.

Lyla is in trouble.

Wait a second.

Another recording device. Just like the one that was left at Wrigley's party. The one where everybody was saying it was Trinity's voice tormenting Lyla. But now I think I know something—that hadn't been Trinity's voice. It has been Sydney's.

I think whoever killed Sydney is going to do something horrible to Lyla, too.

CHAPTER 46

Maddy

I do feel bad for the way things went with Warner this morning. But I don't know what to think. I don't know what to do. So, after he went to school, I did what I felt I needed to. I went to speak to a lawyer.

I spent all day there with him. His name is Theodore Williams, and he seems to really know what he is doing. I don't exactly have the money to pay for him, but I'm willing to take out a personal loan if I need to. Whatever it takes.

While I'm there at Theo Williams's office, I also learn via an automated phone call from the school that Warner did not end up going to school at all today. He was marked absent from every single one of his classes. And then I received a text message from Dean asking if I knew where Warner was because he never showed up to football practice either. I have no way of getting ahold of my son to figure out where he is and why he's not going where he should be, so I have no choice but to wait until I drive home with Warner's jeep later, the lawyer in tow.

Theo and I are sitting on the sofa and chair in my living room when Warner finally walks into the house around eight o'clock at night. I've kept the lawyer waiting for over forty-five minutes.

But he's a kind, patient man, so I'm grateful.

"What's this?" Warner asks as the door slowly closes behind him. He looks like he was about to take his backpack off but has quickly changed his mind. It's like he's going to leave any second if I say one wrong thing.

Luckily, it's Theodore who takes charge. He stands up and walks over to Warner, his hand outstretched. "My name is Theodore Williams, and I am a family lawyer."

Uneasily, Warner shakes his hand.

"I'm here to help you. That's all, Warner," he says. His voice is stern and sincere. "I just want to help."

"Okay..." he trails off. He doesn't move except to put his hand back on his backpack strap, a sign that he's still willing to leave if he finds it necessary.

"I've been talking with Theodore all day," I say from over on the sofa, where I've turned around to look at them both. "He has some really great advice for you."

"Advice?"

"I understand you're going through a hard time right now, Warner, but you're innocent. Innocent until proven guilty, and it's my job to make sure that we never get to the 'proven guilty' part."

"Why don't you take a seat, Warner?" I try. I'm using the nicest voice possible. I don't want him to see me as a threat. I want him to see me as an ally. Regardless of what happened between him and Sydney, he's my son, and I will do everything to protect him. I am on his side.

"That sounds like a great idea," Theodore says, nodding his head. He leads the way back into the living area, hesitantly, Warner follows him. But at least he follows him.

As soon as Warner sits down and takes his backpack off—finally—Theodore gets right down to it. He takes his time explaining everything to Warner that he explained to me this morning and afternoon. He explains the process and how this may or may not go down if they find enough evidence to arrest him. I don't want him to be frightened; I just want him to know what's at stake. And Theodore does a good job explaining everything without making it seem like a terrifying situation, even though it is.

By the end of the conversation, Warner seems warmed up to Theodore. It makes me feel reassured again that I picked the right choice. I just have to figure out how to pay him. But he will be worth it. If need be.

We both shake Theodore's hand one more time before he leaves, then Warner and I are alone in the house.

"That wasn't so bad, was it?" I ask, giving Warner's shoulder a reassuring squeeze.

Warner shrugs and doesn't meet my eyes.

"Everything's going to be fine. You heard him. Nothing's going to happen to you."

"I guess so."

"I know you weren't at school today," I say. But I'm not using my stern-mother voice. I'm trying to be understanding. Would I want to go to school today after this all happened? Probably not. I was young once. I get it.

"What, are you going to ground me now, too?"

I shake my head. "Of course not. It's okay, Warner. I get that maybe you needed the mental health day. I won't ask where you were or what you were doing. I won't try to invade your business. I don't want to do anything that's going to keep you pushing away from me. But if you could just let me know where you are and what you're doing so I'm not worried, I would appreciate it."

He stands there and says nothing, but I get the feeling that it's his way of saying "okay."

I fake a yawn because I know I should probably just get out of his way. "Anyway. I'm going to watch TV in my room. Let me know if you need anything."

He nods soundlessly, so I give him a weak smile and retreat to my bedroom. Seconds later, I hear him go into his own room and close the door.

I feel relatively good about how the evening went. Warner and I didn't scream at each other. He didn't seem to be furious with me. He seemed like he liked the lawyer, and it seemed like Theodore did a good job making him feel a little bit better about everything. I think maybe I started to get the point across that I'm on his side.

I fling myself in bed, knowing I'm not at all tired. I feel this electric energy after everything that just happened. Almost like I'm on adrenaline. I don't know how to describe it.

But as I start flipping through my streaming choices for something to watch, my phone dings with a text message. I pick it up and see that it's from Dean.

When I open it, I see that he has sent me a photo of someone's locker inside Blackfell High. The word MURDERER is written on it in bright, sloppy red paint. Along with the picture is Dean's message.

Dean: Maddy, that's Warner's locker. I think you and I need to have a serious talk.

For once, I think Dean might be right.

CHAPTER 47

Audrey

Usually, I'm pretty proud of the parents that I have. We get along great, and I'm thankful for them and everything they do for me. But this was before things started going so downhill in our lives. Now it seems like everything they do annoys me. It seems like everything they say to me is the wrong thing. And it seems like I can't do anything right by them, either.

However, tonight, they finally seem to have done something right.

They finally agreed to let me join the search party for my sister.

In the kitchen, before we leave, they turn to me with those parental looks in their eyes.

"As long as you stay where we can see you, got it?" Dad says.

"And don't try and pull a fast one on us, either. The second you get out of our sight, we reject our offer, and you will never be allowed to do this again," Mom adds.

"I don't even know if you'll ever be able to leave the house again," Dad throws in.

I roll my eyes. "Oh, come on." But I am grateful. "Thank you."

"Why don't you ride with us?" Mom asks.

"Actually, I want to take my own car. So I can listen to my music." The truth is, I just don't want to feel like I have a parental escort. I know they want to keep an eye on my every move, but I want to feel like I have a little bit of my independence still. I'm really trying not to be mad and annoyed at them because I know they're just worried about me. I know they don't want me to end up like Lyla. But what they don't seem to know is that we're going to get Lyla back. We have to.

"Okay, make sure you stay right behind us," Mom says, then we all shuffle out to the garage together. Their car starts and backs out first. I wave at them before I get into my car and close the door. I start it up, put my seatbelt on, and look over my shoulder while I'm backing out, but my eyes pause on something in the passenger seat, and I slam on my brake.

It's a bracelet. One of those fabric woven ones with three different colored threads. It just lies there, untied. And I know I haven't seen it here before.

I pick it up curiously. How could this have gotten here? Who would've put it here, and why?

Was it you, Ly?

Feeling determined, I follow my parents to the fields where the start of the search party is tonight. When I park my car and get out, I hold Lyla's bracelet securely in my hand. I stay near Mom and Dad, but the second I see the nice cop, Officer Wilde, I make a beeline for him. If Mom and Dad want me to stay in their eyesight, they're going to have to follow where I want to go. Because I am on a mission.

"Officer Wilde, hi," I say, waving at him and giving him a bright smile. I'm glad to be seeing him here and not Detective Fritz.

He gives me a polite smile. "Oh, helping in the search tonight, Audrey?" he asks with a look that's happy yet somber and comforting.

"Yes, actually. And I think I might have something that could help." I hold out the bracelet to him as Officer Wilde looks over my shoulders, where I'm sure my parents are approaching us. Then he looks at the bracelet in my hand.

"What do you got there?" he asks, raising his eyebrows.

Then the exact person I was dreading seeing decides to walk up and interfere in our conversation.

"What's this?" Freaky Fritz asks as he chugs from his plastic water bottle and replaces the cap.

I try to pretend like I don't even notice that Detective Fritz is there and only address Wilde as I speak. "This is Lyla's bracelet. I found it on the seat of my car on my way here. I don't know how it got there, and I don't know when it happened. But it wasn't there before."

In the background, in the distance, I can hear people talking on megaphones, organizing the groups, and giving everybody their vests and flashlights so that the search can get started. I wonder if

Lyla is out there. I wonder if she can hear us calling for her. I wonder if she's able to call back to us.

"You're saying somebody put this in your car for you to find?" Officer Wilde asks.

"I don't see how it's going to be any use to us," Fritz says. "Lyla could've dropped that forever ago. And anybody could've left that in your car."

"Why don't you think it's worth it to try and figure out who that anybody was?" I ask, unable to ignore him any longer. Everything Detective Fritz says irritates me. And I want to ask him what he was doing with my aunt Nora, but I know now is not the time. But something just tells me that he's up to no good and that he can't be trusted.

"Look, little lady," Fritz says. "With your track record, who's to say you didn't just take that out of her room and bring it here to mess with us? To distract us or who knows what?"

"My track record?" I ask incredulously. "What track record? What did I ever do?"

"You're not known to be the most trustworthy and reliable person, Audrey Bailey."

"Yeah, and according to you, neither are Warner or my sister. But I'm telling you this, Detective Fritz, Warner did nothing to Sydney. Or Lyla. Got it?"

"Oh, is that so?" he asks, his eyebrow raising. "Just how would you know that?"

"All right, all right, let's just calm down," Officer Wilde says. He takes a bracelet from me, which makes me feel a little bit better. He's the only one who truly cares. He's the only cop I like. He puts a hand on Fritz's shoulder. "Why don't you go ahead and give us a minute of privacy?"

Glaring at me and then glaring at my parents, Fritz turns and stalks away.

"Thank you for this, Audrey," Officer Wilde says. "Just... ignore him. He's... overly invested in this case. Borderline obsessed, if you will. It's not healthy. That's why I'm doing what I can to step in and help. To see things more clearly."

My chest is heaving rapidly. I'm heated over my conversation with Fritz. It seems like no matter what I say to him, he takes it and uses it against me.

I feel like I have no idea what he's going to do next.

CHAPTER 48

AMELIA

Every single night and day, it's the same old thing. People gather together. People get their vests and their flashlights and group up. People walk around Toxey screaming my daughter's name in hopes that she'll... what? Crawl out of some hidey-hole she's been hanging in?

I am practically numb this time as I do what everyone is instructing me to do. I get my vest and flashlight. I am put into a group with my husband and daughter. We're told which area we're going to be searching. We're given some speech by a cop about how we've all been working so hard and how tonight is going to be the night that we find her. It doesn't restore anything inside of me. It doesn't make me feel any hope.

In all truth, I don't think we're going to find her tonight. I don't think we're going to find her tomorrow night. I don't think doing these stupid little search parties is getting us anywhere. If somebody kidnapped my daughter, they're going to do whatever it takes to make sure she isn't found. They're probably here at the search party, among us, pretending to be just as invested in getting her location figured out as we are, all the while knowing that we're never going to get her.

It's haunting, and it's infuriating.

Gentry rubs my shoulders as if he's trying to warm me from the cold. Sure, it's a little chilly out tonight, but I'm not cold. I'm far from it. The boiling blood inside my body is keeping me plenty toasty on my own.

"Are you okay tonight?" Gentry asks. But he doesn't care. He hasn't cared in a long time. And every word out of his mouth sends me closer to the edge. So instead of risking starting another fight with him, I stay silent and say nothing.

"Okay, are we all ready?" the cop leading this group we're in asks through her megaphone.

Are we ready? Ready for what? Ready for another pointless dead-end night? Is this just some sort of game to them? Like whoever finds Lyla first gets a prize? Like we're on some sort of scavenger hunt?

Who would've thought that it wouldn't be Gentry sending me over the edge tonight? Instead, it's the cop whose name I don't even know that does it.

"No!" I find myself shouting. Then I'm squeezing myself through the crowd so I can get to the front and address the cop directly. "No, I'm not ready."

The crowd gasps and parts for me so I can get up to the front quicker. When I face the cop, a prissy-looking blonde with her hair tightly pulled back; I am pointing a shaking finger at her.

"What do you think we're going to find tonight? What do you think is going to happen?" My voice is loud and angry. I don't care.

"I..." The cop doesn't know what to say.

"You know what?" I snap. "I'm sick of this!"

"Amelia!" I hear a voice yelling behind me. I ignore it. I keep talking to the cop.

"Why do you think this is going to help us find her? What is the point of any of these parties? They're clearly not working! You guys are clearly not doing enough to find my daughter!" I hardly even feel the tears that are streaming down my cheeks. All I can feel is that they come out warm and then quickly turn icy in the breeze around us. "Do your job! Get me my daughter back! The reason she's still out there is all your fault! The reason I don't have her back in my arms is because of you!"

"The cop looks almost frightened. "Ma'am I—"

I don't even hear what the woman is saying as I feel not one pair of hands pulling me away but two. I look over my shoulder and see that I have two people coming to my "rescue." It's both Gentry and Dean.

"I'm sorry," Gentry calls to the officer as they drag me away.

"No!" I scream, trying to break away from both of them. "Let me go!"

"Just...continue with what you were doing!" Gentry continues to her as everyone stares. Because, of course, he doesn't care at all about what I want. Does he even care about finding Lyla? Does he even care about our daughter at all?

I've already lost sight of Audrey, too. What kind of mother am I?

"Mia," Dean tries, shushing me in a comforting voice. "It's going to be okay!" He sounds frantic and worried. Gentry is saying nothing to me.

When we're a far enough distance away from all the crowds, and they've deemed that I'm not going to sprint back over to the lady cop to keep yelling at her, they finally both let me go.

I stand there and try to collect myself. I can't even believe I let that outburst happen at all. And I also can't believe these two men are standing in front of me. Together. At the same time. Both wear equally concerned expressions on their faces. But I know they're concerned about two different things. Dean is the one actually concerned about me and my well-being. Gentry is only concerned about what a mad woman I've turned into.

"I'm sorry," I mutter, not looking at either of them.

"It's okay," Dean says, first to speak. "I can't imagine how stressful and scary this is for you. It's okay."

"Maybe... Maybe you should just go home for the night," Gentry says.

"I'm more than happy to take her," Dean says.

At first, Gentry doesn't say anything to Dean. He just stands there and stares at him. And I watch him staring at him. It makes me incredibly uncomfortable as I'm trying to figure out exactly what Gentry is thinking right now.

But who am I kidding? Why should I even care?

"I... yeah," I say in a defeated tone. "I think I should go home. Gentry, you need to stay. Stay for Audrey. Go find where she is, and don't let her out of your sight."

"And... you're sure you're fine letting him drive you?" Gentry asks.

"Gentry, he is our daughters' teacher. Of course, I'm fine."

Gentry doesn't look the slightest bit happy about this arrangement but nods his head anyway. "Fine." He looks at Dean again. "Get her home safe."

"Will do," Dean says.

I watch as Gentry stares back and forth between the two of us. He's calculating; I just know it. But he doesn't say anything else. He just gives me another quick nod and leaves to find our daughter. Both of our daughters.

It's a shame he'll likely only end up finding one of them tonight.

CHAPTER 49

AUDREY

I watch, frozen, unable to move or even think—or even breathe—as my mom has her meltdown in front of practically the entire town of Toxey.

I almost think it's safe to say that she's lost it.

And I don't entirely blame her. Are the police doing enough? Are all these search parties really going to be how we find Lyla? I'm having a tough time believing it. What do the people of Toxey think?

On top of witnessing the meltdown, I watch my father and Mr. Reeves drag my mom away from the crowd. I watch the three of them talk in the distance, unable to see their facial expressions or hear what they are saying. Then I watch as Dad walks back in my direction while Mr. Reeves escorts my mom toward the parking lot.

I quickly tell Dad I'm fine, then I focus purely on the search, wishing Warner was here with me. It seems like he's the only friend I have around these days. But from what I can tell, he's nowhere to be seen.

I'm searching through a meadow containing a small pond with a group of about thirty people, my dad only a few steps behind me. People are calling Lyla's name every so often, but I don't bother because I know she's not going to say anything back to me. She's not here. I just know she isn't. I think what we really need to start doing is checking everybody's house. Even if it means getting a warrant for every citizen in Toxey and the towns surrounding us. Whatever it takes.

"Hey, Audrey?"

I stop walking and turn around. Danielle approaches me with a sad look, but her head is held high. "Hi," she says when she reaches me.

"What do you want?" I say, not in the mood. My first guess is that she has some sort of stupid message from Sophia. Danielle and Olive do whatever she wants. Whatever she says. They are her little pets.

"How—how are you?" she asks, walking alongside me as I continue with the search—as pointless as it may be.

"I don't really feel like making small talk with you, Danielle. If I didn't make it clear—"

"I know, I know. I'm sorry," she says quickly. "I'll just get right to it. I shouldn't have stayed silent like that when you confronted us before. I shouldn't have let Sophia take control of the situation. What she did was messed up. That whole thing with Ryan? And the fact that she decided not to believe you without even seeing any proof? I just don't get her."

"Join the club," I say flatly.

"But I'm serious, Audrey. I really am sorry. And I'm not playing her games anymore. I miss you. And I don't wanna stop being friends."

"What, did Sophia kick you out of her little clique or something?" I ask, not believing a word Danielle is saying to me. Sure, I guess if either Danielle or Olive were going to stand up to Sophia, it would be Danielle. But still. I am having a hard time trusting anybody right now.

"No. I told her I am done with her. Done with the way she's been acting. I'm not anybody's minion. And just so you know, I talked to Ryan."

This makes me stop walking again. "What?" I snap my head at her.

She nods. "Yeah. I told him the truth. About why Sophia is pretending to be interested in him. And I told him that you never did anything wrong. That you were never talking to Bryson."

"You... you did?"

"Yeah." She reaches out and grasps my forearm. "I just want to make things right. I'll do whatever I can to prove it to you. I'm really sorry, Audrey."

Danielle really talked to Ryan? Does that mean...?

I pull my phone out of my back pocket. Sure enough, there it is.

I have a text from Ryan Copeland.

Ryan: Hey you. Think maybe we could talk?

CHAPTER 50

MADDY

While lying in bed and texting Steven that I can't sleep, I get the invitation for me to go over to his house for the first time. I feel bad about leaving Warner at home because I know he must be feeling pretty isolated not having his phone or laptop and not being able to go to the search party. It was part of Theodore's advice: no going to the search party and no hanging out with Audrey Bailey. He's just supposed to keep his head down and otherwise resume his normal day-to-day activities. Activities that no longer include his assistant coaching job, apparently.

I decide to check on Warner in his room. Depending on what state he is in will determine whether or not I go to Steven's house.

I knock softly at first and don't receive an answer. A little bit worried that he snuck out of the house somehow without me knowing, I crack his door open and peer inside. Thankfully, he's deeply asleep in his bed.

I go into the kitchen, rifle around in the junk drawer for a sticky note, then I scribble with a pen about where I am and when I'll be back, and I tape it to the inside of his door so that he'll see it if he wakes up. Then I borrow his jeep again and go to the address Steven gave me.

I feel completely out of place and a little embarrassed when I pull up to his giant mansion. How is it that he saw what my house looked like when he drove up to it the other day, and yet he still wants to date me? My house is nothing compared to his. In fact, I'm pretty sure my house could fit into one of his garages. That's right, one. Because Steven Hall has two garages. One on either side of his house. And he has the most beautiful, green front garden I've ever seen with gorgeous old trees from which I want to hang a tire swing.

The exterior is well-groomed, too. Like he has a landscaper come once a week.

I roll into the circular driveway, feeling like this jeep is way too old to even be gracing this house's presence. But I swallow my shame and force myself out of the car. Steven knows practically everything there is to know about me, including how much money I have, and it doesn't bother him. He is a man who truly just likes me for me.

Steven swings open the ten-foot-high front door before I can even ring the doorbell. He grins at me and looks handsome in a casual linen shirt and leisurely shorts. He's barefoot, and his hair is a little tousled like he's been laying down.

"There she is," he says to me. I toss some hair over my shoulder and give him my flirtatious smile. He brings me in for a hug and then lets me inside. I marvel at his foyer as he closes the front door. I am in awe of it all. The sophisticated light fixture. The two staircases wrap around to the top floor. The marble flooring. It's incredible.

"What do you think?" he asks as he sees me staring.

"I think that you might have invited the wrong girl over."

He chuckles and then leads me into the kitchen, where I am again in awe. There, he pours me a glass of wine, and we sit in the most comfortable, softest leather sectional I've ever sat in.

"So," I start, wanting to get the topic of conversation on him so that we don't have to go over how my day has been. "What have you been up to today?"

"Not a whole lot. Spent most of the day at the restaurant. Came back and unwound. I was thinking about you the whole time, though." He shoots me a wink. It makes my heart melt.

"How is The Viper these days?" I ask.

"It'd be better if you popped back in for another visit."

I sigh. "Trust me; you have no idea how good that sounds."

"What's stopping you?"

I give him a look. It seems all I need to do to get him to understand.

"Oh, I take it the family drama. How is all of that going?"

"No, no," I say, shaking a finger at him. "Please don't make me talk about myself. I came here for a good distraction."

He chuckles, and the two of us sip our wine.

"It's quiet around here. Where is Wrigley at tonight?" It's a school night, and it's kind of late. But Steven doesn't seem to mind that he isn't at home.

"He went out to that search party for Lyla Bailey," he says. "You've been going to those, haven't you?"

"I... I have. They're kind of pointless. I feel horrible for Mia, but I really am starting to think they're never going to find her. I feel like it's going to turn into figuring out what happened to her instead of trying to locate her. It's really sad."

"That is sad. Imagine: having a twin who disappears and is never found again. Her poor sister. I can't imagine what she's going through."

Yeah, I feel a little guilty about that, too. Would I have messed with Audrey for trying to tell Warner about his father if I had known this was going to happen to her? It feels a bit childish, looking back at it. But it felt like the right thing to do at the time. I truly felt that Audrey needed to be punished. That I needed to stick to my word. I told her if she ever told a soul the truth about who Warner's father was, she would have to pay. I hate that one little girl has the power to upset my entire life.

"What are you thinking about?" Steven asks me, knocking me out of my trance. I shake my head to get the thoughts away; then, I smile at him brightly. My feet are tucked under my butt as I lounge on his sofa and lean in a little bit closer to him. I want Steven to know just how much I've been thinking about him lately. So I tilt my head. Then I lean in a little bit more. And Steven, seeming to get the idea, follows suit and leans toward me.

Just as my lips are about to touch his, I hear the front door open and close.

"Dad?" a young-sounding voice echoes through the foyer. "Why is Warner Carpenter's jeep out front of our house?"

Steven and I quickly separate on the sofa as Wrigley appears in the kitchen with a full view of us in the living area. "Oh," he says quickly.

Steven swiftly gets to his feet, so I do, too.

"Wrigley, this is my friend, Madeline Carpenter."

We both start walking toward him, and then I hold out my hand for him to shake it. He takes it, looking me up and down with a little bit of reservation about him.

"It's nice to meet you," I say. "I've heard a lot about you."

"I thought you'd still be at the search party," Steven says.

"I was, but... Lyla's mom had sort of a freakout, and she brought up a lot of good points. It seemed kind of pointless to be out there. We're not gonna find her just searching through fields." He looks at me. "You're Warner's mom, right?"

"I am," I say confidently.

Wrigley nods, then his shoulders sag slightly. Steven puts a hand on one of them and grasps it firmly. "Keep your head up, kiddo. She's out there somewhere. They're going to find her."

"Yeah. Maybe..." he trails off, looking at his feet. Then he starts to walk away. "Nice to meet you, Mrs. Carpenter," he says over his shoulder as he goes toward the staircase.

When we're alone again, Steven gives me an apologetic look. "I'm not sure if you were ready to meet him yet or not..."

"Oh, it's okay. It happens. You never know what to expect with teenagers."

"You got that right," he agrees. "Anyway. Shall we go back to the couch?"

"I'd love to," I say with a smile. As we walk back over to it, a thought crosses my mind. "Wrigley seems really sad about Lyla. Is he okay?"

"He's been out of sorts since she disappeared. That kid has it bad for her. Poor guy."

That's when it really clicks. Now I get why Warner doesn't like Wrigley. It's because Wrigley likes Lyla. So that must mean that Warner likes Lyla, too.

CHAPTER 51

AUDREY

Lyla's Fifth Day Missing

I know I'm not going to school right now, but I wake up early, shower, and get ready like I am going anyway. I made up my mind last night while I was lying wide awake in bed scrolling through my phone, my eye continuously catching one text thread with one specific name of somebody I really need to talk to. Somebody who doesn't seem interested in talking to me back.

Jackson.

Dad is already gone, doing who knows what, when I get downstairs. Mom is sitting on the couch, holding a cup of coffee and staring at nothing. Joey is in the kitchen making himself a bowl of cereal.

"Where are you going?" Joey asks, seeing that I have my shoes on and my car keys in my hand.

"Don't worry; I won't be gone long," I say. "I'll probably even be back before Joey leaves. I just have to make a quick errand to talk to a friend."

At this, Mom turns her head to look at me.

"Don't worry, it's not Warner or anything like that," I assure her.

"Who is it?" she asks.

"Danielle. We got in a fight recently, but she tried to make up with me yesterday. Dad can tell you—he saw us together. I just need to hash out some things with her really fast. It's always better to do these things in person, you know?" I don't want to tell her about Jackson because I don't want her to tell me not to get involved. I'm way too past that.

If there's one thing my mother might have been right about yesterday, it was how pointless the search was. How pointless all of them have been. But still, I felt good being out there. Like I was actively trying to get Lyla back instead of just sitting around the house doing nothing.

Five days, Lyla. You've been gone for five days. I think that's long enough, don't you?

"Okay," Mom says quietly. "Um, drive safe."

I don't like seeing her this way. I go over and kiss her on the cheek. She gives me a one-armed hug and sips her coffee but doesn't even look at me.

"I will," I say. Then I give Joey a playful shove on my way to my car. I owe him big time for not spilling the beans about how I snuck out the other night.

When I get to school, I roll up to the curb and put my hazards on. I don't bother going to my parking spot. I know usually, Jackson arrives at school in Warner's jeep, but I don't know how he'll be arriving today. So I'm waiting by the entrance to make sure I don't miss him.

When he arrives, it's via his skateboard. He rides up to me, kicks the board into the air, and catches it. I get out of my car and practically slam the door shut.

"Hey," he says. "You're back."

"I'm not staying," I reply. "Why haven't you texted or called me back?"

"I didn't realize you were calling or texting me," he says, smoothing his hair back like the cool guy he is. "I've been busy."

"Whatever. Can you talk now?"

I know people are looking at us as they walk by. They're all surprised to see me at school.

"I... I really need to get to class early, actually," he tries.

"It won't take long. Why don't we talk in my car?"

He looks over his shoulder like he'd rather be anywhere else but reluctantly follows me into the car.

I turn to him sharply, one of my hands on the steering wheel. "Do you have a car?" is the first thing I ask.

"What?"

"I... I saw you driving a car past our house during the press release. At first, I wasn't sure if it was you, but the more I think about it, the more positive I am that it was you. Did you get a car?"

"No," he says sharply.

"Are you sure?" I ask. "You don't drive an old gray Mustang now?"

"No. I don't. Besides, why would it matter if I did?"

Because you could've taken Lyla in it somewhere.

"I just wanted to check. I'm just worried about this whole Lyla thing. Aren't you?"

"Of course I am; how could you even ask?"

It appears to be true. Jackson does look really beat up about it. He looks tired and not as well-groomed as he normally does.

I sigh deeply and look through the windshield, staring blankly at all of our peers as they head into the school. "It's just really... it's really bad, Jackson. Do you know it's been—?"

"Five days. Yeah. I know."

So he's been counting, too. I don't really know what to make of that.

"I'm scared."

"So that's why you want to talk to me? Because you're scared?"

"I just..." How do I put this without making him think I am suspicious of anything? "Do you know anything? Have you heard from her at all? Did she say anything before she left that struck you as odd?"

His expression darkens. "You don't think I had something to do with it, do you?"

"I—no!" I say, a little bit too defensively.

"Look," he snaps, "the boyfriend is always a suspect. Of course, he's always a suspect. So in case you're wondering, I've already talked to the police. People at school are already looking at me like I did it. I don't need it from you, too."

"Jackson, I'm not saying that; I—"

But he's not listening to me anymore.

He gets out of the car and slams the door closed behind him.

Great. That conversation got me nowhere.

CHAPTER 52

Amelia

Mom comes over again a little bit after Audrey leaves to talk to her friend. She's here to make breakfast. But I know my mother. So I know that's not the only reason why she's here.

She and Joey talk nonstop in the kitchen while I stay in the living room and drink my coffee. Then after we all nibble on pancakes, bacon, and eggs, she sees Joey off to the bus stop while I do some light dishes. I think it might be the first bit of housework I've done since Lyla went missing. But I just don't want to hear my mother saying anything about it or giving me a look if she were to come back and see that I hadn't done anything with myself since she left.

When she returns, it's only her and me in the house.

"So," I start. "What's going on?"

"How are things going around here?" she asks in a casual tone. Then it gets more worried-sounding as she continues. "Any better? How are you doing, sweetie?"

I sigh, stop doing the dishes, and take my gloves off. Then I turn around and lean against the counter as I stare at her. "It's miserable around here. What else would you expect? I am miserable."

She nods her head understandably, takes a seat at the counter, and folds her hands carefully across the countertop. "I'm sorry," she says. "Have you talked to your sister yet?"

Again with the Nora thing? What is her deal about it? Why does she care so dang much about my younger sister?

I remember what it was like when things first started going badly with Nora. After that day when she claimed she saw Carson Price's body in the woods. How broken she was. How upset and unmanageable she was. When Nora started losing it, my entire life was put on hold. Everything I had planned. The reason why I had a job and was saving up all my money. It didn't matter anymore. Suddenly, Nora needed to go to this institution to get better, and suddenly, my parents expected me to help pay for it. I didn't even get to go to the college I wanted to go to. It was all about Nora. All the time.

"No," I say snippily to my mother. "I haven't talked to her. Why? Have you talked to her? Has she been trying to get a hold of me or something?"

"Um, well, I don't know..." she trails off, looking away for me. But I'm irked now. I am hurt that my daughter is missing, and my mom has the audacity to want to talk about Nora instead. It's just like it always was. Or at least how it always was when Nora started her mental health decline. And I suppose I have a lot of built-up resentment about it all.

"What is it with her?" I decide to ask. "Why is it always about Nora with you? Mom, have you forgotten that my daughter is missing? Who cares about whatever little spat I might have gotten into with her? My daughter is missing!"

"I know!" she snaps back, putting a hand to her chest like she can't believe I'm behaving like this. "Honey, I know."

"Then what? Why do you always want to talk about her? Is she the reason why you're here? Do you even care that Lyla is missing?"

"Of course I do!" A tear falls from her eyes straight onto the countertop. "I've just been meaning to talk to you about something, and I haven't been sure about how to bring it up, okay?"

"Talk to me about what?" I ask, my voice quieting down. Still, my arms are crossed in front of me.

"Do you remember much about your grandmother, Patty?"

"Her? Not really, why?" My grandma Patty is from my mom's side. I think I've only met her twice in my entire life. My only memory of her is that her house smelled like burnt chestnuts and was covered in floral wallpaper.

"Well, the reason you didn't see her much while you were growing up was that she... she had some issues, Amelia."

"What kind of issues?"

Mom wipes her eye before continuing. "Some deep, deep mental issues. And that's why I worry about your sister so much. I'm worried that... I'm worried that those issues your grandma Patty had were passed on to Nora. That she has the same issues now."

This is news to me. I never knew there was any history of mental health issues in my family. It was never talked about. Never discussed. We simply never even talked about Grandma Patty. I don't know why I never even tried to bring her up when I was younger. Wasn't I ever curious as to why I never saw her as much as I saw my other grandma?

I'm stunned. "I... I don't even know what to say." Could Nora have mental health issues just like Grandma Patty had? I don't think so. Nora is normal. She had her first love ripped away from her. I think that's enough to make anybody go crazy.

"I think maybe prom was what caused her... mental health decline... in the first place. I... I know they never found Carson Price's body. And I don't know what happened to him. But sometimes I just worry... maybe seeing Carson as dead was easier than accepting the fact that he might've just run away. Does that make sense? In her head, I think she truly believes that she did see him dead. That her mind made it up as a coping mechanism because she can't handle the fact that he would ever willingly not want to be with her."

But the thing is... Carson Price really is dead. Because Maddy and I really did kill him. So no, Nora isn't crazy. But I can't say that to my mom without telling her how I know she's not. So instead, I just have to stand here, letting guilt and shame nearly consume me.

Grandma Patty didn't pass her crazy genes down to my sister.

But what if she passed them on to me?

CHAPTER 53

LYLA

I feel strange today. Off. And I've never felt more alone.

Everyone must think I'm dead, right? How likely is it for a kidnapper's victim to remain alive when it's been five days?

What if I am dead?

What if none of this is really real?

Because this can't be my life, there's no way this is my life. Before Trinity's accident, I would've never thought anything like this could happen to me. I had a good life. A normal life. A normal family... as far as I knew.

"Maybe this is my karma," I say to no one. Why not talk out loud? Am I worried someone is going to hear me talking to myself? No. If anything, it would be nice if someone could hear me talking to myself. If someone heard my voice and came to my rescue and I didn't have to sit here screaming and shouting and begging and pleading and banging on the wall.

So I keep talking. I'm my only company.

"I was texting Wrigley while driving. I'm the reason Trin is... dead. Sydney wanted me to meet her out in those woods. And I went too late. I'm the reason she's dead. I am a terrible person. Me being in this shed is all my fault."

What if this shed is a metaphor for something? What if I died originally when the masked man first caught me? And this is where I went after?

Feeling a little crazy, I realize that maybe there's one way I can find out for sure.

I get up off the ground and stretch. My entire body is stiff from my lack of movement. Mostly I just lay on the floor all day and night and stare at the dust and cobweb-ridden ceiling.

I walk over to the table and dig around until I can find something sharp enough to use. I pick up the least rusty-looking nail there is. Then I hold out my arm.

It's been a while since I felt any pain. A new wound will surely be enough to convince me that I still am here.

I take a deep breath, hold it, then bring the nail down and press deep enough to cut skin as I drag it horizontally across my forearm. I gasp as I feel the sting and watch the blood bubble out. Then I drop the nail and step backward, shocked at what I'm seeing. It hurts. And I'm bleeding.

So I am still alive.

"When am I ever going to get out of here?!"

I walk over to my little crack in the wall. It's daylight out again. "Why are you doing this to me?!" I call out. I know that I'm in a shed at our tormentor's property. Some old cabin. He must be inside there now. He must be able to hear me, right?

"Just tell me!" I continue. "You don't even have to let me out! Please just tell me why!"

Just as I was expecting, nothing happens.

"I said, 'Why?!'"

Nothing.

"Hello? Come on, answer me!"

It just goes on like that while my arm bleeds onto the ground. I stand there at that little crack in the wall and ask the same question over and over.

Why?

CHAPTER 54

WARNER

We are released from First Hour about twenty minutes into the period. It's time for us all to make our way to the gym for some sort of safety assembly. I haven't heard much about it, but I'm pretty sure it has to do with all of the scary stuff that's been happening around Toxey to teenagers lately. I wonder if they held one of these assemblies back when my mom was in high school. After Carson Price disappeared.

MURDERER is still written on my locker, and everybody is staring at me because of it. But heck, they were already staring at me before then, too. They're all thinking it anyway. It just took someone with the guts to actually write it out for everyone to see.

I'm a suspect. Not just to the police but all my peers as well. As people move around me, I repeatedly get shoulder-checked. People keep whispering, "Murderer," as they pass. People keep shooting me dirty looks. But I'm trying to take that lawyer's advice—just keep my head down and resume activities as normal.

Just ignore them, Warner.

The next shoulder check I receive is a bit more aggressive than the other ones, and as the person passes me, they turn sharply on their heel to stop in front of me. It's Wrigley Hall, and he looks angry.

"Murderer, huh?" he asks.

Around us, people are already stopping to watch, probably hoping a fight breaks out between us.

But I have no idea what Wrigley's problem is.

"It's not true," I say, keeping my head held high.

"Bull," he snaps. "Tell me what you know. What happened to Lyla?"

"If I knew, I wouldn't be here right now. I would be out there bringing her back." I can't believe anyone thinks I would hurt her. I'm crazy about her. I just want her to be okay.

"Why would somebody write that on your locker, then?" he asks. "Tell me. Why?"

"Dude, what is your problem? I already told you I didn't do anything!"

So much for keeping a low profile.

"My problem is that Lyla's been gone for five days! I want to know what happened to her, and if you have anything to do with it, or if you know anything at all, you need to tell me!"

Suddenly, a voice is shouting behind me. "Hey!" They sound angry. We both turn and see that Jackson is storming up to us, pushing his way through the throng of students.

He steps right in the middle of Wrigley and me. "What's going on?" he demands, shooting Wrigley a dirty look.

"He thinks I did something to Lyla," I inform him.

Now Jackson seems even angrier. "Why would he have done something?" he snaps to Wrigley. "Warner is my best friend. And he's one of Lyla's good friends, too. You don't know what you're talking about. Stop barking up the wrong tree."

"I don't think I'm far from the right tree at all, actually," Wrigley says, not backing off.

Jackson raises his eyebrows. "Why do you care so much, anyway?" he asks him. "Huh? Since when are you and Lyla even friends? When did you start talking to her in the first place? I know you're the reason she got into that car accident. Maybe you did something to her."

Wrigley takes a step closer like he's ready to take a swing at Jackson. I am honestly surprised that he's this angry. He seems as angry as I feel, but he's just not doing as good of a job keeping it in as I am.

"All right, break it up!"

The voice belongs to a freshman teacher who is carefully pushing his way through the crowd to get to all three of us. "Everyone get to the assembly! NOW!" Then he pushes Wrigley, Jackson, and me apart from each other when he reaches us. "You guys better knock it off, or you'll find yourself at the principal's office."

"We're not done here," Wrigley says before shooting me another look of hatred. "I'm going to figure out what you did."

WARNER

Needless to say, I'm in a pretty foul mood when I get to the assembly. I try to sit in the middle of the crowd and blend in with everybody, and I keep the hoodie over my head even though technically we're not allowed to inside the school. I don't know if this is drawing more or less attention to me, but I don't really care. Because the second Dean Reeves walks up to the podium and speaks into the microphone, I'm even more angered. Just the sight of him makes my teeth clench.

"Thank you all for coming today," he says.

Like we had a choice.

"As you well know, some tragic events have befallen our beloved school. And even though we have lost two cherished peers of ours, one of them is still missing. I appreciate everybody's efforts. I've seen you all out there searching for Lyla Bailey. Your actions don't go unnoticed, and her family really appreciates it. And I'm sure Audrey Bailey, and her parents and brother, appreciate their privacy during a time like this, too. So thank you."

This is so pointless. I don't want to be here. Him talking to us all about this isn't going to bring Lyla back. It's not going to stop people from thinking I had something to do with it.

"We've called you all here today to go over some ways we can prevent more tragic things from happening. I just want to review some safety protocols and give you all some tips on how to protect yourselves. I think it's important."

Sitting in a chair behind him, Principal Mathers is nodding his head grimly, agreeing with every word Mr. Reeves is saying.

I can barely bear to look at that man. Up there, seeming like he's this totally cool guy who everyone at school loves. But he's not deceiving only me; he's deceiving all of them. What would they think if they knew the truth about him? That he's known he's my father and hasn't done anything about it for nearly eighteen years?

You know what?

I think I want to find out.

I get up from my seat in the stands and step over people until I'm going down the steps and walking on the wooden floor of the basketball court. Then I go up onto the platform, and Mr. Reeves, finally realizing what I'm doing, stops his stupid speech abruptly and looks at me with wide eyes.

"Warner, not now," he says. "We can talk after." He's speaking away from the microphone, so not everyone can hear.

But I nudge him out of the way and stand in front of the microphone directly, eliciting some gasps from my peers.

"I think I want to talk about this now, actually," I say, making sure everybody can hear me loud and clearly. But as I speak, I only look at Dean Reeves. My father.

"Mr. Carpenter, sit down," the principal says, getting to his feet. But I ignore him as well.

Mr. Reeves is looking at me with a shocked expression. Like he has absolutely no idea what's coming. But I don't even pause to consider that maybe he doesn't know.

Because I know. Deep down, I know the truth—he's known all along.

"This'll just take a second, Principal Mathers," I say. "Mr. Reeves. Don't you think to start the safety meeting, we should all address how we need to feel safe around our teachers? How we need to be able to trust them?"

He opens his mouth, but it's clear he has no idea what to say.

"Like you, for example," I continue. "You'd like us all to trust you, right? You'd like me to trust you?"

"Warner, please," he says softly.

"That's a yes, right?"

He hangs his head and nods glumly.

"But the thing is, Mr. Reeves—I don't know how we're supposed to do that. How I'm supposed to do that. How can we trust you when you've spent your entire life living a lie?"

"Warner, that's enough!" The principal is approaching me. I have to do this fast.

"When were you ever planning on telling me that you're my father?" I look him directly in the eyes as I ask it. Then, unexpectedly, my own eyes well with angry, hurt tears. "Huh? Tell me that, Mr. Reeves." Then I push the microphone away as hard as possible and jump off the stage as it screeches with feedback. I don't look to see what anyone is doing about my outburst. About my big reveal. I just look straight ahead and run right through the metal double doors, getting the heck out of there.

CHAPTER 56

MADDY

I know somebody is repeatedly calling me, but I'm in the middle of giving one of my clients a hair trim. And wanting to be professional and respectful, I calmly have to stand there and continue cutting their hair like I'm not worried at all that something horrible has happened. Why else would my phone be vibrating so much?

"It looks like somebody would really like to get a hold of you," the sweet older lady says to me as I work.

I wave it off with the hand my scissors are in. "I'm sure it's nothing. I've been getting a lot of those spam calls lately," I reassure her. But I am nervous.

And when the lady finally pays and leaves, I all but run back over to my station to pull my cell phone out of my purse.

Seven missed calls from Dean. Several texts, too. Most of them say something along the lines of, Madeline, call me now. It's an emergency.

"I have to step outside for a moment," I say to my coworkers. Then without waiting for them to tell me if it's okay or not or if I have another client waiting to get their hair done with me, I dash out the glass door and make sure I'm far enough away from where anyone might be able to overhear me before I press the button to call Dean back.

"Geez, Maddy, there you are!" Dean says in a frantic voice that I don't think I've ever heard before.

"Dean, what's going on?" I ask. "Is Warner okay?"

He doesn't have his phone. What if something happened to him, and he had no way of letting me know?

"He's... I don't know how he's doing, in all honesty," Dean tells me.

"What are you talking about?"

He takes a deep breath. "Maddy. I have no idea how. I swear to you. I said nothing. I told no one."

Stones drop in my stomach. My hands grow clammy. I can hear the sound of my own heart beating.

"Dean. What. Happened." My tone is very careful. Very direct.

"He... oh, Mads, he knows I'm his father."

There it is. The words I never wanted to hear out of Dean's mouth. Ever.

Am I that stupid not to think this was inevitable?

I don't know what to say. I don't know what to do. I feel like I can't breathe. I'm seeing dark spots in the corners of my vision. Great. A panic attack is about to start.

"Are you there?" he asks.

"I'm—yeah," I say, sounding as if there's a frog in my throat.

"I don't know how this happened," he assures me. "I swear to you. But not only does he know—now the entire school knows, too. He... he took it upon himself to announce it to everyone at the school assembly today."

This makes my mouth drop open. I can picture it. An angry, fed-up Warner, just having learned the truth somehow, so blinded by his rage that he storms up to the microphone in that smelly old gym and tells everyone Dean's and my dirty little secret.

What am I going to do?

"Mads?"

"This... this is your fault, Dean."

"How? I just told you I never told him. I don't know how he found out, Maddy, but I didn't do this."

"Still! It's your fault! If you would've just been there from the beginning, none of this would've ever happened!"

I have so many emotions in my body that all I can do is press the END button. I can't talk to him any longer.

I sit down at the picnic table Amelia once confronted me on and tug at the roots of my hair as I try to breathe. I don't know what I'm going to do. I don't know how I'm going to handle this. All I know is that I have to face Warner sooner or later. And I have to face the truth.

It takes me a good twenty minutes to calm myself down. Then I walk back inside my salon and tell my coworkers that I have a family emergency and that I need to leave. And I know, I know I shouldn't be leaving work early again. I know we need the money. I'm already late with the electricity bill and the mortgage. But I can't worry about that now. I have to go home and prepare.

I have to go home and face my son.

CHAPTER 57

AMELIA

I don't know where my mom is, but she told me she just had some errands to run and that she would be returning to my house soon. I told her I don't need her to be keeping me company twenty-four-seven and that I am doing okay on my own, but she isn't having it. She won't listen to me—but that's nothing new. She's never been one to listen to me much. She just does whatever she feels like. Whatever she thinks is right, regardless of what anyone else thinks or wants.

I honestly wonder how she and my father are still married.

It's quiet in my house this afternoon. I am all alone.

Again.

But I should be grateful for this little time I surely have. The weird thing is that I have no idea where Gentry is, and I don't much care, either—the not caring part isn't weird to me. It's the norm for me now. I don't care where Gentry goes, what he does, or who he talks to. As long as he's not around me.

Is that horrible? I don't know.

I get up from the sofa in my favorite front room with a heavy sigh. I know my mother will be disappointed with me if she comes back and sees that I haven't moved from the same spot she left me, and as much as I don't feel like doing anything right now, I don't feel like seeing that dumb look on her face either. So I decide I'll catch up on some laundry.

I walk up the stairs to Joey's room and grab his hamper, and then I hear a creaking noise coming from the loft, and it makes me freeze. But it's probably just one of those noises of the house settling, right?

Still, I am slightly more cautious when I leave Joey's room and head to the staircase. I realize just how alone I am. Did I make sure all the doors and windows were locked? I know we remind the kids to do it, but I didn't even think to make sure for myself.

You're being silly. No one is here. It's just you.

But the uneasy feeling doesn't leave me as I load the clothes into the washing machine and start the load. I still have this bizarre feeling that someone is watching me. But how would that even be possible?

I leave the laundry room, peering around both corners of the doorway before I do so. Then when I step, I realize I am tip-toeing, not wanting the sound of my footsteps to be heard.

No one is here. No one is watching you.

Despite the thoughts I am thinking to try and calm myself down, I am not satisfied.

Especially when I walk to the front door and see that the deadbolt is unlocked.

Great.

My uneasiness turns to fear as I stand there in the foyer. The door was unlocked. That means my instinct could be right.

Someone could be in here with me.

I make up my mind quickly and go into the kitchen. I grab a long butcher knife out of one of the drawers, and I figure I better start upstairs, where I first heard that creaking noise. I ignore the fact that my hand holding the knife is shaking as I move about the house.

When I make it up the stairs, I start checking every room, even the closets, terrified of what I am going to find when I swing each door open. But each bedroom, each walk-in closet, is so far empty.

I'm beginning to think I have officially gone crazy. I mean, really crazy.

I go back down the stairs and pause. Should I check the hallway with the study and master bedroom next? The hallway with the guest bathroom next to the laundry room? The mudroom and the garage?

I take a left back into the family room and kitchen, where I just recently got the knife and hadn't seen anyone. Still, as I stand between both areas of the house, I see nothing.

Until suddenly, that nothing turns into something.

Right there, written on the window above the kitchen sink—it's a note in black ink. It's sloppily written, and as I get closer to it, I realize that the note was written backward, from the outside of my house:

YOU DESERVE WHAT'S COMING TO YOU

I cry out in fear and drop the knife to the floor. When I can't bear to look at the message any longer, I run into the front room and fall back into the couch, feeling more terrified than I have ever felt in my entire life. I don't know if whoever wrote that is still here or if they're watching me. And I don't know what to do. Where to hide. So I just sit there shaking.

My first thought is that I know who left me that note.

Carson Price. It was him. He's alive. And he did this to mess with me. He's always been out there, hiding in the redwoods, just waiting for this moment.

What am I saying, though?

No. It's not him. It can't be him.

Carson Price is dead.

CHAPTER 58

MADDY

I think I'll have some time when I get home to prepare myself for what it is I am going to say to my son when I see him. To try and plan out ahead of time some sort of speech. Some way I can say everything to him just right to where he isn't so furious at me that he never wants to talk to me again.

But the second I walk through my front door, I realize that preparation isn't going to be possible.

Warner is already home.

I clear my throat and drop my keys on the catch-all on the small sideboard overflowing with books along the wall next to the front door. "Wh-what are you doing home?" I ask my son, my voice not sounding the least bit casual. He can tell that I know what happened. I know he can.

"I got sent home," he says to me as he sits in the armchair in the living room, his head down and his voice flat.

"Wh-why's that?" I ask.

"Oh, ya know—interrupted the school's assembly about safety."

I slowly step toward him. "And, uh, why did you do that?"

"Come on, Ma," he says darkly. "I find it hard to believe that you really don't know. I'm sure it's all anyone in this whole town can talk about. It is quite the scandal, after all. And this town loves getting something juicy to gossip about."

"Warner." I don't sit down. I can't. I am too terrified. Too worried about what he's going to do or say to me.

"What?"

"Why... don't you tell me what happened?"

"Guess."

"Just... just tell me."

He sighs heavily and shakes his head slowly. Back and forth. "No, Mom. For once, I think it's time for you to tell me something."

A single tear falls from my eye to my cheek. I sniff. "You're right, Warner. You're right."

"So?"

I take another step toward him. "I, uh, I talked to Mr. Reeves on the phone not too long ago. It's why I left work early."

"And?" he asks. "What is it, Mr. Reeves told you?"

More tears fall. It feels like my heart is being crushed into a million pieces. And it doesn't even make sense. I am the one who did this to him. I am the one who kept his father a secret from him his entire life.

"Warner, I just wanted the best for you," I say. "That's all I ever wanted. You... you have to understand."

"What are you talking about? Just. Say. It."

"Warner..."

"TELL ME THE TRUTH!"

A sob escapes me. I was trying my hardest to keep it in, but I just can't do it. "He's your father, okay?!" I cry. "I'm sorry, Warner! I'm so, so sorry!"

He gets up from the chair. Tears are streaming down his cheeks, too. "You've known. You've known all this time, haven't you? My entire life!"

"Yes! I have! I'm so sorry, Warner, I have!"

"H-how could you do this to me? Why didn't you ever tell me? I just don't get it! Why?!"

I step toward him again. I just want to throw my arms around him. I want to get his crying to stop. I want to do whatever I can to take his pain away.

But Warner backs away from me so abruptly that he trips over the leg of the chair, falls back, hits his side on the armrest, and lands on the ground.

"Warner!" I reach a hand to help him up, but he scrambles backward toward the dining area.

"Stay away from me!"

"I'm sorry, okay?!" I plead. I'm full-on sobbing now, and there is nothing that can stop it. "I didn't want to tell you because I thought that would mean you would want to try and find a way to have him in your life, and he doesn't deserve you, Warner. He doesn't!"

"Why not?"

"Because he... he abandoned you! He abandoned us!"

My son wipes snot from under his nose with the sleeve of his hoodie and stays on the ground. "What are you talking about?"

"The second Dean found out, he was scared. He didn't want any part of it! He... he broke up with me and left me to raise you all on my own. I never wanted you to find this out. I never wanted you to know you had a father who didn't want you. I'm so, so sorry!" I sink back into the couch when my knees buckle, and I can no longer hold myself up anymore.

"He...didn't... want me?"

I continue to cry. I can't believe this day has finally come. I should have always known it would have.

"No," I say, "he didn't."

CHAPTER 59

MADDY

I don't know how it's even possible. But somehow, eventually, Warner and I calmed down. We calmed down enough to where he even let me hug him. He actually let me hug him, there on the floor in the dining area of our small, crappy house that I bought all by myself. Because I didn't need anyone to help me raise my son, I did it all on my own, and I am proud of it.

After we held each other, I helped him off the ground, and we walked over into the living area and sat down. There is where he told me how he found out.

Craig Fritz.

We both cried a little more; then Warner told me he needed some time alone. I found this completely justifiable, given everything he had just learned. So I let him retreat into his room, where he softly closed the door. Then I put my head in my hands, and I've been sitting here like this ever since.

Eventually, I make myself get up. I can't just keep sitting here feeling sorry for myself. I can't sit here waiting for more fireworks. For another explosion to erupt in my life. For another bomb to drop. And I'm terrified that while I am sitting here, I am going to start hearing Warner sobbing in his room. I don't think I can bear it.

"Warner, I am going to Steven's, okay?" I call down the hallway. When he says nothing, I don't bother going to check on him, and I just take the keys to his jeep and leave.

I'm not going to Steven's. Not right now. There's only one thing in the world I want to do.

I speed down the dirt roads of our neighborhood. I roll stop signs and take sharp right turns. I barely pay attention to stoplights, and I recklessly drive the whole way there.

The whole way to Craig Fritz's house.

He lives in the house his parent's lived in. He bought it from them ridiculously cheap before they moved to some sunny city in Arizona. I've always known how to get to it.

I peel loudly into his driveway and slam the jeep's door when I get out of it. I know he might be at work right now, but for his sake, he better be home.

I pound on the old dusty screen in front of his front door. "Craig?! Get out here! Now!"

I keep pounding on it. I'll keep pounding on it, and I'll never stop until he answers.

Thankfully, it doesn't take long for him.

"Maddy, what on earth?" he says when he opens his front door and sees me behind the screen.

"How could you do this?!" I shout. He's lucky this screen is between us, or else I think I would hurt him. Shove him. Kick him. Something. "You had no right!"

"What are you talking about?" he asks sharply. It smells strange inside his house. Strong.

"What are you even doing at my house right now? Have you lost your mind?"

"Why did you tell him?!"

"Tell who?!" His voice is getting defensive.

"My son! How could you? How dare you!"

To my horrified astonishment, Craig stands there and smiles at me. Actually smiles!

"So, he finally told you, huh?"

"This is my life you're messing with!"

"Maddy, Maddy, Maddy. I'm sorry, but someone had to tell him."

I slap my hands on the screen and growl. "The decision was not up to you! If I wanted to tell him, I would tell him! In my own way. In my own time!"

Still, the jerkwad is smiling. "Sure, sure," he says. "But tell me this: what great lengths would you have gone to make sure this secret... stayed a secret?"

"What?" I am almost speechless. "Are you kidding me?!"

"I'm just curious."

"LEAVE ME AND MY FAMILY ALONE!"

"Ah, you see? I'm afraid I can't do that," he says, chuckling. "Your son, Warner, is a person of interest in a murder investigation, Madeline. Don't you forget. I'm not going to be leaving you or your family alone until I get the answers I'm wanting."

"Why you—!" I grab the handle of the screen door to try to pull it open as I scream some more in frustration. To my dismay, it does not budge.

"Ah, ah, ah," he says, shaking his head. "I think it's better if you stay out there. Don't you?"

I slap both hands on the screen again. "My son did nothing, Craig! I did nothing!" I want to break the door down and tackle him. I'm quite certain I've never wanted anything more in my life.

"Sure, sure, Mads." He steps away and begins closing his door.

"NO!" I bellow. "I'm not done with you!"

"Have a good rest of your day, Maddy."

He closes the door, and I hear it lock, too.

"NO!" I slap the screen. I kick it. I jiggle the handle. And I scream. But it's no use.

Craig Fritz has made ruining my life one big game to him.

And right now, he's winning.

CHAPTER 60

AUDREY

I was too stressed out and anxious to come home after my failed attempt at confronting Jackson outside of school this morning. So I drove around Toxey and tried to distract myself. I went downtown and shopped in some boutiques. Then I went into Delilah's and had myself a root beer float, which I sipped ever so slowly as I sat there at the counter and watched an old couple split a sundae. I texted Warner a bit, too, while I was there, to check on him, but he never messaged me back.

It's not until I get in my car after Delilah's and go to play a song on my Spotify that I see on social media the horrifying video someone captured of Warner telling the whole school that he knows Dean Reeves is his father. It makes me audibly gasp and drop my phone on my lap.

How could this have happened? How could Warner have found out?

Instantly, I think of his mother. Does Maddy know yet? Does she think I told him? And if so, what is she planning on doing to me to retaliate?

I can feel myself beginning to panic. Should I say something to Warner? Should I tell him how I knew and how she made me swear not to tell him?

No. He'd hate me forever. No way he'd ever forgive me.

Still, I'm nervous. Maybe Maddy is the one I need to talk to. But how? I can't just show up at Warner's house and tell him I'm not there to see him but to see his mom instead.

Ugh!

I take a few deep breaths and force myself to drive home, where I planned on going originally. When I park the car in the garage and walk inside through the mudroom, I freeze because I can hear my mom talking to someone on the phone.

"I just don't know what to do, Maddy."

She's talking to Maddy? Right now? After this stuff with Warner's father and my English teacher going down?

It's clear she's too distracted talking to her friend that she doesn't realize I have walked into the house. I can see her in the living room, sitting on the sectional, her back to me and her phone to her ear.

I decide I have to stay quiet and eavesdrop.

"I just... I keep having this horrible thought. An insane one, really. I mean, it wouldn't even make any sense..."

What is she talking about? And why is the window cleaner sitting out on the counter? Since when has Mom decided she's finally okay enough to start doing some housework around here?

"I know," she says after Maddy does some talking. "I just can't help but feel like I'm being messed with. And today isn't the first time I've felt this way, too."

She feels like she's being messed with? By who?

More silence as Maddy talks. Then she speaks again. "Yeah. And I know this sounds crazy, but... I feel like I'm being... watched. God, how paranoid am I?"

That sentence makes me feel a little afraid and kind of guilty. But it's true. right now, she is being watched. By me. But if it's not me she's worried about, who is it?

Mom sighs and runs a hand over her face. "I don't know. What if... what if it was Carson?"

What?

Why is my mom saying that? Why is she even talking about Carson Price? He's dead, isn't he? Missing.

Isn't he?

Whatever happened to him, wasn't the last time anyone heard from him years ago, back when my mom was in high school?

And isn't it possible—at least according to what I heard Craig shouting at my mother when I followed her to their confrontation that one night—that she and Maddy killed him?

Mom chuckles pathetically. Meanwhile, I have my hand over my heart to try and calm the fact that it's started beating rapidly. "Oh, I know," she says to Maddy. "It's silly. How crazy would that be, right? I know, I'm being ridiculous."

Yeah, Mom. You got that right.

So many questions are running through my mind right now that I can barely even process them. Why would my mom be talking to Maddy about Carson? Especially if they didn't have anything to do with him being dead or missing? And why would she be casually mentioning to Maddy—whom she doesn't want anyone knowing she's friends with again for some reason—that she's worried Carson is messing with her? Especially if she didn't do anything to him?

I shudder and keep listening.

"You just need to be careful, okay? I know you're dealing with a lot already. Just... take precautions. Because if I'm being messed with, and my girls are being messed with, and Warner is being messed with, then you might be messed with next. Not that I'm trying to scare you or anything. I'd have you come stay with me if it was possible, but..."

But you just don't want anyone knowing you and Maddy have rekindled your friendship, do you, Mom? You don't want anyone knowing that there is a reason you're concerned about Carson coming back from the dead—or wherever he's been hiding all this time—and "messing" with you.

But if she and Maddy never harmed Carson, then why do they both seem so suspicious?

CHAPTER 61

AMELIA

"**A**re you sure you're okay?" I ask Maddy as we continue to talk on the phone. I called her almost immediately after cleaning off the writing on the window outside. It came off easily—I'm thinking it was written with a dry-erase marker of sorts.

Maddy lets out a slow, long breath. She's definitely not okay. I wonder if what I have told her has gotten her all worked up.

"I have to tell you something," she says.

My stomach dips. "Okay."

"Um, the thing is, Mia, I haven't exactly been honest with you about something. And I don't have a clue how you're going to react once I tell you..."

"Tell me what?" I ask. "It's okay. You can tell me anything. We're in this together. You know that."

"Mom, I'm home!"

I jump and look behind me to see Audrey walking into the kitchen through the mudroom. I hadn't even heard the garage door open.

"Who ya talking to?" she asks casually. I stand up and start walking away from her toward my bedroom.

"Just one sec," I say to Maddy as she begins telling me the thing she's scared to say. Then I look back at my daughter. "No one," I lie. "I'll be out in a bit."

I walk to my room and shut and lock the door behind me.

That had been close. What would Audrey have to say if she found out Maddy and I were friends again?

"Sorry," I say to Maddy. "You can tell me now."

"Um, okay. Well, the thing is... I have sort of always known who Warner's biological father is."

Whoa. This is definitely not the confession I had been expecting. I thought maybe she was going to finally tell me that she and Nora had stayed friends all of these years since everyone seems to want to talk to me about her today and all.

"What?" I ask, wondering if maybe I didn't hear her right. But I already know who Warner's father is. It's Dean.

"I know, I know," she says, talking quickly now. "I just didn't know how to tell you. We weren't friends anymore at the time anyway, and it happened so long ago, and I've been so ashamed..."

"Wh-who is it, then?"

"Um, it's Dean Reeves. He's the father."

I have to pretend to be surprised. But I am far from it. Instead, I find myself in a trance as a memory takes over my brain.

Dean and I were sitting on a bench under a shady tree at my college's campus, and he was acting weird. It was my sophomore year there, where I was diligently studying interior design. Dean was a freshman at a different college a few hours away. But he had driven all the way out here to spend time with me for Spring Break. Up until that point, we had had an amazing time. But that morning, he asked if we could go on a walk, and then we ended up quietly sitting on that bench.

Gentry had been pursuing me since he first found out we were both attending the same college together, and we even shared a few classes. And I liked him enough, but there was just something keeping me from settling into what would surely be a comfortable relationship with Gentry. And I knew that something—or someone—was Dean.

Dean and I had first been weirdly calling each other nonstop. And then one weekend, back toward the beginning of the school year, we decided to drive halfway to each other in nearly the dead of night, just because he had dared us to. And it had been one of the best nights of my entire life. We had talked and laughed as we sat on the hood of his Bronco and looked up at the brilliantly shining stars in the middle of nowhere. Then he told me how much he had missed me since I went away for college and how much he still had remaining feelings for me. We had kissed then—our second time ever. And it had been just as magical—if not more—than the first time, when I had been a freshman in high school and he in the eighth grade—the secret kiss we had shared that I made him promise never to tell anyone about. That I never told anyone about, either. My little sister had a massive crush on Dean, and I knew it would break her heart if he found out what we had done.

But things were different after Nora went away. And since she had turned eighteen and was on her own, and she and Dean hadn't even so much as shared a phone call in forever, it seemed like maybe it was finally going to be okay if I let Dean pursue me like he had told me he always wanted to.

After that weekend, there were more weekends. And Dean and I continued talking nonstop. But still, something was holding me back from making it public and telling anyone about how I was romantically involved with him. Although I was sure if he could, Dean would shout about it from the rooftops. He was absolutely smitten with me, and he made it clear.

"What's going on with you today?" I decided to finally ask him as he looked at anything and everything but me on that shady bench.

"Mia, I have to talk to you about something. It's kinda... big."

"Okay," I said, reaching out and taking his hand because he looked so nervous about it. I had absolutely no idea what he was going to tell me. None.

Finally, he looked at me. "You know that I really like you, right?"

I giggled. "Yeah. I think so."

"I mean it. I really like you. You're... you're all I think about."

I could feel myself blushing. I wondered if maybe he was about to officially ask me to be his girlfriend.

Boy, how wrong I had been.

"I really like you, too," I told him. Then I gave him a small, playful shake. "Just tell me what's on your mind and why you're being so weird already!"

"Okay, okay." He looked away from me again and cleared his throat. "I don't even know where to begin."

"Whatever it is, I'm sure it's okay."

"It's not, though," he argued. "It's really not."

His words made my heart fall. "Oh."

He sighed before he continued. "You know how I started dating Madeline Carpenter again at the end of high school?"

My stomach dipped, and my face turned red at just the sound of her name being said out loud. Madeline Carpenter, his ex-girlfriend and my ex-best friend, was one person we never talked about. And I didn't want to start now. "Yeah," I said anyway.

"Um, it didn't last long. I swear to you. I don't even know why I agreed to get back with her. She and I just don't... we don't make sense."

"What is this about, Dean?" I fidgeted in my seat. My body was no longer turned toward him.

"You mean a lot to me, and that's why you deserve to know the truth, Mia."

"What truth?" I asked, my voice hoarse. Was he still seeing her? Had he been seeing her without telling me?

Or... wait a second. Hadn't I heard a rumor about Maddy from my mother not too long ago...?

Oh.

My.

God.

"No," I breathed as he struggled to find the right way to tell me. He turned to look at me again, and his eyes were welled with big fat tears.

I couldn't believe it.

"Dean, you didn't."

He hung his head and nodded. "I... I got her pregnant, Mia."

Suddenly, it felt like all this time we had been together, every romantic moment we had shared had been one big lie. None of it felt real anymore.

Dean Reeves was having a baby with my ex-best friend.

"This... this can't be happening," I said, not looking at him. Now my eyes were tearing up as well.

"I-I can't be a dad, Mia. I'm only eighteen!"

"Dean, please!" I got up from the bench. I couldn't take hearing any more of this. "Just... stop." All this time, he had been courting me and spending this time with me, and meanwhile, back home, Maddy was there carrying his child. No one in the town even knew, as far as the rumor went, who the father of Maddy's baby was. I knew right away that I was one of the only people in the world who knew the truth.

Dean got to his feet as well and reached out his hands to hold mine, but I backed away from him. "Mia..." he trailed off, sounding broken.

"Whether you want to be a...a dad or not...that sounds like a personal problem. Y-you should really go home and take care of that."

Then I started walking away.

"Mia, don't!" he called after me. "Please! Don't do this!"

I couldn't even bring myself to look over my shoulder at him one last time. But from that moment on, I knew.

Dean and I would never have a future.

CHAPTER 62

MADDY

I sit there in my car after I finish talking on the phone with Mia, revealing to her the truth. It feels weird to have it all out in the open like this with her. Especially when I know, she has a secret about Dean, too. One she hasn't told me about yet.

I know Mia and Dean had some sort of fling or relationship with each other when they were both in college. I didn't learn the info from Dean, either. I learned it from an anonymous piece of mail sent to my house, with a picture of the two of them kissing inside of it. In the photo, both Mia and Dean look young, and Dean is wearing a college sweater.

I want Mia to tell me the truth. It hurts me a little that she hasn't yet. But I know we haven't been friends again for very long, and maybe she will tell me. Maybe it will just take a little more time.

I just hope it happens soon. I love Mia. And I love that we're friends again. But I know if the truth doesn't come out, resentment is going to build, and it's going to put a heavy strain on our relationship.

I still have so many questions about her and Dean's fling. When had they even started developing feelings for each other? Back in high school, when Mia and I were best friends, she had seemed mad at me for dating Dean when we both knew how in love with him Nora was. But Nora wasn't my best friend or sister, and she had told me personally that she was totally fine with Dean and me dating, so I went for it. Was it way back then that Mia had feelings for him? When we were teenagers? Had she used Nora as a cover-up for the real reason why it bothered her that we were together?

And when had Dean started getting feelings in return for her? It makes my stomach roll to think about it. What if they had started talking when Dean and I got back together at the end of high school when Mia went away for college? What if Dean had completely played me?

And what if Mia was the reason Dean didn't stick around when I told him I was having his kid?

I think back again to the conversation I just had with Mia. I know I should be thinking more about what she told me about Carson. The ridiculous thing about how she's worried he is still somehow out there, messing with her. But I don't think there's any possible way that's true—seeing as we killed him—so it's easy to brush aside and ignore. Instead, I'm obsessing over what I told her about Dean.

Had she seemed really all that surprised?

What if she already knew?

What if, while they were having their fling, Dean had already told her?

God. I think I'm going to be sick.

CHAPTER 63

WARNER

It's out there. It's all out in the open. Everybody knows. My mom knows. Mr. Reeves knows. My entire school knows. And I know Audrey wasn't at school, but she's probably figured it out from social media by now, too.

Dean Reeves is my father.

I guess the only person that doesn't know is Lyla.

I can't believe it's true. I don't know what I was expecting when I confronted Mr. Reeves like that on stage. Or what I was expecting when I got home later and talked to Mom about it. Maybe part of me thought she would tell me I was wrong. That she would tell me it was impossible. That Craig Fritz got it all wrong. But I had also been expecting the conversation with my Mom to go sort of just like it had.

My mom.

I can't believe that after such a huge revelation and the ginormous fight we had just gotten into, all she wanted to do was go to Steven Hall's house. Wrigley's dad's house. It makes me mad because it's as if she doesn't care that much. As if she doesn't understand that my world was just completely turned upside down. That the rug was pulled out from underneath me, leaving me in a heap on the floor. Either she doesn't understand, or she doesn't care.

I sit there in my bed and think it over.

My mom is a liar.

What else has she lied to me about? What other secrets are there?

I get out of bed and peek my head out my door just to make sure Mom is really gone. The coast is clear. So I walk a few steps down the hall and stand in front of her bedroom door.

I want answers.

And a distraction from everything that has happened today would be nice, too.

Carefully and slowly, I push her bedroom door open. Her room is a mess. There are clothes all over the floor. The bed is unmade. Cups from the kitchen are piled up on the nightstand. She acts more like a teenager than I do.

I can't believe I'm doing this.

It's not me. I don't go snooping through my mother's room.

Usually, I act more like a parent than she does.

But still. It needs to be done. I'm only snooping because I know I'm going to find something. I know I am. I have to.

I start with her dresser. I rifle through each drawer to see if I can find a box. A folder. An envelope. Something she doesn't want to lose but doesn't want anyone to come across, either.

That "anyone" mainly being me.

I don't find anything, so I move on to the armoire. I swing it open and scoff at what a mess it is inside. Out of all the clothes she has, only two shirts are actually hanging up. I rifle through everything, and I don't find anything secretive here, either.

I walk through the archway into her small bathroom. I start opening up the drawers on the vanity. It's not until I get to the skinny one cut out to go underneath the sink—that's when I see an envelope. And I know without even looking inside it that it has to be something. I pick it up, turn it around, and pull out the content inside. All that's in it is a single photo.

I don't know right away who it is. I see a blonde and a brunette standing beside each other, kissing. But then I realize that the brunette kind of looks like me. And that's when I figure it out. It's Mr. Reeves.

And he's kissing Amelia Bailey.

The photo drops out of my hands as I stare at my horrified expression in the mirror.

"What?" I mutter, in complete shock. Mr. Reeves had been with my mother. That's how I came to be. So when was he with Amelia Bailey, too? And why doesn't anybody seem to know about it? And if my mom knows about it, why is she still friends with Amelia?

I step backward into Mom's bedroom and sit on her unmade bed. I know I wanted a distraction. I know I wanted answers. But now I'm more confused and scared than ever. I can think of a reason why Mom would be friends with Amelia again—because she got this photo. Because she somehow got her hands on this photo, and she's always had feelings for Mr. Reeves, and now she wants revenge for Mr. Reeves cheating on her with Lyla and Audrey's mom.

And what better way to get revenge on Audrey and Lyla's mom than pretending to be her friend so that Amelia will never suspect it when my mom kidnaps her daughter—or possibly kills her?

Just like she killed Carson Price.

What if my mom is responsible for all of this?

CHAPTER 64

LYLA

I'm in the woods in the middle of nowhere. I'm in a shed at a lake house with a pool. The lake house is old and black and A-framed. It has a pool in the backyard. Nobody is around for miles. I know because no one has been able to hear me screaming.

It doesn't feel like I'm that far from home. I don't think it took a very long time for us to get from that random parking lot to here. You have to find me. You have to understand me so that you can come and find me. I can't spend the rest of my life in here. I can't keep living like this.

I'm mentally talking to Audrey. I'm trying to use my twin telepathy. Maybe it's not real. But maybe it is. Maybe there's something magical about being a twin. Maybe she won't hear the exact words I'm saying to her in my head, but maybe she'll feel something. A surge. A sensation. Something that'll tell her in her heart where she needs to go in order to get to me.

After all, anything is possible, right? If I somehow ended up in this situation in the first place, then it has to be true.

Come on, Audrey. Give me something to let me know you understand. To let me know that you're there. And that this is working.

I don't feel anything, but I don't want to lose hope, either.

Help me, Audrey. Just, please. Come and find me.

I scratch another tally into the wall, and then I open a small bag of trail mix because even though I don't feel hungry, my stomach is growling so loudly I bet my kidnapper can hear it from inside his cabin.

When that's gone, I sit down on the floor and make a smiley face in the dust around me. Then I stare at the dust on the pad of my index finger.

Who is my kidnapper? Who could've done this to me? And how long is this going to keep going? Forever? What if my kidnapper keeps taking care of me, but then something happens to them? What if he leaves, gets in a car accident, dies, and then never comes back again, and I'm left here to starve to death? Is that how it's going to end?

I'm in a shed in the middle of the woods, in the middle of nowhere.

Audrey, please hear me.

The things I would do if I could get out of the shed. They're endless. I'd reinvent myself. I'd bring more of the old Lyla back. The livelier, the happier me. I'd be the best daughter. I'd do all the chores asked of me and then some. I'd always get all my homework done. I would never have an attitude with Mom or Dad whenever they asked me to do something. I'd get good grades and get into a good college just to make them happy. I'd be a good big sister to Joey—someone he could look up to. I'd join any club or afterschool activity they want me to, just to show them what a hard and dedicated worker I am.

I would be the best friend, too. I'd apologize to Sophia, Danielle, and Olive. I'd get back in their clique. I'd even become a cheerleader again if I needed to. Sure, my body doesn't quite work the same since the accident, but I could get back into going to physical therapy every week, and I could get back into shape. I'd be closer with Audrey, too. Hanging out with the same friend group and cheering together would help with that.

I'd do right by Trinity, too. I'd go to her parents. I'd give them my confession. They deserve to know what really happened that night. And if I went to jail, I went to jail. I can't worry about the what-ifs anymore. I just have to do the right thing. And I would do the right thing.

If I could just get out of here.

No more mopey, sad girl. I'd be friendly to everyone at school. I'd be nice to my teachers. I wouldn't ignore people who were trying to talk to me. I'd be a ray of sunshine. Even if it killed me.

If I get out of here, maybe I'd finally go for Warner. Life's too short not to be with who I want to be with. I know it would hurt Jackson, but I'm not responsible for his happiness. I'm responsible for my own. And I think being with Warner would make me happy.

But I also think being with Wrigley would make me happy. I know I have a crush on him, despite everything that happened. And despite the fact that it had been him, I had been texting the night Trin died. He's a good guy. And I'm one of the few people who get to see that.

In all truth, I had been crushing on Wrigley way before I started liking Warner. I had been crushing on Wrigley when I was still with Jackson—there's no point in denying it to myself. We had flirted during our texting conversations. We had flirted over Snapchat. All of our texts had not been harmless and friendly. We had both hinted at being interested in more than just being friends, but I was too afraid to break up with Jackson and go for him because I didn't want to hurt Jackson. And we had been together for so long that I didn't know if I knew how to not be with him. I didn't go for Wrigley because I was too scared.

So I just texted him in secret behind Jackson's back instead.

If I can just get out of here, I'd no longer be a coward.

If I could just get out of here.

CHAPTER 65

AUDREY

The phone rings. And rings. And rings.

Then it goes to my aunt Nora's voicemail.

"Hi, Aunt Nora. I don't know if you have my number saved, but this is Audrey. Your niece. And... I just had a couple of questions to ask you. I was wondering if you could help me with something. I... I hope you're okay, and I'm sorry I didn't get a chance to say goodbye to you before you left. But call me back if you can. Soon, please."

I hang up, not feeling satisfied. I just feel like she's not going to call me back.

I text her, too.

Me: *Hi, Aunt Nora. It's Audrey. Can we talk?*

I stand there and stare at my phone. Who am I kidding? She's not going to text me back, either. At least not right away.

Probably not at all. She doesn't even like me.

I try calling her again. No answer. I don't leave a voicemail this time. Instead, I just text her again.

Me: I just have some questions to ask you. And they're sort of really important. Please, call me.

"Come on!" I groan as I sit in one of the armchairs in the upstairs loft and want to toss my phone at the wall.

"Who are you talking to?"

I jump and turn around and see that Joey has come up the stairs.

"Joey!" I cry out, startled to see him. "When did you get home?"

"Just now."

"Oh. Uh, how was school?"

"Stupid."

"Why?"

"Because it's always stupid. Everything's stupid."

"Everything? What's wrong?"

"It must be nice knowing that with everything going on with our 'parents' and with Lyla missing, you don't have to worry about being taken away."

"Taken away?" I ask. "Joey, what are you talking about?"

"I'm not exactly safe here. Not with Mom and Dad fighting all the time and never being home because they're out looking for Lyla. I'm not getting taken care of as well as I should be. It doesn't look good. I don't want to go back."

With everything going on and Joey having been a part of our family for three years now, I haven't even really thought about this. This isn't a happy, healthy, safe environment for Joey to live in. What if he does get taken away? What if I never see him again?

I get up from the chair, quickly rush to him, and hug him. He doesn't hug me back. He just stays limp in my arms. "Nothing's going to happen to you, Joey. I'll... I'll make sure of it. Whatever I have to do. You're not going back there."

He shrugs out of my grasp. "Whatever." Then he sulks away into his room and closes the door behind him.

I sink back into the chair and bite my fingernail. Great. Now Joey is starting to spiral, too.

I'm beginning to think I can't hold his family together like I thought I could.

But I still have to try. It's still up to me.

I check my phone again. No response from Aunt Nora.

"Why won't you reply?!"

I quickly go down the stairs and into the study. I hop on the computer and open up my mom's email account even though I know I shouldn't. I go to her address book, type in Aunt Nora's name, and then get her email address. I get back on my phone and compose an email to her. I'm trying every avenue. Anything to get her to give me some answers.

Hi Aunt Nora,

You're not answering my calls or texts. But I really need some help. I don't know who else to ask, and it's kind of important. I can't exactly explain why right now, but I just need some answers. Like about what happened to Carson that night? I know you found his body. But I know that when the police went to look for it, they couldn't find it. But that's all I really know. I was hoping you could tell me more. I just need answers and explaining why is far too complicated.

Also, while I'm at it, I was curious if you've been talking to Detective Craig Fritz. I know he's talked to Mom a few times, and he's working on the case of what happened to Lyla and Sydney. But I also know that he wants to know what happened to Carson, too. So have you talked to him? And what have you told him?

Again, explaining is complicated. But I would really like your help. If you can give it to me.

Your niece,
Audrey

I send the email and sit in the rolling chair at my parents' desk. I wait about ten minutes, constantly refreshing my inbox, but no email comes through. However, if Aunt Nora is going to answer my questions, I can't expect her to do it right away. I have to keep myself busy, and maybe she'll email me back later.

I make it a whole two hours before I drive myself crazy enough to where I sent her another text in frustration.

Me: It's not fair. If I were Lyla, you would reply to me.

I know I'm right, too.

WARNER

My world just keeps getting rocked—and not in a good way—and I am completely unqualified to deal with it. So when there is a knock on the screen door on my porch, I'm not exactly in the mood to be dealing with houseguests.

"Who could that be?" I mutter through my clenched teeth as I leave my room again and head to answer it. For their own good, it better not be Mr. Reeves, Craig Fritz, or Wrigley Hall. I can't promise that I won't explode again if it is.

I throw the door open aggressively and see Jackson standing on the other side of the screen.

"Oh," I say. He definitely isn't who I had been expecting. It makes me calm down a little to see him standing there. It's also been a while since he's come over to my house. My house that's a mess, and I would be embarrassed to let him see the inside of. "What's up, Jackson?" I open the screen door, and he steps back; instead of letting him inside, I walk out on the porch to talk to him.

"This not a good time?" Jackson asks with his hands in his pockets. He looks slightly sunburnt like he just walked all the way home from school from football practice.

"Uh..." I trail off, thinking that it is a bad time. That I'm not in the mood to see anybody.

"I can come back if it is," Jackson says. But he seems down. Off. Like he could use a friend. And after what I've done and everything that's gone down between us, I owe it to him to try to be a friend.

"No, man, you're good," I tell him. "What's up?"

"The stuff going around the school is crazy, dude," he says. "I... I don't think you did anything to Sydney. Just so you know."

"Oh... thanks."

"And... what you said about Coach—is that true or were you just pulling some sort of stunt to get everyone talking about something other than the fact that you're a person of interest in a murder investigation?"

"It's true," I say stiffly. "And I'm not a murderer."

"I know, Warner," Jackson says. "I know."

"Good. Now get the rest of the school to believe it, too."

"Why do they think that, though? You can tell me. You can tell me the total truth, Warner, and I won't judge you. And I won't tell a soul, either."

"What does it matter?" I ask. "I just told you I'm not a murderer. That I didn't do it."

"But something had to happen between you and Sydney for the police to think you did."

"You just said you don't believe I did it," I remind him. A fresh bout of anger is flooding my body now. I don't believe Jackson for one second. I think he just came here to see if he could get a confession out of me.

"Look, I'm on your side," Jackson tries. "But... we're supposed to be best friends, ya know? We're supposed to tell each other stuff. I feel like I don't know what's going on with you."

"Because you don't," I say quickly. "There's so much, Jackson. Things are bad. And I feel like they're only going to get worse."

"What do you mean?"

Before I can even answer him, I hear his mother calling his name. We both look over and see that she's standing on her driveway with her hands on her hips.

"Get your butt back here!" she calls to her son.

"Hi, Mrs. Mullens," I say, giving her a friendly wave. She doesn't wave back. She doesn't say hi back. She just stands there, and I can't tell if she's glaring at me or if the sun is just in her eyes.

But I'm pretty sure she's glaring.

"I'm coming!" Jackson shouts.

"NOW!" she shouts back.

"What's her deal?" I ask.

"She..." Jackson sighs. "She doesn't want me around you."

Mrs. Mullens doesn't want me around Jackson?

"Are you serious?" I ask, deeply offended. "She knows me. I've been in your house, like, a hundred times."

"Things just don't look good right now. I'm sorry, dude. I tried to talk to her."

"Dude. Try harder," I say. Mrs. Mullens has always liked me. "This isn't fair."

"I—"

"JACKSON!"

"I gotta go." Jackson hangs his head, turns around, and jumps off the porch to go back home.

And replacing him, headed towards my front porch from her car on the street, is a very shaken-up-looking Audrey.

AUDREY

"Everything okay?" I ask as we watch Jackson retreat into his house with his mom. "What was that all about?"

"Um... nothing. Are you okay?" Warner asks me in return. "You look pale."

I walk up onto the porch and stand in front of him. "Not really," I say. "I know I'm not supposed to be here. But... I have to talk to you."

"You're fine. My mom's not home."

I nod and put my arms around myself as if I'm cold, even though I'm not. I just don't know what to do.

"What's going on?" Warner asks in a timid voice. He seems genuinely worried about me, and it's nice. It feels nice to be worried about. And Warner has always been so nice to me. It kills me that he's going through what he's going through. And that we're supposed to stay away from each other. He's all I have right now.

"I overheard my mom on the phone talking to your mom today," I begin.

"Great," Warner says flatly.

"Yeah. I—my mom said she's getting worried that Maddy is going to be messed with, too. And she said that she's worried that Carson is the one doing it."

"Wait, hold on," Warner says. "Didn't you tell Lyla and me that our moms killed Carson?"

"Exactly," I say, tugging at my hair in frustration. "That's why I am so confused. It doesn't make any sense. And I don't know what my mom means by 'being messed with.'"

"Is your mom being messed with like we're being messed with?"

"I don't know."

"I don't think she has to worry about my mom," he says. He walks over to the porch steps and takes a seat on them. I join him. Our knees touch.

"What do you mean?" I ask.

"I... I found a picture in my mom's bathroom. It was of your mom and Mr. Reeves kissing. And they looked like they were young. Like high school, or college even."

"What?" I ask loudly, jutting my chin out. "My mom?"

"Yeah. I just—Audrey, what if it's my mom doing all of this?"

"All of what? The tormenting? Kidnapping my sister? Do you really think that?"

"I don't know anything for sure," Warner says quickly. "It's just a thought. Nothing makes sense. I'm just trying to see what fits together. What makes sense."

"Oh my God." I put my head in my hands and stay there like that for a while.

"I know. We thought maybe it was Mr. Reeves. We considered the fact that it was Jackson. Now I'm thinking it could be my mom. Who knows who is truly behind all of this? I wish we could just get answers."

"This is too much." My voice is quiet as I speak into my legs. Aunt Nora still hasn't messaged me back, and I'm losing my mind over it.

"Well, to hurt it, even more, I sort of found out that Mr. Reeves is my biological father, and I sort of told the school about it today at the assembly."

I lift my head and look at him. "I heard," I admit. "It's sort of all anybody can talk about."

"Figures."

"I didn't know if you wanted to talk about it, so I didn't want to say anything. But... holy cow, Warner. Are you okay?"

"I don't know. No."

"Did you tell your mom?"

"Yeah. We talked about it. I don't really know how things are going to be now. She's lied to me my whole life. How do I forgive that? How do I move past that?"

"I'm so sorry. This is horrible. I can't even imagine... How did you find out?"

"Detective Craig Fritz."

I gasp. He nods as if he was expecting me to have that reaction.

"How?" I manage to squeak out.

"He's been doing his research, I guess. He thought it was strange how invested in me Mr. Reeves seemed to be. I don't know. I've known for a while now. It's just taking me a little bit to say anything."

"I don't know how you're dealing with it so calmly."

"Hah. I'm the opposite of calm." He chuckles weakly, and I can tell he's just using the pitiful laugh as a mask to cover up how much he wants to burst into tears again. Knowing what he needs, I wrap my arms around him. He hugs me back and rests his chin on my shoulder. I rub his back soothingly, and we sit there like that for some time.

"It's going to be okay," I whisper. He says nothing.

It's the sound of leaves crunching somewhere nearby that makes us break apart.

"Did you hear that?" Warner asks. He gets to his feet and then holds his hand out to help me to mine as well.

"I did," I say. We step off the porch and walk around the house toward where we heard the sound of the leaves. I expect to see somebody standing there. To find that somebody has been spying on us.

Instead, I see absolutely nothing.

CHAPTER 68

LYLA

It's dark out when I hear the sound of footsteps crunching on leaves getting louder and louder. Closer and closer to the pool shed.

I stand and press myself up against one of the walls. As far as I can get away from the door as I hear it being unlocked on the outside.

The man in the mask is back.

When the door opens, he stands there with a knife. There's no point in me trying to run now. I've already tried that. It just doesn't work.

But what else can I try? How can I get myself out of here? He clearly doesn't want me to die. That's why he's been giving me food and water and checking on me so often. He doesn't want me to go home, but he doesn't want me to die, either.

What does he want?

Thinking quickly, I cough. He just stands there in the doorway, holding the knife, staring at me. I don't know what he wants.

But I know what I want.

"I... I hurt myself," I say. Then I show him the nasty, messy cut on my arm. All the blood has dried off, and I haven't bothered to wipe it with anything, so it looks pretty gnarly. "I don't feel so good. I think it's getting infected."

Still, he stands there and doesn't move. He's not even holding any more drinks or snacks for me. So if he's not here just to refill my goods, then what does he want? Why is he just standing there like that?

Still, I keep trying. "I think it's making me sick. I need a doctor. I probably should've gotten stitches." I continue to cough. Then I slide down the wall and fall onto my butt. I want him to think I'm so sick that I can barely even hold myself up. That I'm so sick, I need to see a doctor unless he wants me to die there in his shed.

"Can you please just help me?" I ask. "Look, I don't know why I'm in here. I don't know who you are or what you want with me. But—" I cough some more. "But I really need help."

I think maybe I'm getting through to him. Maybe he's thinking through all his options. Seeing if there's a way he can get me some sort of treatment without having to reveal who he is.

"Please," I say softly, letting my eyes drift shut.

When I peek through them, creating the tiniest slits with my eyelids, I see that he's walking toward me. He still has a knife held out. And in his other hand, he's taking something out of his pocket.

It's the opposite of what's going to help me. It's that disgusting, odorless white rag.

"No," I gasp out, pushing up against the wall farther and getting slowly back to my feet. "No, please."

But it doesn't stop my kidnapper. He comes at me again, and as the rag is placed over my mouth and my nose, the chloroform enters my body, and everything goes black again.

CHAPTER 69

WARNER

Without knowing when Mom is going to return, and without really caring either, I decided to invite Audrey into my house after our talk on the porch. She looked like she wanted to do anything besides go home, and I didn't exactly want to be alone. So we sat on the couch in my living room, put on some mindless funny TV show, and snacked on the little bit of junk food I had in my pantry.

I think I read the clock wrong at first when I look and see that it's nearly nine in the evening. Audrey's been over at my house for nearly five hours. And I haven't heard a word from my mom.

"Does your mom know your here?" I decide to ask Audrey as the most recent episode of our stupid TV show ends, and the streaming service we're using asks if we're still watching.

For the second time.

"Definitely not," Audrey says. "But she thinks I'm with girlfriends. I lied to her. But why shouldn't I? She lies to me about everything."

"I know the feeling," I say.

"You know what I want to do?" she suddenly asks, sitting on the edge of her seat. She looks wide awake. Like an idea has made a little lightbulb turn on over her head.

"What?"

"I want to go to the library."

"The library?" I ask, thinking about going into Blackfell High this late at night. "Uh... it's definitely closed."

"Not the one at school," she says. "The public library is twenty-four-seven."

"Okay...why do you want to go to the library?"

She gets to her feet. "Come on," she says. "Let's go. I want to do research on Carson Price."

"Right now?"

"Got anything better to do?"

I'm tired, but if I picture myself trying to go to bed, it doesn't work. All I picture is myself lying in bed, staring at the posters on my walls, thinking about the horrible, horrible day I've had.

So I stand. "I guess not," I say to Audrey.

We take her car and drive to the public library. We sit at some open computers next to each other and start googling. We also try to find old news articles. We ask the librarian if she has any information on any student that attended Blackfell High in the years Carson Price would have. Unfortunately, we don't get any helpful information about it.

A couple of hours go by before Audrey gasps so loudly that it makes me jump in my seat.

Maybe I had been dozing off a little bit.

"Warner," she hisses, grabbing my forearm. "Look at that."

I lean over and look at her computer. I also notice that she smells like strawberries.

Concentrate, Warner.

I shake my head, blink my eyes, and focus on the words on the screen. "Um... what am I looking at?"

"This is big," she says. "At least, I think it is. It's the house where Aunt Nora claimed Carson Price's body was found near. In the middle of the redwoods."

"No way," I say, suddenly feeling more awake. I look closer at the image. The house is old.

When Audrey scrolls down the web page a little more, there's an older photo of the house, where it looks to be in much better shape. A black A-framed cabin with a pool in the back, right in front of a lake.

"Where did you find this?" I ask.

"It's sort of... a conspiracy theorist's blog. But you see the balcony?"

I look closer. In the older photo, where the house is in better shape, the railing on the balcony is broken. "Yeah?"

"This person is saying that there are all kinds of different rumors going around about why the balcony is broken. One of them being that Carson Price was pushed out over it. Or that he fell over it. That his death was either a murder or a simple accident. Or that it was a lightning strike. Or just bad weather."

"Oh my God," I say, staring at that broken balcony even harder now. "If our moms killed Carson Price... do you think that's how they did it?"

"I don't know," Audrey says, turning and looking at me with her big blue eyes. "But anything is possible."

If my mom was capable of pushing a classmate over the railing like that all those years ago, did that make her capable of doing something as equally horrible to Lyla?

"We need to figure out why Carson Price died," I decide. "I don't know if I'm gonna be able to sleep until we do."

AMELIA

Lyla's Sixth Day Missing

It's nearly impossible to get out of bed this morning.

Another day has passed, and we still don't have my Lyla back. I don't know what I'll do if we never find her. I don't know how I can continue life. I don't know why the world hasn't stopped. Why everything is still going. How can everything still be going when I don't have her here with me?

I'm slow after I get out of bed. I take my time in the bathroom pretending that I'm getting ready when really I'm just running the faucet and half-heartedly putting a brush through my hair. I'm afraid to look at my reflection in the mirror because I know I'll see how sad I am, and it will only make me burst into tears again. I've been doing a good job so far this morning—even if I've only been up for a little while—of not crying. Not breaking down. I have to keep this going.

When I finally look at the clock, I know that Joey has to leave for school soon. And I want to see him before he goes. I feel terrible because I haven't been spending that much time with him. I don't even know if I've been checking up on him as often as I should be. I know I'm not the only one hurting, but sometimes it's hard to remember that. Sometimes it's hard to think about anything other than my pain and Lyla.

I walk carefully down the hall in my warm, fuzzy socks and fluffy robe toward the kitchen. But I pause when I hear Gentry talking. I hear his voice, and I hear the sounds of my kids sniffling. I pause, not wanting to reveal myself. I want to hear what it is Gentry is saying to them. So I stay in the hallway, out of sight, and listen.

"I know it's hard right now," he is saying to the kids. "And I know you don't want to have hope. I know things seem hopeless. I feel that way, too, sometimes. But feeling that things are hopeless isn't going to get us Lyla back. If we lose that hope, they will never find her. So, as much as we may want to let go, we can't. We have to hold onto that hope. It's all we have right now."

"What if she never comes back?" Joey asks, hiccupping as a sob catches in his throat. Audrey's sniffle is loud and watery.

"We just can't think like that, buddy," Gentry replies. "All we need to rely on is the fact that Lyla will be found. It's just a matter of when. I know we all miss her very much."

"I don't want to go another day without her being home," Joey continues. "I just want her back. I want everything back to the way it was. It's not f-fair."

"Everything is going to be okay, Joey," Audrey joins in. "I know it... it really sucks right now. But just you wait. Things will go back to the way they were. It's just like Dad said. We have to have hope."

"We just got to take it one day at a time," Gentry continues. Even he is sniffling snottily. All three of them are crying in the kitchen together. "Come here, you guys," he says, and then I hear all of them embracing and crying into each other's shirts.

I give myself some support by leaning against the wall. Then I slide my back down it and find myself crumpled on the floor. Tears start streaming down my cheeks, and I sit there and cry silently. So much for holding it together. But hearing my family so broken like that, so desperate for their sister and daughter to come back, it's all too much. How can anyone handle that?

I don't want to intrude on the heart-to-heart they're having, so I stay like that in the hall. Maybe I could use a hug, too, but that doesn't matter right now. I'm glad the kids have their father at this moment. I'm glad Gentry was able to say something comforting. I know I wouldn't be able to. How can I be comforting when I feel just as helpless as my kids do?

What if I never get my daughter back?

CHAPTER 71

AUDREY

Dad is out at work, and Mom is holed up in her room when, later in the afternoon, there is a knock on the front door, followed by the doorbell ringing.

I, having been in the living room trying—and failing—to distract myself with TV, am the closest one to the door, so I get up and hurry over to answer it. I never know what to expect when I answer the door these days. But every time I do, I'm hopeful it's Lyla I see waiting out on our front porch.

When I swing the door open this time, I see Ryan Copeland standing on my doorstep.

"Ryan?" I ask, my eyes turning to saucers. "Wh—what are you doing here?" I check the time on my phone and see that school is not even out yet for the day.

Ryan smiles at me sheepishly, revealing his super white, straight teeth and the cute little lines at the corners of his eyes. I never texted him back when he asked if we could talk when I had been at the search party. As happy as I was to know that he had come around to seeing my point of view with everything that went down with Sophia, I needed to remain focused on finding Lyla. That's all I wanted to do.

Standing in front of me at my actual house, Ryan isn't exactly a text message I can ignore now.

"I'm sorry for just swinging by like this," he says with his hands in his jeans pocket. "I've just been really wanting to talk to you. To clear the air and make sure you don't hate me, and to check up and see how you're doing with everything going on. Are you okay?"

The hottest senior at Blackfell High is on my doorstep asking me how I'm doing.

"Wow, did you ditch school just to do this?" I ask.

"Sort of, yeah. Once I made my mind up that I wanted to come over here, it was all I could think about. Don't worry. If I get in trouble, it'll still be worth it. Even if you do tell me you hate me. It's just... it's good to see you."

"I don't hate you," I confess. "I was a little hurt when I found out you and Sophia were hanging out, but probably more at the fact that my best friend stabbed me in the back than the fact that you were with her."

"I should've never listened to her. She told me that you were leading me on and that you've always had your sights set on that Bryson dude. It bummed me out, but I should've just talked to you."

"Yeah," I agree. "You should have."

He drops his head for a moment, and the two of us stand there wordlessly.

"I'm sorry, Audrey. I really am. And—" He quickly takes off his backpack, unzips it, and starts rifling through it. "I know this isn't the best thing to receive, but I did take the initiative to figure out your class schedule and to go around to all your teachers to pick up your homework."

He pulls out a folder and hands it to me. As much as I don't want to catch up on my homework, I'm touched that someone would do this for me.

"Oh. Thank you," I say, feeling stunned.

"Don't mention it. Again, I'm sorry it's not flowers or something better."

"No," I say. "This is definitely a good start."

He smiles, and I watch his shoulders relax a little.

"Everything is forgiven," I say to him. Then I smile back. It feels strange and slightly foreign on my face. I think it might be the first time I've smiled since Lyla went missing.

If only she could see what was happening now.

"Awesome," Ryan says. Then he goes back to looking slightly nervous again. "So then... do you think sometime you'd be free for me to take you out on a date?"

"Oh..."

I don't know how to answer that one. A week ago, if Ryan had asked me on a date, I would have probably screamed the word, Yes! and jumped into his arms. Then I would have bragged about it to my friends and Lyla, and I would have written about it in my journal.

But things are so much different now.

"If that's pushing it too far, and you just wanna go back to being friends for now instead, that's totally cool," Ryan says, looking flustered.

"Ryan, I... It's really sweet that you asked. But I'm not in any position to date anyone right now. Not with so much going on with my sister, ya know? I can't think about anything else but that right now."

"Oh, yeah," he says, blushing. "Of course. I totally get it. I shouldn't have even asked. I probably shouldn't even be bothering you right now. I can't imagine what you're going through."

"It's really hard," I admit. "But we're just trying to take it a day at a time."

"For sure."

There's another moment of awkwardness as we stand there and look at each other. Eventually, Ryan itches the back of his neck. "Well, I'll get out of your hair then. Just text me or call me if you need anything. I'm serious. I don't care what time it is."

"Thank you," I say.

He nods his head and turns away from me.

I step over the threshold and onto the patio. "Ryan."

He turns back around.

I throw my arms around him and give him a tight hug. I want him to know how much I appreciate him coming here and apologizing and bringing me my homework. And maybe I want him to know that I do have feelings for him, but that now is just not a good time for me to do anything about those feelings.

He's stiff in my arms at first, but then he loosens up and hugs me back.

Come on, Lyla. You have to come back. I want to be able to think about something other than how hard this all is without you.

I want to be able to think about a potential future with Ryan Copeland.

CHAPTER 72

LYLA

"Hey, Lyla. It's me again. Warner."

I knew he was there, but I was on some strong drugs, and it was hard to keep my eyes open. So I just let them rest. I let Warner think that I was asleep.

I was still in the hospital. It was a little bit after my and Trinity's accident. Usually, Warner came to visit me with Jackson, but this was the first time he had shown up on his own. I wanted to ask what he was doing here without Jackson, but I also didn't want to spoil this moment, either. I wanted to know what Warner wanted to talk to me about. Why he was visiting me alone.

"I don't know if you can hear me. But I don't wanna bother you or try to wake you up either." He used the softest of voices. He sounded so gentle and worried about me.

"I really hope you get better soon. It really sucks that this happened to you. I saw photos online, and... remind me never to do that again. I don't even know how you survived. But I am... I'm really glad you did, Lyla."

I'm glad I did, too. I'm glad you're here, Warner.

He cleared his throat. "Uh, I'm not really sure how to do this. It's not often I visit people in the hospital, ya know? I just learned that every time they play that baby lullaby over the speakers in here, it means somebody has just given birth. Did you know that?"

Everyone knows that.

"Geez. Imagine having a baby. A literal, physical human being that you have to watch over. My mom was only nineteen when she had me. I am only a couple of years away from being that same age. And if I had to become a dad at nineteen?" He made a noise to show he was shuddering. "It is just a horrible idea for me to be a father. Then again, it was also a horrible idea for anyone to make my mother a mother. But here I am. I guess I'm not so bad, right? She didn't mess me up too much."

She didn't mess you up at all. You're great.

"School is weird," he said, changing the subject. "Everyone seems miserable. And then the ones that aren't miserable are getting talked badly about because everyone is personally offended that they're not more affected by your accident. It's weird. School without Lyla Bailey and Trinity Cruz galloping through the halls with their arms linked together? It doesn't even make sense."

You're right. It doesn't. And it'll never be something Blackfell High gets to see ever again.

"We all miss you. Sure, Audrey's around, but it's not quite the same, you know? She's... she's not you."

Does somebody other than Jackson actually think I'm better than my sister?

"I guess I don't really know what else to talk about. But I don't know when the next person is coming to visit you, and I hate the idea of you sitting here all alone, so I'm going to stay."

Good. I don't want you to leave.

And so Warner stayed. He talked to me for over an hour. He talked to me about anything and everything.

And I loved every single minute of it, even if I kept my eyes closed and said nothing in return the entire time.

My eyes flutter open, and for a moment, I think I've found myself in that same hospital room. But I'm not there. I'm on the floor in the shed. I don't know what's happening, and I don't know how much time has passed anymore. But now, my kidnapper keeps coming in here and drugging me. It's like he wants me to stay unconscious. I'm so so weak that I don't even bother to move off the floor. He'll be back soon, anyway. Besides, time goes by quicker when he puts me under. And I get to go into dreamland and relive flashbacks from precious moments in my life. Moments like when Warner had visited me in the hospital.

I want to stay in those flashbacks.

CHAPTER 73

WARNER

School is absolutely miserable. At this point, I don't even know why I continue to go back. I don't even have my phone to pretend to look at to keep myself distracted from the fact that everybody is staring at me and everybody is talking about me. I am the teenage kidnapper and murderer who has a screw loose and is lying about one of the high school teachers being his father just so he can get attention. That's what I'm gathering anyway from all the talk I hear.

That's me. Crazy Warner.

When the bell rings, I keep my head down and try to get out of the school as quickly as possible. But I don't even make it out of the hall of my last class when a loud voice is calling my name.

"Warner!"

I turn around, dread filling me. Dean Reeves is standing a few yards away in the middle of the hall. He waits for me to follow him into a classroom that's not even his.

"Got to have a good old fashion father-son talk?" Cody Lawson jokes as he passes me. I'm tempted to shove him, but I hold my composure and see what it could possibly be that this guy wants from me now.

The classroom we enter is unused. Some desks are stacked on each other and pushed aside, and every surface seems to be coated with a layer of dust.

Mr. Reeves shuts the door as soon as we're inside. Then he turns around and crosses his arms.

"Don't we have to get to practice?" I ask.

"I wanted to talk to you."

"Clearly."

"Warner... the way you left things yesterday—after you told the entire school..."

"Don't even worry about it. Most of the kids don't believe it, anyway."

"I don't care about that," he says. "Because the fact of the matter is that it is true, Warner. You're my son."

Every time I dreamt of this moment as a kid, of someone saying that exact sentence to me, it was always a happy scenario. I always ran into their arms afterward, and we embraced, and then we went and played catch in the yard. I should've known it would turn out to be nothing like that if it ever happened.

"Great," I snap, not wanting to hear it. "Can I go?"

Coming in here to talk to him had been a bad idea.

"Warner, I—"

"Do you know who is behind all of this?" I ask abruptly. While I have him here, I might as well try to get the answers to some questions that have been bugging me, especially today. I haven't been able to stop thinking about that lake house near where Carson's body was supposedly found since I saw the photo of it in the library with Audrey.

"What do you mean?" he asks.

"Who killed Sydney? Who kidnapped Lyla? Who is messing with Audrey and me? Do you know who's behind it?"

"I wish I did," he says. "But I don't believe you had anything to do with what happened to Sydney or Lyla."

"I don't care what you think. You dated my mom once—clearly. And you were seeing Amelia Bailey for a moment at least, too."

"What—how did—I don't—"

He's clearly flustered because I've found another one of his secrets. The one about him and Audrey and Lyla's mom.

"It's the least of my concerns right now," I say quickly, just wanting to get to the point. "You were clearly close with them in high school. Which means you know Amelia Bailey's sister. Nora Flynn."

"Why are you talking to me about Nora?"

"The expression on your face tells me I'm right. So you had to be at least somewhat closely involved with what happened to Nora Flynn's boyfriend. Carson Price."

"Carson Price?" Mr. Reeves takes a step back. "Warner, what is all of this?"

"Nora thinks Carson Price died. But what if he didn't? They never found his body, right? What if Carson never really died, and what if he came back to Toxey? Would you happen to know anything about it?"

I see his gears turning as he stands there, not saying anything. It makes fear course through my veins. Because if his gears are turning, that means he's considering it. That means he's thinking about how it might be an actual possibility.

Maybe we got it all wrong.

Maybe we're finally getting closer to the right answer.

AUDREY

Dad comes home from work early, having picked up Joey from his junior high. He seems a little off when he walks in, barely greeting me as he gives Joey's shoulder a squeeze and then leaves the two of us in the kitchen to go into his office.

"Is he okay?" I ask Joey, who grabs a granola bar out of the pantry and sits with me at the table. I am attempting to do some of the homework Ryan has given me, but it's easier said than done.

"I don't think so," Joey answers. "He was all fidgety the whole car ride back. And he kept checking his smartwatch like he was waiting for a message from someone. Do you think it's the foster care agency?"

"Definitely not," I lie.

"It probably is." He stops unwrapping his granola bar and slides it far away from him across the table.

I stand up. "Do you want me to give you proof?" I ask. "You stay right here. I'll go find out."

I have to give my brother some sort of peace of mind. So I head over to the study to press my ear against the door and try to see if I can listen to whatever it is my dad is doing in there. Even if I do find out he is talking to Joey's case worker, it'll at least buy me some time to come up with a lie about how it was something completely unrelated to Joey that dad was doing. Joey doesn't need to be more worried about anything than he already is.

I'm careful to make sure my feet don't cast a shadow under the door as I lean against it to try to hear what Dad is doing. I'm satisfied when I can tell he's on the phone with somebody instead of just typing away an email to somebody at his desk.

"I know," my dad says. "There's just been a lot going on."

Pause.

"I've been trying to call you back. I've really been trying. It's not that I don't care; I just—"

Pause.

"Yeah. Exactly. I promise it's just that and nothing else."

Pause.

"Yes. I can make dinner work. Not tonight. But maybe tomorrow."

Pause.

My dad chuckles.

Then there's another pause.

"Sounds terrific. I'm really looking forward to it."

I step away from the door. I think I've heard enough.

First, I discovered the dating profile on my mom's laptop.

Now it sounds very much like my dad is scheduling a date with another woman.

Could both of my parents really be cheating on each other?

CHAPTER 75

WARNER

After the sun sets, I go to my spot and wait to see if Audrey shows up. I had sent her a message from my mom's ancient computer over social media. But after I sent the message, I had to get off the computer, so I have no idea if she even received the message or not.

As I sit there and wait for her at the abandoned train station, I think about how when I was here before; I saw Nora and Detective Fritz together.

Fritz. Nora. Carson Price. My mom. Amelia Bailey. Sydney Hutton. Dean Reeves.

All these names are connected somehow.

And we're getting closer to figuring it out.

A car pulls into the grass-filled lot and out climbs Audrey from the driver's seat of her Mini Cooper.

"Warner?" she asks, walking toward me as I sit on the bench. "What is this place?"

"You can't tell a soul about it," I say. "It's my secret."

"Is this a train station?"

"Yeah. Trains still come by, but they never stop here anymore."

She joins me on the bench. "This is creepy."

"Maybe a little," I agree. "But I never see anybody here. Usually."

"Huh. So, what's up?" she asks. "My parents didn't want me to leave tonight, so I snuck out. I really shouldn't be gone too long."

"I can't stop thinking about what we researched last night. About that house."

"Me neither," she agrees.

"Who's cabin do you think that was?"

"No idea."

"Me neither. I think we should go to it."

"What?"

"Yeah. I've given it a lot of thought. And I mapped it out. I found the location. I think we need to check it out. See if we find some sort of clue as to what went down that night when Carson Price did or didn't die."

"Warner, if the police couldn't find anything, what makes you think—?"

"I just want to go, okay?" I interrupt, sounding a little harsh. "I'm sorry," I say quickly.

"It just seems kind of pointless. Don't you think?" she continues. "It's already dark out, and won't it be like over an hour's drive just to get there?"

"It will, but I think it would be worth it. Will you come with me? I want you to, but you don't have to. I'll go alone if I need to."

She rolls her eyes. "You're not going alone, Warner."

"I will. If you don't come with me."

I just... I'm going to be in so much trouble if I go."

"Who cares? We're trying to figure out what happened to Lyla. All of this is for Lyla, remember?"

"Okay. You're right. We'll go to the creepy old house. For Lyla."

"I don't want to join any more of the stupid search parties."

She nods in agreement. "Absolutely not."

"And I've been thinking something else," I add, having no idea how she's going to react to it once I tell her.

"Okay?"

I wince before I say it. "How would you feel about maybe giving yourself a little bit of a haircut?"

CHAPTER 76

MADDY

I get home from work later than usual, and I barely get a freezer meal popped into the microwave and my shoes off of my feet before my phone is ringing.

"Can't I sit down for two minutes?" I ask to no one. I hear the TV on in Warner's room, and his bedroom door is closed, so I'm assuming he either isn't ready to talk to me yet or that he's fallen asleep.

I check my phone and see that it's Dean calling me.

I'm not even hungry anymore.

"Dean?" I answer.

"Hey, Mads."

"Hey. Funny, you should call. I wanted to ask you: is Mia the reason you bailed on being a dad all those years ago?"

"What? Maddy, I didn't call you to talk about any drama."

"I don't care. I still want to know."

"Okay... I don't know where this question is coming from, but I'm calling to ask if you know why Warner didn't show up to practice again."

"He didn't?"

"You didn't know?" he asks. "Is he home now?"

"Yeah. He's in his room," I say.

"Have you talked to him? Is he okay?"

"Stop acting like you care, Dean."

"For the last time, Maddy, I do care. Knock it off."

"Don't talk to me that way," I snap defensively.

"Have you talked to him or not? Can you just check on him? I'm not telling you how to parent here, but I am worried. Something's going on, and... please, Maddy."

I roll my eyes. "Fine." I trudge down the hallway and knock on Warner's door. "Warner?" I call. "You okay in there?"

I don't get an answer. I knock again and still don't hear anything. I try the handle and find it locked. But it's easy to just use the pad of my thumb to turn the lock on the handle. Then I push the door open.

My stomach dips.

"Great," I say.

"What is it?" Dean asks.

"He's... he's not here."

"Well, where is he?"

"I don't know, Dean!"

And I don't know how I'm going to find out, either. Warner still doesn't have his phone. He has no way for me to contact him at all.

Immediately, I'm worried. Immediately, I can tell something is not right. I need to find Warner.

CHAPTER 77

AMELIA

I'm lounging on my bed watching an HGTV show when Maddy calls me.

"Hey, how are you?" I say as a way of answering. I know she's also going through a lot right now.

"Hey, Mia," she says in a rushed tone. "Uh, is Audrey home?"

"Audrey?" I ask, confused as to why she would even care.

"Yeah," she says. "Is she?"

"I... I think so. Why?" I haven't left my room practically all day. But Audrey asked if she could go to a friend's house a little bit ago and I told her no. So she should still be home.

"Is Warner with her, perchance?"

"Warner?"

"Yes, Mia," she says, sounding exasperated. "Is he with her?"

"Is everything okay?" I get out of bed. Audrey knows she's not allowed to be around Warner right now. But still, I leave my bedroom and walk up the staircase to check her room, just to be certain.

"He's not home, and the police took his phone, so I'm trying to figure out where he went," Maddy explains.

I get a bad feeling in my stomach. What if something very similar to what happened to Lyla happened to him?

"I'm sure everything's alright," I say as I reach the landing of the stairs and walk to Audrey's room. I push the door open and peer inside, but nobody is there.

"Audrey?" I call out. But I receive no answer.

"Wait, is she not there?" Maddy asks on the other line.

"I... I thought she was," I say. "Gentry and I told her she couldn't leave the house tonight." I walk back down the stairs. There's another way I can check for sure.

"I'm worried, Mia," Maddy says. It is clear that she is. I can hear it in her voice plainly.

"Just try to breathe and stay calm," I say. I walk through the mudroom and into the garage.

My heart skips a beat, and my stomach falls to my feet.

Audrey's car is gone.

"Did you find her? Is she there or not?" Maddy asks.

"Um... Maddy? Audrey left. Her car is gone." Where would she have gone? Why would she have disobeyed us and left when we told her no?

What is happening?

"I'm coming over," Maddy says to me. "I'll be there in ten minutes. Don't move."

I don't even have time to tell her it's not a good idea before she ends the call.

"Who was that, sweetheart?"

I spin on my heel and see my mom folding laundry in the living room.

"Mom?" I ask, shocked to see her there. She didn't even tell me she was coming over. She didn't even check on me in my room. How long has she been here?

Great.

It looks like it's only a matter of time before Gentry is officially not the only person who knows that Madeline Carpenter and I are friends again.

CHAPTER 78

MADDY

Amelia greets me at the front door with an orange prescription bottle in her hand. She pours out a pill and tosses it into her mouth, not even needing a liquid to swallow it. She doesn't even say hi to me. She simply leaves the door open so that I can come inside.

We walk toward the kitchen, and I am greeted by not only Gentry, sitting on his sectional looking apprehensive, but Susan Flynn, whom I haven't seen in many years.

"Maddy Carpenter?" Susan asks, getting to her feet with her eyebrows sky high. "Is that really you?"

"Guys," Amelia says. "You remember my friend Maddy?"

"I... I didn't realize you two were still friends," Susan says, walking over to me and giving me a friendly hug. She had always been so nice to me when we were younger. I always liked going to Amelia and Nora's house. It felt so much more like home than my place did, even if it was smaller and even if they didn't have as nice of things. Sometimes I wished I could live with them. Sometimes I wished I could have Amelia's life.

"What are you doing here, Maddy?" Gentry asks in an unfriendly tone. "It's kind of late, isn't it?"

"Um, Audrey's gone," Amelia tells her husband.

"What?" Gentry and Susan say at the same time.

"Yeah. And so is Warner."

"And I think they're together," I say.

Gentry gets to his feet. "Or Warner did something to her!"

Oh no, he didn't.

I step toward him sharply and narrow my eyes. "How dare you?!" I snap.

I really hate this man.

"Stop!" Amelia bites out loudly. "For whatever reason, the two of them are friends. I don't think Warner did anything to Lyla. But we need to find them."

"Easy," Gentry says. "I put a tracker on her car the day after Lyla disappeared so that I would always know where she was at all times in case I ever felt like something wasn't right."

"You are tracking our daughter's car?" Mia asks.

"Lecture me about it later," Gentry replies with an eye roll. "But now, it could be the only thing that saves her life."

She gets on his phone and starts looking something up.

"Put that app on Mia's phone right now," I say.

"She's driving," Mia says as she looks at her husband's phone. "We're going to go follow her."

"No. I should go," Gentry says.

"No," Amelia disagrees. "You are going to stay here with your son. And Maddy and I are going to go."

She hands her phone to Gentry. With a scowl, he downloads the app on her phone and logs into it. Then Mia snatches it back out of his hand and grabs onto my arm. "Come on, let's go."

She drags me through the kitchen and into the garage, and then we get into her car.

I don't know where Audrey and Warner are going, but they are about to be in some huge, huge trouble.

CHAPTER 79

AUDREY

"**D**id you notice anything weird about this drive?"

Warner is in the passenger seat, and we are going through the winding, narrow roads of the Boldosa Redwood Forest.

"You mean like how close that house is to where our upperclassmen camping trip was?" I ask.

"Yeah," he says. "These roads look really familiar."

I shudder and don't reply. I have a horrible feeling in my stomach. Not just because I lied to my family and snuck out and because I know they're going to be worried sick about me and because I hate the way I can feel cold air on the back of my neck now that my hair has been cut to the same length of my sister's, but because I don't know what is going to be waiting for us at that house. I am desperate to find some information. To get some sort of clue. But I'm also scared of what I am going to find. Scared of what might happen.

I just really want to find my sister, and I don't want this to be another dead-end road.

"Hey, you okay?" Warner's voice has turned soft.

I grip the steering wheel harder and nod my head. He can clearly sense that I'm feeling off, and I don't want that. I want to appear strong and able, and ready.

"Yeah. Totally," I say, using a fake confident voice. I don't know why I can't just show him how I'm really feeling. I can't seem to show anybody.

"I'm feeling really good about this," he continues. "I really think we're going to find something here, Audrey."

"Are you scared of what it is we might find?"

He takes a second to think about it. "Maybe a little," he says carefully. "But it'll be worth it. I just know it."

"Yeah. Totally worth it."

"Hey, I can drive if you want."

I smile at him. "Warner, I'm totally fine. Don't worry about me. I'm not gonna kill us."

But somebody else might.

I shake the thought out of my head. Everything is going to be fine. Just like Warner said.

I decide to play some music from my Spotify app over the speakers in my car. I keep the tone upbeat and pleasant. I don't like sad music anymore. I much prefer to be distracted by happy sounds.

We drive in silence until the map app on my phone tells us that we are close to the destination.

"I don't see the house anywhere, do you?" Warner asks as he peers through his window. I peer out mine, and it doesn't seem that there is a house—or lake—on either side of the street.

"No," I say. But then the app tells me we've arrived at our destination, so I pull over and turn off the car.

"Should we get out and walk, then?" Warner asks.

I swallow. "I... I guess."

We unbuckle our seatbelts and cautiously step out of my Mini Cooper. We seem to be completely in the middle of nowhere. No cars are driving by. No houses are lining the trees. It's nothing but wilderness. And it's dark.

Very dark.

"There's a pathway right here," Warner points through the trees. I follow his finger and see that it's not so much a pathway as it is just a spot in the dirt where several people seemed to have walked in the same spot over time.

"Great. Should we go that way then?"

"I think it's worth a shot."

I stand very close to Warner as we begin our journey through the woods. I feel like we should've brought weapons, but I don't want to say anything because I don't want Warner to know how scared I feel. But we have nothing out here to protect us. Nothing but our phones and my car keys.

Something cracks behind us, and we whip our heads around.

"What was that?" I ask quickly.

"Probably just... an animal or something," Warner says. But the fact that he looks slightly uneasy now only makes me feel more worried.

"Right," I say. "A bunny. Or something small and not ferocious."

"Exactly."

We keep on.

After a few long moments of silence, Warner speaks again. "Not to freak you out or anything, but... does it feel like to you that somebody... I don't know. Never mind. I'm being stupid."

"What?" I ask.

"Does it seem like somebody knows we're here?"

The hairs on the back of my neck stand up.

"You mean... like, somebody's watching us?"

"I'm probably just being paranoid."

"Maybe," I say. "But I don't know. There could be anything in these woods."

"Yeah. But it's probably nothing."

But now I feel it, too. I feel the noise behind us wasn't an animal or a small rodent. I feel like somebody's watching us. Following us, even.

And I don't like it one bit.

Amelia

"If you get a speeding ticket, I'll pay for it," Maddy says to me as we're in the car to go chase after our son and daughter.

"You're sure Warner's with her?" I ask, ignoring her.

"Yes. I think they've been hanging out with each other all this time. And that they've been keeping it a secret."

"Kind of like you and I have been doing with our friendship?"

"Exactly. They're just like us."

"Yeah."

We're silent for a moment. Both of us are on the edge of our seats. We just want to get to our children. We want to know what it is they're doing, and I want to make sure that my daughter isn't in any danger. As much as I don't want to think that Warner could actually be a bad kid who has done something to Lyla—and now Audrey—I just can't put it past him. I keep replaying Gentry's words in my head. I shouldn't be trusting anybody right now. Nobody knows what happened to Lyla. So every avenue is still open to explore.

But I don't say anything to Maddy about it. I don't want to upset her.

"So," Maddy says after some time of being quiet. "Why is your mom at your house?"

"Oh." I don't even know where to begin with that. "She's been helping us out. With everything going on lately."

"I see. Are you guys close?"

"Definitely not."

"Because of what happened with Nora?"

I squint as if I can't see the road clearly even though I can. I have excellent vision. "Yeah. Because of that."

She's the one who brought it up. So she's why I can't stop thinking about it now and why I'm suddenly fixated. Suddenly, I need to get an answer from her. "Listen, I know you've stayed in touch with Nora all these years."

"What?"

"You heard me, Maddy."

She stammers, me having completely caught her off guard. "I... What are you—where did you even get that from?"

"It doesn't matter. Why would you lie to me about it?"

"I don't think you want to be talking to me about what a liar I am, Mia," she says, her voice suddenly turning darker.

"What are you talking about?"

She crosses her arms and says nothing.

"Maddy. What are you talking about?" I repeat.

"Oh, you know... I'm just not the only one who's been keeping a secret."

"Oh, yeah?" I ask, my stomach dipping. According to the app on my phone, we're getting closer to my daughter's car. I am going twenty miles over the speed limit, even though it's really unlike me. "What secret am I keeping then?"

"You know. The one where you and Dean had a fling all those years ago."

My mouth drops open, but I quickly snap it shut.

How did she find out? I don't even know what to say back. I can't believe she knows. I never intended on that happening. I never got with Dean to hurt her. It just... happened.

Before I can say anything, she shakes her head.

"Honestly, it's not really anything we need to be discussing right now," she tells me. "We just need to focus on getting our kids back. Can we just do that?"

"Yes," I say. "Definitely."

I'm afraid if I start telling her everything right now, I'll tell her way, way too much.

CHAPTER 81

MADDY

"Up there!" I suddenly shout to Amelia. Up ahead, I see a familiar baby blue Mini Cooper pulled over on the side of the road.

In the middle of nowhere. In the deserted redwood forest.

"What on earth?" Amelia mutters as she pulls up behind the car and shuts hers off. "What are they doing out here?"

"No idea. Let's go."

I get out of the car, and it takes her a second, but then she follows suit.

"I don't like this," she says.

I swallow and look around. One of us has to be brave. And I know it's not going to be Mia.

"Which way do you think they went?" I ask, searching the ground for signs of their footprints.

"I think they went this way," she says, looking at the ground by her feet where she's standing. I walk over to her and see some footprints that look fresh. And they lead through a narrow pathway into the woods.

"Great," I say. "Let's go, then."

"We should've brought a flashlight," Mia says, sounding like she wants to do anything except going into these woods. But we have to get to our kids, and she knows that.

"It will be okay," I say. "We have a flashlight app on our phone in case we need it. But I don't think we should use it. Maybe our kids don't want to be found. And we don't want to spook them and make them run off."

"Good point."

We start walking. It is terrifying being in these woods so late at night with no sign of life around.

As we go, we don't say anything to each other. I think we're both mad at each other. We don't want to talk about anything unless we have to. We just want to find our kids. And then once we do that, maybe we will try to reconcile later. She knows about my and Nora's friendship—not that I know how. So I'm going to have to apologize and come clean about it. But I know her dirty little secret, too. And I want answers. I want to know when she and Dean were together and why. I want to know how long it lasted and why it ended. I think I have a right to know. Dean is the father of my son. Not of her daughters. It's not right that they ended up together.

"How much longer?" Mia asks.

"How should I know?" I snap, not meaning to sound so rude. "I just... I don't even know where this trail will lead us."

"I sort of... have a feeling I know where."

"What are you talking about? You know where we are?" Hope fills me.

"Maybe. I'm not one hundred percent positive. But... Maddy, I think this is where we followed Carson Price that night."

CHAPTER 82

Audrey

Finally, after what feels like a good mile at least of walking, we enter a clearing of trees and come upon the front of the A-framed lake house.

It looks just as it did in the photo.

But no lights are on. No signs of life are inside. It looks completely deserted. There's furniture on the patio. There are no curtains hanging over the windows. It's just pitch black, like everything else in these woods.

"Whoa," Warner says quietly. I'm too afraid to speak. Too afraid of what is waiting for us here.

"Should we go inside?" I eventually squeak out.

"Maybe," Warner says. "It might be worth it to check it out. To find out whose house it is and what Carson Price would've been doing here all those years ago."

I nod, but that's the last thing I want to do. Who knows what could be waiting for us inside? Who knows what type of squatters, hunters, or killers are in there?

I approach the house slowly, and I think Warner is right behind me.

When I turn around, suddenly, he's gone.

"Warner?" I whisper. I don't want to be heard by anybody in case there is somebody around here. We can't be spotted. "Warner?"

Where could he have gone? He was literally just here.

Now I'm alone.

My heartbeat picks up speed. We came here for answers. I can't just stand here and be a baby about it. I'm sure he's around here somewhere.

I decide that before I'm going to try to get into the house, I'll check the perimeter of it. I take a right and walk around the house. No signs of open windows or any easy way to get in.

When I round the back of the house, that's when I see the pool and the lake beyond that.

The pool is disgusting. It doesn't look like it's been cleaned in a decade. Its surface is mainly covered in leaves, but I also see lots of green from moss and algae and twigs floating around from trees during storms.

There could be living creatures in there... or dead ones.

The smell is horrible, so I cover my nose with my shirt when I step on the edge of the pool. Then I look up at the back of the house and see the balcony. It's still broken at the railing. And I have to agree with some of those conspiracy theories—it looks like somebody fell right through it. And if that's the case, what happened after? Why didn't anybody ever come to repair it?

If there were ever a place to film a horror movie, this would be the perfect one. Heck, with somebody wearing a mask and tormenting my sister and us missing, I am living in a horror movie. How many people can say that?

"Warner?" I whisper-yell again. Still, there are no signs of him. And everything seems still around me.

To the house or toward the lake?

I turn toward the lake. I can see it only barely through the trees, lit up by the moonlight. There's a dock down there. Maybe I should go, just in case.

I step away from the pool and back onto the mixture of crunchy and damp leaves on the forest floor. I take a few steps through the trees and then pause.

A few yards away, nearly obscured by the overgrown greenery and trees in front of it, there's a run-down, old, eerie-looking pool shed.

CHAPTER 83

WARNER

I walk around to the left of the house to see there's an unlocked window we can crawl in through. It slides open with ease, which surprises me a little bit. I thought it would at least be rusted shut since it doesn't seem like anybody's been here in a long, long time.

But maybe I'm wrong about that.

When I walk back around to the front of the house to tell Audrey that I got a window open, I see that she's disappeared.

What the heck?

I look around myself. "Audrey?"

She doesn't seem to be anywhere in sight.

Did she get spooked and go back to the car?

It would be really nice if I could have my phone right now. Then I could just call her. Text her and ask her where she went. Make sure she's okay.

I wonder if maybe she walked around the right side of the house and found another way in. Maybe she's already snooping around the interior.

I go back to the open window and climb my way through it. I enter the house through the kitchen. The disgusting, dirty, hasn't-been-used-in-a-hundred-years kitchen.

Every surface is coated with dust. There's mold on the walls. Some of the cabinets are hanging off the hinges. The refrigerator looks ancient, and I'm terrified to even try and open it. What if there's expired food in there? I can only imagine the number of maggots and rodents that could be living inside of it.

It looks completely deserted. Like nobody's been inside for years. But maybe they just don't use the kitchen.

I walk through it, careful not to step on anything that will make a noise to let anyone know I'm here. Just in case. I think we're alone, but you can never be too certain.

I want to call out for Audrey again, but I also don't want to be heard by anyone. So I stay silent and move to the next room.

At first, it all looks the same as a kitchen. Just a little less grody. There is still dust on everything. There's some furniture, like an old table and a chair that only has three legs. But other than that, it's empty in here.

Well, almost empty.

I pause in my step when I look over at the corner, on the far side of the house, where a sleeping bag is on the floor. Next, that sleeping bag is a small lantern. And the floor around it looks like it's been swept and scrubbed. There are also food wrappers and empty water bottles by it.

It's evidence that somebody has been staying here. And based on the lack of dust around the area, that person staying here was here recently.

"Oh my God," I breathe, realizing what this might mean. Sure, it could be anyone staying here. A squatter. A hunter. But we're in the middle of nowhere. So it could also be somebody else.

I'm about to approach the sleeping bag corner so I can snoop through everything there to see if I can get any helpful information on who the person is that might be staying here, but then I hear a noise. It sounds like footsteps walking up the steps to the front porch.

"Crap."

I look around wildly. I have to hide!

I'm closest to the staircase, so I take off up it, trying to be as quiet as possible while also moving as fast as I can. I still hear the footsteps out on the porch. Somebody is definitely here. And it could be Audrey, but for some reason, I'm scared that it's not.

It looks even more lived-in up here. There are boxes and boxes with unknown contents inside, cases of water, more lanterns, and a couple of folding chairs. There's also an old bookcase, and it's perfectly angled in the corner of the room, so I run over to it and squeeze myself behind it, covering myself in old cobwebs and nearly choking on the smell of the musty, damp walls.

I keep an ear out and cover my mouth so that my breathing is hidden. The sound of the footsteps has grown louder. That can only mean one thing.

Somebody is inside this house.

CHAPTER 84

Audrey

I don't expect to find anything inside the shed other than rodents, like raccoons or skunks. Lots of bugs, too. But maybe, just maybe, I'll also find a clue. Some sort of evidence. A document or a receipt for tools or something that has a name on it. Something that will tell me who this cabin belongs to. If we can find that out, I know it will be a great start.

I stand there, a good distance away, staring at the shed for a long while before I'm finally brave enough to walk toward it. I go to play with my hair around my shoulder, something I always do when I'm nervous, but I remember it's not there anymore. How long is it going to take me to get used to that?

The reason we decided to chop my hair off—and we did not do a good job—was so that I could impersonate my sister. Just in case anyone spotted us out here—that anyone being the man in the mask—so he would think I was Lyla. And if the masked man does see me and has Lyla captured somewhere, then he will probably think that Lyla escaped. And then he will come after me.

It was a risky and terrifying maneuver to make, and I never wanted to lose my long hair, but it had to be done. And I'm willing to do whatever it takes. Anything to help Lyla.

A tree branch rustling behind me makes me stop walking. A chill runs down my spine, and even though I'm terrified to do it, I turn around to see what's behind me.

I turn around at the same time that somebody grabs my hand with both of theirs. I nearly scream out, but then I realize who it is.

"Mom?"

"Lyla?"

"I'm not Lyla," I say quickly. "I'm Audrey."

"Audrey?" she repeats, looking like she's never heard that name in her life.

"Your other daughter," I remind her. "What are you doing out here?"

"What—what is this?" She takes some of my hair in her fingers. "Why did you do this? What are you doing out here?"

"We're... we're just looking for answers."

"What kind of answers?"

"Hello?"

We both freeze.

What was that?

It hadn't been Mom's voice.

It hadn't been my voice.

We wait, and then we hear something else.

"Is someone there?"

We turn toward the shed. That's where the voice had come from.

That familiar voice that makes my stomach feel like it's going to fly right out of my mouth.

"Lyla?!" Mom and I call at the same time.

"Yes!" Lyla suddenly screams from inside the shed. "It's me!" Then she pounds on the door. It makes me jump. "I'm in here! Oh my God, I'm in here! Help me!"

Together, Mom and I sprint toward the shed. I can't believe this is real life. I can't believe I've found my sister.

Mom grabs my wrist harshly and stops me when we're just a few feet in front of the shed.

In front of Lyla.

"What are you—?!" I'm about to ask her what the heck she's doing and why we're not rescuing my sister, but I stop in my speech because suddenly, I smell something. Something strong and unfamiliar in the middle of the woods like this.

Gasoline.

Then I hear the click of a lighter.

And suddenly, the entire perimeter of the shed is up in flames.

LYLA

"**M**om?"

"Lyla?"

The voices I hear wake me up again from my chloroformed slumber. Everything is hazy and unclear. I don't even think the voices were real. I think I was dreaming that Audrey and my mom were here.

Even though my eyes are blurry and out of focus, I look around the shed, expecting to see that the masked man is still in here. Waiting to drug me again.

"I'm not Lyla," a voice says to someone outside the shed. "I'm Audrey."

Or, maybe the voices aren't outside of the shed. Maybe they're in here. Maybe they're in my head. Maybe I'm having a wakeful dream. The chloroform has been really messing me up.

"Audrey?"

What a strange conversation for me to be dreaming about—my mom mistaking Audrey for me. It used to happen all the time, but not since I changed my hair.

Where did the kidnapper go? Why did he chloroform me all day long and then disappear? What was the point of it?

"Your other daughter," Audrey's voice says. "What are you doing out here?"

"What—what is this? Why did you do this? What are you doing out here?" My mom's voice says to her.

"We... we're just looking for answers."

"Mom?" I say, my voice incredibly weak. I clear my throat and try to push myself up to the seated position. "Audrey?"

"What kind of answers?" My mom is saying to Audrey.

"Hello?"

Finally, my voice is louder this time. More clear.

Now, no voices are talking. Maybe I did imagine at all.

"Is someone out there?" I ask anyway as I crawl toward the door. It's hard to do, but I manage.

Please let this be real. Please let there be somebody out there to save me. Please let it be my mom and my sister.

"Lyla?!"

My heart soars, and my throat tightens. I cling to the wall and pull myself up.

They're here. They're really here!

"Yes!" I shout as loud as I can. "It's me!" Then I hit the door as hard as I can. I slap it with both of my palms, making the whole thing shake. "I'm in here! Oh my God, I'm in here! Help me!"

I continue banging and pounding on the door. I can't believe it. I'm being rescued! And so what if I'm locked in here? They at least know I'm here! They'll be able to get help, and they'll be able to get me out of here!

But then suddenly, something feels off. I stop pounding on the door and turn my head. It sounds like somebody is standing on just the other side of the shed, behind it. And why does it sound like there's a water leak somewhere suddenly? Like something is pouring out on the leaves around the shed?

Then I breathe in the strong scent of what is unmistakably gasoline.

"No," I breathe out, my stomach twisting violently.

My kidnapper knows my family is here.

And now he's doing what he can to make sure I don't escape.

With a click of a lighter, I hear a whooshing noise, and then I feel the heat all around me. I see the orange glow through the cracks in the old shed.

My kidnapper is going to burn me alive.

CHAPTER 86

WARNER

The footsteps of the unknown person still wander slowly around the house. How long are they going to stay here? What are they doing? Who are they?

I'm still behind the bookcase in hiding. My heart is hammering in my chest, and I'm terrified of what could be waiting for me out there. Of what's going to happen if I am found.

Please don't come up here, please don't come up here, please don't come up here.

But naturally, it's as if me hoping that the person didn't make the way up the stairs was exactly what willed it to happen anyway.

I'm so scared that it hurts to think. It hurts to breathe. I feel frozen to the spot. Like even if whoever it is catches me behind this bookcase, I'm not going to be able to try and run away. I'm just going to be stuck here like this. I'm going to be an easy target.

The footsteps approach the bookcase.

Please don't look behind here, please don't look behind here, please don't look behind here

I hold my hand tighter over my mouth. I hope they don't hear me breathing. I hope I haven't given myself away by having to push the bookcase out a little bit to be able to stand behind it in the corner of the room.

The footsteps stop.

They're literally three steps away from me. Just on the other side of the bookcase.

What are they doing?

I wait. Wait for the unknown. Wait for the horror.

But then, the footsteps start again.

Whoever it is is walking away from the bookcase.

But they're still here on the second floor. What are they up to?

I came here for answers. I can't stay here behind this bookcase, too afraid to figure out who's been squatting here and why. We came this far. We literally came all this way to a cabin in the middle of nowhere to get some answers. To get to the truth.

If they go back down the stairs and disappear, and if I miss my chance to see who's out there, I might regret it for the rest of my life. And I can't live like that. I want to know where Lyla is. I want to know what happened the night Carson Price died. I want to know who killed Sydney Hutton. I want to get to the bottom of all of it.

So I have to stop hiding.

Careful to remain quiet, I slide out from my hiding spot behind the bookcase. I don't know who I'm going to find out there. Carson? Dean? Audrey, even?

I look around but don't see anyone. Outside the window, there's a strange glow. And when I inhale, I smell smoke.

The door to the balcony is open. Whoever was up here went out there.

So without thinking any more about it, I cross the room and go through the open door.

My heart stops in my chest when I see who is standing there, close to the railing in the area where it isn't broken.

I can barely speak. "Mom?"

Has it been her all along?

CHAPTER 87

LYLA

"NO!" I scream inside the shed. "HELP ME!" I am not only banging on the door with my fists now. I'm slamming my entire body into it now.

I can hear my mom and Audrey on the other side, crying out to me and trying their best to get the door open, even though the whole place is practically engulfed in the flames.

"GET ME OUT OF HERE!" I beg. "PLEASE!"

"Just hang on, Lyla!" Mom calls. "We're gonna get you out!"

"It's going to be okay!" Audrey calls, then she coughs, and it sounds horrible.

I continue ramming into the door. I have to be able to break it open. At some point, the flames have to start breaking down the wood, right? The flames have to start making it easier to break through.

"Please don't let me die in here!"

That's when the smoke fills the shed so much that I can hardly see, and I start to cough. Then I'm coughing so violently that I can no longer focus on anything else. I can no longer ram into the door to try to break it down. What I do instead is drop to my knees. Then I keep coughing.

"Lyla!"

I can't even say anything back to them. The smoke is too thick. I have no air.

I'm not ready to die, but I don't think the fire cares about that.

CHAPTER 88

MADDY

It's so weird being back in this house. It looks nothing like it did all those years ago. None of the furniture is inside it. Everything is coated in dust and cobwebs. The wood is rotting. There's mold on the walls. It smells so bad that I want to keep my shirt over my nose.

The second I step foot inside the house through the open window in the kitchen and walk into what used to be the living area, I can see that there has been somebody squatting in here. I can tell by the sleeping bag on the ground and the lantern. And how that one little corner of this entire house is the only spot that is clean.

I wonder who it is. I wonder if maybe Warner has been coming out here. If maybe this is his and Audrey's little secret hangout spot. But it's too much of a coincidence. They have to know more about what happened with Carson Price that night than I realized. That can be the only explanation as to how they ended up at this exact house.

Eventually, I start up the steps. I have the strangest urge to go back up there. Back to where it happened.

Back to where we killed Carson.

I think back to that night.

"Where is he?" I had mouthed to Amelia as we stood in front of the staircase. Then we heard a noise upstairs, and we knew our answer. I went up the staircase first. I was the one with the weapon.

As I go up the stairs, it creaks heavily underneath my feet. I am a little bit worried that I'm going to fall right through it. But as I get higher up and see what's in the loft, I realize that the stairs have been used frequently over the years. They must be safer than I thought.

There are boxes of food and supplies up here. More than enough for one person.

Nothing here is the same except the bookcase in the corner of the room. I approach it slowly. The last time we were here, it was full of books. Now there's only an old encyclopedia and a dusty hardcover of a Hardy Boys.

I look at the back door leading out to the balcony. I think back again to that night.

Amelia had nudged me. We had gotten to the landing at the top of the staircase, but Carson wasn't around. The reason why Amelia had nudged me was that the back door was wide open. Carson was out there.

And I went first.

"What are you guys doing here?" Carson asked us when he turned and saw that we were there.

"We know what you did, Carson," I said. When I went to look behind me, Amelia was further back than I thought.

I thought she was a coward.

I stare at that same back door now. It's closed this time. Nobody is out there.

But for some reason, I want to go out there and see for myself.

I leave the bookshelf and walk over to the door. I find it unlocked, so I push it open and walk out.

I freeze when I see the broken railing. The spot where after Amelia ripped the shovel from my hand, she screamed wildly and ran toward Carson. Then she whacked him across the side of the face, and he fell back into the railing, where the whole thing gave out.

This is where he died.

This is the last place Carson Price was alive.

I peer down over the broken railing, careful to stay a far enough distance back, and I look into the pool. It's different than it looked all those years ago. The pool light isn't on. The water isn't clear. If a body fell into it now, it would probably get swallowed by all of the leaves and sludge inside of it now.

"Oh my God, what did you do?"

I can still hear the horror in my voice when I asked Amelia that question after Carson went through the railing.

We hadn't wanted to kill Carson. And as far as I knew, we weren't going to hurt him, either. We were just going to act very threateningly and demand he left Nora alone. He was a horrible person. He abused her. He deserved to have a little fear put into him.

But that's all I had wanted to do. It was Amelia who took that next step.

After it happened, I pulled Amelia down the stairs, and together, we ran over to the edge of the pool and pulled Carson out of it. I remember there being so much blood. And he had a gash on the back of his head, with even more blood pouring out of it. Along with a cut on his face where Amelia hit him.

Mia whimpered, terrified. I shook him and tried to wake him up. He couldn't be dead. We couldn't have killed him. I continued shaking him.

"Maddy!" Mia shouted, grabbing my shoulder and shaking me to get me to stop.

And so I did.

I stood up next to Mia, and together we looked down at his dead body.

"What do I do?" Mia asked. "Do we... do we call someone? We have to call someone, right? I didn't mean to kill him, Maddy! I didn't!"

"How were you supposed to know that the railing wasn't safe?" I asked, trying to make her feel better. But I felt like I was going to be sick. Still, I didn't want Mia to know it. She was terrified, and I didn't want to make things worse. If I acted calm, maybe it would help her be calm, too. "We need to run," I decided.

"What? But we... Maddy, he's dead!"

I grabbed her shoulders. Then I look deep into her eyes. "You were never here, Mia. Okay? We were never here. We need to leave, and we need to leave now."

"No," she whispered. "No, Maddy. I can't do that. I... I killed him!"

"Be quiet!" I demanded. Then I started pulling her along. I brought the shovel with us. "Come on. We have to go!"

She started sobbing, but she went with me. "No," she cried. "Oh God, no."

I swallowed back my own sobs. I just kept telling myself everything would be fine. Nobody would ever know we were out here. Once his body was discovered, no one would know how it happened. In fact, they would probably just assume he fell to his own death. That he got too close to the railing, and it broke on him. The whole thing would be ruled an accident. No one would know that we murdered him.

It sucks looking back to that night right now. Now, I wish we had told somebody. I wish we had just come clean. Because I could've never expected everything that was going to happen afterward.

Now, someone is onto us. And if the truth comes to light, we're not going to get out of it so easily.

As I stand out on the balcony, staring at the pool, I suddenly see a bright light in the distance to my right.

A fire.

Mia.

I quickly turn back around to leave and check on her. I don't know why the fire started or how, but I need to make sure Mia is okay.

I freeze when I see my son standing behind me. He has a horrified expression on his face, and he's staring right at me.

"Warner," I gasp, putting a hand to my heart. "Warner, someone started a fire. We have to get down there."

"What are you doing here, Mom?" Warner doesn't seem like he's going anywhere.

"I—the real question is, what are you doing here? How did you find out about this place?" I ask.

"How did I find out this is the house where Nora Flynn claims to have found Carson Price's body?"

"Warner, I don't know how you found out all of this information, but—"

"What are you doing here?" he asks again.

"I... I followed you."

"Is that the truth?"

"What? Warner, we really need to get down there."

"Where is Lyla, Mom?"

I freeze in my step. "Where is Lyla? I don't know, Warner. Why... why are you asking me that?"

"I know a lot more than you think. I know why you're angry. Why you might want your revenge. But this isn't the right way, Mom."

"Warner, what are you talking about?"

"Just tell me where you put her."

Wait a second.

Does my son think I kidnapped Lyla?

"Warner..." I trail off, not because I don't know what to say, but because I smell something.

Gas.

Before I can even react to it, before I can even tell warner that we need to get off of this balcony right this second, suddenly, there are more flames. And they're right underneath the balcony, galloping upwards and jumping at me.

And this balcony wasn't sturdy when Mia and I were on it twenty years ago.

"Mom!" Warner cries out. He goes to step further onto the balcony to grab me. But the whole thing creaks violently under him.

"Don't move!" I shout.

He freezes.

The creaking is loud. There are snapping noises, too. This balcony is going to break at any second. I'm going to fall into those flames.

"Mom, what do I do?" Warner asks, realizing that the balcony is unsafe. I start to cough as smoke fills my lungs. I don't know what to do. I don't have an answer for him.

"Mom!"

"Warner, get out of here! Go get help!"

"No," he says sternly. "I'm not leaving you!"

"It's going to collapse at any moment!"

"Run, Mom! Come on!"

It creaks and groans so loudly that it makes both of us hold our arms out in brace for it to break. But by some miracle, it doesn't.

Warner runs back inside the house. For a moment, I think he's left me. But when he quickly returns, he's gripping a broom. He holds out the bristly side to me. "Grab onto this!"

I do as I'm told, some of the flames leaping onto the balcony. Now the broken part of the railing is on fire. Flames are leaping at my arms. The creaking and groaning continues.

"Warner," I say. I want to tell him that I'm scared. But I am his mother. He's supposed to be the one saying that to me.

"Come on, Mom! Even if it falls, just hang on, and I got you!"

Then right in front of me, the ground splinters. It looks like the balcony is opening up a hole right in the middle. This is my only chance.

I scream out and run for it. Warner holds the other end of the broom and pulls back as hard as he can, and then suddenly, there's no more ground underneath my feet. I scream some more, and Warner jumps backward. Holding the broom, I jump through the air and barely make it through the open door onto the ground beside my son.

The balcony outside is no longer there. Warner has just saved my life.

CHAPTER 89

Amelia

"Why isn't she saying anything anymore, Mom?" Audrey asks me as we stand outside the flaming shed.

"Lyla?!" I call. "Are you okay?"

She doesn't answer. She just keeps coughing.

Audrey is a wreck. "She's going to die in there!"

"No, she's not!"

I don't care if I get third-degree burns. I don't care if my entire leg melts off of my body. I approach the flames, the heat burning my face and my lungs burning from the smoke. I lift my chunky-heeled black boot in the air, and then I kick the door through the flames with all my might.

"Lyla, stand back!" I shout. It didn't break open, but it definitely loosened it. I step away from the flames for a moment and cough some more. I have to try it again. "I'm coming!"

Again, I lift my leg and kick hard and fast as I can through the flames.

The door bursts open.

"Lyla!" I scream. "Get out of there!"

At first, I don't see anything but the flames.

Then I hear a scream, and after six days, six long, agonizing, endless days, Lyla flies through the opening and is finally back in my arms.

We're all coughing, choking, and sputtering, but we're all hugging each other and standing in the woods. I almost feel like this isn't real. I didn't realize until this moment how much I truly believed I would never see her again.

"I'm so sorry, Lyla!" I say as I cry into her hair. She doesn't say anything. She buries herself in my jacket and cries.

"Mom," Audrey gasps. Lyla and I look up and see what Audrey sees. Not only is the shed on fire. But the house is on fire. The woods around us are on fire. Everything is engulfed.

And we're right in the middle of it.

"Let's get out of here," I say.

"Warner's here!" Audrey says. "We have to find him!"

Maddy and I had split up. She said she'd check the house, and I said I'd check the backyard.

Maddy could be trapped in that fire.

"Let's go!" I say to the girls; then I make sure I have both of their hands in mine as I pull them back toward the house.

"Wait!" Lyla suddenly screeches, making us all stop. I look at her and then see she's staring at something in the trees. So I follow her gaze.

There, coming out from behind the burning shed is a man. He's coughing loudly and covering his face. Then he pulls something off, and at first, I'm horrified, thinking he's pulling off his own skin. But then, when it drops into the leaves, I realize it's a mask.

The man stumbles around and continues to cough. And then he drops his hands, and his face is revealed.

"Carson?"

When he sees the three of us standing there, staring directly at him, he doesn't wait around. He turns sharply on his heel, then takes off at a run and disappears into the trees.

CHAPTER 90

LYLA

"**W**hat did you just say?" I ask my mom as I turn to look at her after the man disappears into the woods.

She looks like she's seen a literal ghost. She shakes her head quickly, ignores me, and then continues tugging on Audrey and me.

"Come on."

But I know what she just said.

Carson.

That was my kidnapper? Carson Price has been alive all this time, and he locked me in that shed?

We hurry past the pool and around the side of the house, and out in front of it, Warner and Maddy are standing huddled together in a clearing of trees that aren't on fire.

"Thank God," Amelia says, running over to Maddy. The two of them hug.

I stand there and stare at Warner. He stares back at me.

Then he's running.

He slams into me so hard that we nearly fall over. He hugs me tightly and holds the back of my head with one of his hands.

"I can't believe it's you," he says.

"Hi," is all I can think to say back. But it feels so, so good to be held by him like this. It feels so good to see all of them. Even Maddy.

I never thought I'd see any of them ever again.

I never thought I'd get out of that shed.

When Warner and I pull away, he has tears in his eyes. "This doesn't feel real."

"I know," I say. I feel the exact same way.

"Maddy," Mom says to Warner's mom. "It was Carson. Carson did this."

"What?" Maddy asks sharply. "He's dead, Mia."

I look at Warner and Audrey. They look at me.

I think we're all thinking the same thing. We can't believe our parents are talking about Carson's death right in front of us.

I also notice briefly that my sister looks a lot like me again.

"I'm telling you," Mom continues. "It was him. We need to go. Now."

"I'm with Amelia," Warner says. He takes my hand; then he reaches out his other one to take Audrey's. "Let's get the heck out of here."

Together, all five of us run through the woods in the opposite direction of where we saw Carson Price disappear.

CHAPTER 91

MADDY

We end up waiting there on the street by our cars, far away from where the fire is and where Lyla's kidnapping location is, for the firefighters and police to get onto the scene. We all get checked out by paramedics, and when it's determined that we're all okay—except for Lyla—and the firefighters have mostly gotten the fire out, they insist that we go to the hospital to get more thoroughly looked at there.

Amelia, Lyla, and Warner all pile in her car and take off before even waiting to see if I want to ride in there, too, and it leaves Audrey and me alone, standing by her car.

This should be fun.

I get in the passenger seat of her cute little Mini Cooper that I once vandalized, and we drive in silence through the redwoods.

"We really saw Carson," she decides to say to me after quite some time. We're both covered in soot, and Audrey looks exhausted.

"I just... I don't know," I say. "I guess it's possible. They never did find his body."

"So does that mean that Nora made it all up, just like people were saying she did?"

"I... I don't know," I say. It still makes no sense to me. Mia and I stood over his dead body. Mia and I saw the amount of blood that was pouring out of his head. He didn't move. He didn't stutter. No matter how much I shook him.

How did he survive that?

We drive in silence some more. I think about what a good thing it is that Lyla was found. It at least clears my son of one problem. Warner is no longer going to be a person of interest in Lyla's disappearance. People will stop thinking he's a kidnapper. And maybe, if this all is tied together, people will stop thinking he's also a person of interest in the murder of Sydney Hutton.

If Audrey and Warner hadn't decided to come out here, Lyla would still be in that shed.

And we would still be in the middle of a huge mess.

"Audrey, listen," I say, not really thinking about the words that are about to come out of my mouth. "I saw the letter you wrote to Warner."

"What?" Audrey asks, looking thoroughly confused. "What letter?"

"What do you mean 'what letter?' The one where you told my son who his father was. Luckily, he didn't read it. I got to it first." Not that it matters now.

"Miss Carpenter, I never sent him a letter. I... I kept your secret. I swear I did. I didn't tell a soul. "

"If you didn't tell a soul, then who wrote that letter?"

"I honestly don't know. Maybe Freaky Fritz?"

"Freaky Fritz." I chuckle slightly. I like that name for him.

But now I feel even more terrible. Audrey had held up her end of the deal this whole time.

I sigh. "I thought you wrote it," I admit. "And... I told you you'd regret it if you did. So, I'm sort of the one who ruined things with your friend, Sophia, and that boy, Ryan, that you liked."

"Wait... what?" Still, she looks confused.

"I did some stalking on your social media. I'm not proud of it ." I figured out that she liked Ryan Copeland. I figured out that her best friend likes Bryson Anthony. I made it so that Sophia thought Audrey and Bryson were hanging out together. And then I wrote "Boyfriend Stealer" in the red paint on her car.

And I admit it all to her now.

"You're... you're crazy," she says, pain in her voice after I finish. "Do you have any idea how hurt I was by all of that?"

"I was in high school once. I do know."

"I thought Sophia wrote that on my car."

"I'm sorry," I say. "I really did think you tried to tell Warner about Dean. I just... I wasn't ready for that yet. I wasn't sure if I would ever be ready. "

"I'm sorry he found out anyway," she says. For some reason, she's not nearly as mad as I expected her to be. And a huge weight is lifted off my shoulders from having told her the truth.

"I guess I am a little crazy," I say. "Because I'd do anything to protect my son. And that's what I thought I was doing. But it's still not a good excuse, and I'm sorry. At least now you don't have to keep that secret anymore."

"Actually, I would prefer if it stayed a secret that I ever knew at all," she says. "If Warner finds out, I knew way before he found out, and I never told him…"

"Deal," I say. "I won't say anything."

Now the roles are reversed. But I sort of owe it to her to keep her secret.

CHAPTER 92

AMELIA

Lyla received pretty bad carbon monoxide poisoning from inhaling all the smoke inside of that shed, and she has some other old injuries, so she's the only one who has a stay at the hospital overnight.

But still, Maddy, Audrey, and Warner all come to the hospital and sit with me in the waiting room. I appreciate their being there. And I'm so glad that everyone is okay. I know Lyla's going to be okay, too. She just needs some rest and an IV.

Maddy and I are exhausted as we sit in the chairs of the waiting room, so we say nothing for a long, long time. But then I can't go any longer without talking about it.

"We thought he was dead all this time," I say to her in a quiet voice. Warner and Audrey are sitting in some chairs in a grouping away from us, so they can't hear our conversation.

"You're sure it was him, Mia?" Maddy asks me.

"I know it's been... what, twenty years? But it was him, Mads. Of course, it was him. He's been... he's been hiding out in those woods all this time."

"I just... I don't get it. Why did he kidnap your daughter? Why now, after all this time? Why hasn't anyone found him? Why hasn't anyone heard a peep? Do we tell Nora?"

You mean your best friend?

I want to say it, but now is not the time to be snooty.

"I don't know," I say. "You saw how the police acted when we tried to tell them that we saw Carson in the woods. I don't think they believe us."

"Of course not. We're just a couple of liars. No one ever believes anything out of our mouths."

"Uh-huh," I agree.

She chuckles lightly.

"Thank you for coming with me tonight," I say. "Thank you for making me realize that Audrey left the house at all. Things could have ended a lot differently if we hadn't followed them."

"I'm glad we were there," she says. Then she reaches over and squeezes my hand. There are still a lot of words left unsaid. About my secret and her secret. But still, now is not the time to discuss it.

Her phone vibrates in her purse, and she pulls it out. She lets go of my hand, and her brows furrow as she reads the message on her screen.

"Everything alright?" I ask. She looks concerned.

"I... I'm so sorry," she says, getting to her feet. "But I really need to go."

"Maddy, wait," I try, getting to my feet as well. But she's already rushing out the door.

"Where'd she go?" Warner asks from his seat next to Audrey.

I stare after her, wondering what on earth just happened. "I have no idea."

CHAPTER 93

AUDREY

S omehow, through all the chaos of the night with people asking us millions of questions and the media being all up in our faces and following our every move, I miraculously end up in Lyla's hospital room alone with her.

She's smiling at me as I walk in and sit in the chair by her bed. She doesn't look the greatest. She's bruised and scratched and tired. More than anything, my sister just looks tired.

"Glad we're finally alone," I say to her.

"Why did you cut your hair?"

"I just missed you so much that I thought if I looked at myself in the mirror with your haircut, I would think I was seeing you."

She rolls her eyes, not believing me for a second. I scoot even closer as if I'm worried about being overheard by anybody when I talk to her about the reason why I'm glad that we're alone.

I hate being in hospitals. I hate the smell of old people, sickness, sweat, and sterilization that mixes in the air. I hate the furniture and the bright lighting. I hate the various colors of scrubs the nurses and doctors wear. I hate the various beeping machines that go off at random times and cause me to worry about what they mean. I hate how, for the most part, the hospital is where you're born and where you die.

"Do you want to know the real reason?" I whisper, reaching one of my hands to grab her forearm.

"Duh." Her voice is hoarse, and she speaks.

"I didn't do it to look like you," I admit. "I wanted your kidnapper to think you escaped if they saw me. To go after me so that Warner could free you. We also didn't know if you were even going to be at the house at all. It was more a precaution than anything."

"How did you find out about the house?"

"You probably don't know this yet, but that house is where Aunt Nora claimed to have found Carson's body."

"So it was really him then?" she asks. She looks like she wants to sit up straighter in her bed but is much, much too weak to do so. She braces herself and then drops back down onto her pillow with a sigh. "He's been alive all this time, and he kidnapped me?"

"That's what Mom seems to think. That's what she's telling the police."

"And I highly doubt they believe her."

"Who knows? A lot of people didn't believe Aunt Nora when she said she saw Carson dead."

"Why now?"

That's the question. Why now?

It's been twenty years since he disappeared. Why would he start messing with us now? What would he have to gain?

I let go of her and sit back in the chair. It's hard as a rock, but I could still easily sleep in it. On the other hand, this hospital bed is probably the most comfortable thing Lyla has slept in for nearly a week. My stomach lunges at the thought. The thought of her in that shed. The thought of her all alone. Of her thinking, she was never going to get out of it.

"I don't know." I shake my head slowly and stare at nothing because I'm in deep thought about it.

"Cutting your hair was dangerous," she suddenly tells me, sounding a lot like Mom. "And stupid. You love your hair."

"Obviously I do," I say. "But I kind of love you more, dummy."

She smiles again at me, only the corners of her mouth barely turn upward. It takes effort just for her to do that.

"I know you're tired," I continue. "But I want to talk to you before we're interrupted again."

"What's up?" She looks as if she struggling to keep her eyes open.

"Ly, the police found a long blonde wig during their search for you. Did you... did you go somewhere pretending to be me?"

Instead of answering, she turns her head toward the window.

"Lyla," I repeat, my voice a little more determined.

"I just wanted answers," she says without looking at me.

"So that's a yes, then?"

She says nothing.

"It was supposed to be me?"

"Whatever happened in the past, it doesn't matter now." She closes her eyes, and her shoulders relax. "I'm going to try and get some sleep now."

"What? No, you can't just leave it like that," I complain. "What happened that night?"

"Don't make me call the nurse and have her escort you out of here, Ree."

I cross my arms and frown. "Fine. Sleep. But this conversation isn't over."

"Sure it is." Her eyes are still closed, and I want to keep arguing with her, but I know that she needs her rest.

Just like I know that she went somewhere posing as me. That all this horrible stuff that happened to her was supposed to have happened to me. And if I had been in her shoes? I don't think I would've been as brave. I don't think I would've survived out there like she did.

I sort of think I owe my sister my life.

CHAPTER 94

MADDY

My hand grips the armrest on the door of the backseat of my rideshare tightly. My stomach is rolling, and I can hear my heart beating in my ears. It's as if I have to put out one fire—literally—after another tonight.

"I'm so sorry, but if you could go any faster, I'm kind of dealing with an emergency," I say as I lean forward to talk to my driver.

"I'm going as fast as the speed limit will allow," the old man says patiently. His Buick is so clean inside, and his skin is so wrinkly that I'm reminded of the hospital. They could recline the passenger seat, and the doctors could perform an operation on someone right here in this car, and it would be more sterile than being inside one of their operating rooms.

"Okay, thank you," I say, trying to use a deeply disappointed voice to sway the guy to speed it up a little. The text I had gotten from Steven had been pretty unnerving, and I want to make sure that he is all right.

After a lifetime of going at a speed I'm pretty sure toddlers could outrun, we pull into Steven's neighborhood. Before we even round the curve to his mansion, I can see the glow of red and blue lights in the distance.

The police are at his house. But I already knew that. Because that's what the text message he sent me had mentioned.

"Uh oh, looks like someone's in trouble," the old man says jokingly. But then his chuckling turns into a deep-throated, hoarse cough. It makes me cringe and lean back further in my seat.

As soon as he's hardly even in PARK, I have the back door open, and I am lunging out of the vehicle.

"Thank you!" I call over my shoulder. Then I slam the door shut and take off at a slight jog. Steven is at one of the two police SUVs, nodding his head at something one of the cops is saying as they get into their vehicle. Then the door closes, and both cops drive off, turning their lights off as they go.

In the shadows, facing away from the lights emitting from the front of his house, Steven looks alright, but I can't make out his facial expression.

When Wrigley runs out the front door, yelling, "So, what happened?" and Steven turns around to face him, that's when I get a better view of him. He looks awful.

His face is swollen and bleeding in a couple of areas. Already, bruises are forming along his jawline and around his eyes.

"Wrigley, not now," Steven says to his son.

"No!" Wrigley argues, still approaching his father. "I wanna know what happened." He stops in his tracks when he sees me standing there. "What is she doing here?"

"Wrigley, go to bed," Steven repeats, not even able to talk properly because his mouth is so swollen.

"No," he continues to argue. "Besides, they found Lyla. So I'm gonna go see her, anyway."

"Fine. Just go. We'll talk about it later. I'm fine."

"So you can tell this woman that you've been seeing for two seconds what happened to you, but you can't tell your own son?"

"Wrigley. Go."

He looks at me with an expression I'm not fond of getting, and then he hops in his vehicle and drives away. I stand there in front of Steven, the both of us silent until his son's brake lights are barely visible in the distance.

"Steven..." I can't wait any longer to say something. "What happened?"

He walks over to his patio and sits down on the curb of it, wincing in pain as he does so. I stand in front of him, too anxious to sit.

I want to help him. I don't want him to be in pain. I feel scared and worried.

"Let me get you some ice or something," I try.

"No. I don't think it's a good idea for you to be going in there right now. The house isn't in the best shape."

"Were you... robbed?" I don't really understand why he wanted me to come here. Unless maybe he wanted some comfort.

Or unless this robbery and why he's so badly beaten is because of me.

That's what I'm most afraid of.

"Yeah. But nothing super valuable was taken. And that's sort of the least of my concern right now," he says.

"I don't understand." I'm wearing short sleeves, and the October air is chilly outside. I cross my arms and try not to shiver.

He looks like he's about to get back to his feet, but then I realize he's just pulling something out of his back pocket. It looks like a folded piece of paper.

"Here." He holds it out to me. His knuckles are bloody. I think whoever he got in a fight with took a couple of hits himself.

"What is this?" I don't want to take it. I don't want to touch it.

"Just read it," he says.

I do as I am instructed, not wanting to upset him further. I slowly begin unfolding it. It takes me four times until I can read what it says.

"I kept this private from the police," Steven says to me. "For now, at least. I wanted to talk to you first."

I'm staring at the note, barely even hearing anything Steven is saying to me. Fear is coursing through my body. Guilt. Shame. Confusion. Desperation. So many emotions that I almost want to turn around and just start running.

"Maddy, you hear me?" he asks, his tone flat and even a little dark. He's mad at me. He's distrusting. He's unsure of me now.

Not that I blame him.

"I... I hear you," I say, still not looking at him and still staring at the note.

"Maddy, someone broke into my house and jumped me in my bed. While my son was home, it could've been him who got hurt. Are you understanding me?"

"Yes." I swallow.

"So then, do you wanna explain that note to me?" he asks. "Do you maybe want to tell me what the heck is going on?"

But how can I even explain this? What can I even say to him?

For the twentieth time, I reread the note.

Stay away from Madeline Carpenter. Far away.

"Well?" he asks again. "I don't want something like this ever happening again, Maddy. Not when I have my son to protect. So, are you gonna tell me what's going on or not?"

CHAPTER 95

AMELIA

Gentry rubs my arm comfortingly. I open my eyes and find that we're still in the hospital. I have no idea what time it is, but I know that it's late.

"You should go home and get some sleep. Some real sleep," Gentry tells me. "Now that our daughter is safe. I'll stay here all night with her. I'll have one of the nurses roll in one of those reclining chairs."

"No, I can stay," I say. But the truth of the matter is, I don't want to stay. I very much want to get out of this hospital.

"I won't let her out of my sight, Mia," he says, still trying to push it.

I pretend to think it over for a little longer. Then I sigh and stand up from the small armchair. "I guess... some actual sleep does sound nice."

"If you see Audrey out there somewhere, tell her she should go home, too."

"You sure you'll be alright here?"

"Better than alright. Mia, you got her back."

I smile lamely, not feeling very much like a hero. How can I feel like a hero when seeing Carson Price in those woods made it very clear that I'm why this even happened to Lyla in the first place?

I turn and leave him there, stepping out into the night air in the parking lot of the hospital.

I still smell like smoke. It's in my hair and all my clothes. My lungs ache, too. My eyes are tired from watering. My nose is dry from how runny it has been. I know I don't look good in front of all these cameras as they try to snap pictures of me, record me, and ask me a million questions.

I really didn't think this through. My car isn't exactly close by.

"How did you know where the kidnapper was keeping your daughter?" a reporter asks.

"Mia, if we can just get your comment!" another one calls. I try to rush past them.

"Is Lyla going to be okay?" another one asks. Part of me wants to answer some other questions, but I'm also exhausted, and I look like death and don't want to be seen by everybody in the country on their TVs. So I make it to my car and drive off, not giving them anything.

Instead of going to my house, I drive in a different direction. To an address, I have been texted.

When I park the car and get out at my destination, there doesn't seem to be a soul around. But why would there be? It's the middle of the night. I know reporters and police officers aren't expecting to find me here.

I walk up the pathway toward the front door of the two-story house. Since it's late, I knock instead of ringing the doorbell.

I don't even think I wait a full second before the front door opens and arms are reaching out to me.

I quickly fall into them and let them catch me. We stand there at the doorstep like that for quite some time.

Being in Dean Reeves's arms is quite the stress reliever. It seems as if all of my troubles are finally, finally melting away. I have my daughter back, and I am in Dean's arms.

Everything is just the way I want it.

Almost.

"Let's get you inside," Dean says when he gently pulls away. "You must be freezing." He brings me in and shuts the door behind me. We go into his living room and sit in front of his small electric fireplace on his cream sectional. I've never been in Dean's house before. It doesn't look anything like the bedroom he had in high school. There aren't posters all over the walls. I don't see endless stacks of CDs. Instead, he now has endless stacks of books.

Everything is well organized, neat, and clean. All of his books are the most cluttered thing about him. Otherwise, his decor is very sparse. But it works well. And I would know. I'm an interior designer.

He reaches over and takes my hand. "Can I get you something to drink? Some coffee? Something stronger?"

I shake my head and cough.

"That doesn't sound good," he says.

"It's just from the smoke."

"I'm so glad you found her."

"It almost doesn't even seem real still." And he doesn't even know the worst part. I don't think anybody has reported it to any news outlets yet.

"Did they catch who did it? Do you know who it is?"

I don't know if he will think I'm crazy. When I told Gentry, I could tell he thought I was. So, I'm not expecting a much different reaction from Dean. But still, I want to tell him anyway.

"They didn't catch him," I say with a deep, careful breath. I'm having a hard time looking into his eye as I tell him the truth. Or what I saw as the truth—others would say it was just what I was seeing in my hallucinations from the smoke. "But... it was Carson Price."

"Cars—but... I thought..."

"You thought he was dead," I finish for him. "Everyone did. Or they didn't. They simply thought he ran off. But he was never found. Not until tonight."

"I don't understand."

"I can't even begin to understand," I say. "But I know what I saw. I got a good look at his face before he disappeared into the woods after lighting everything on fire and trying to kill us all."

He shakes his head and holds my hand tighter. "I guess I just... I have a lot of questions. But I'm not going to bug you with them right now."

"That's kind of you," I say. "I wish others would do the same."

"I wanted to come to the hospital as soon as I found out," he says. He looks genuine. His honey-brown eyes are wide, and his brows are furrowed, showing all the worry lines on his forehead. Even making a face like this, it almost hurts to look at him because of how beautiful he is.

"No, it's okay," I say. "It would've just complicated things. Things with Maddy and I..."

"It's okay," he says quickly. "You don't have to explain anything to me now. I'm sure that must've been awkward and tense between you two."

Dean doesn't know that we're friends again. He also doesn't know that Maddy knows about our fling. But I suppose he's right. He doesn't have to know everything right now.

"Thank you for letting me come over," I decide to say, changing the subject.

"You're welcome anytime."

"You say that now..." I sneak a peek at him. The last time I tried to mention to Dean that I had been enjoying seeing him and that I would like to spend more time with him, he freaked out at me, and we got into a fight.

"And I mean it," he says. He scooches a little closer to me on the sofa. "Mia, I don't really know what's going on with your life and in your marriage, and I've tried to be respectful. I've tried to behave myself. But you have no idea how hard it is. You have no idea how much I think about you every single day. I just..."

I think the look in my eyes is what has made him stop talking. I'm surprised to hear him saying all these words. I truly am.

But it's not that I don't dislike them.

He shakes his head quickly. "I shouldn't be saying all of this," he says. "As a friend, I'm here for you. I just want to make sure you're okay."

But I'm more than okay. Ever since I was little, there's only been one person that's ever made me feel more than okay.

And that person is Dean Reeves.

It's always been Dean Reeves.

So, without thinking about anything except that, I lean forward and kiss him.

CHAPTER 96

LYLA

The next morning, after I've barely woken up, a shadow looms in the doorway of my hospital room, and I think it's my dad returning from getting some coffee or taking a phone call.

To my dismay, a disheveled but exuberant Craig Fritz strolls in with an almost playful expression on his face. When he meets my eyes, he raises his eyebrows. "You're awake!" he calls excitedly. Nobody's with him. Nobody had been in the room with me before he walked in. It's just him and me.

"What do you want?" I ask, making it very clear with my tone that I have no interest in speaking with him.

But, of course, Freaky Fritz doesn't care about that.

"Boy, you went through quite an ordeal last night, didn't you?" he asks, reading something over on his notepad.

"I did. And since it took me so long to be found—not even by the police, might I add—I need lots of time to rest and recover. So if you'll excuse me..."

"I heard you're being released today," he says, looking like he's trying to fight off an eye roll. "I think you're a lot better off than you are trying to tell me you are. Besides. I won't take long."

"Can't I speak to someone else?"

"Just me."

I press the button to summon the nurse. Maybe she'll get him out of here.

"So, you were trapped in a pool shed at a house that burnt to the ground last night," he says, staring at my hand that just pressed the button. He knows his time is limited. Good.

"Yes. Carson Price had been staying in that house. And Carson Price put me in that pool shed. And Carson Price started that fire."

"You really want to say that to my face?" he asks, squinting.

"What are you talking about?" I snap. "It's the truth."

"You can't just spit out all the lies your mother is already spitting out. You're telling that to the wrong person, Lyla. Tell me what really happened. Tell me what you really saw and what really went down that night."

"Are you kidding me?" Where is that nurse? "I just told you."

"Carson Price is dead."

"Did you ever see his body?"

He doesn't have anything to say about that. He just stands there glaring at me. He detests me just as much as he detests my mother and Maddy Carpenter.

"And you didn't do this for attention? You didn't just go hide out in the woods for a few days and then start a fire, commit arson because you weren't getting enough attention back home?"

"I don't want attention."

"Says the girl who has the world following her every move."

"Why would it be so hard to believe that Carson is alive?" I ask.

"Tell me this: what do you even know about Carson Price, Lyla?"

I don't answer him. He smirks at me and continues.

"What has your mother ever told you about him?"

"Nothing."

"Exactly. And that's for a reason. Because your mother doesn't want you knowing the truth."

"My mother isn't a liar."

But even saying the words, they feel funny in my mouth. Because that's not exactly true.

My mother is a liar.

Everything I found out about Carson Price, I didn't find out from her.

"Take it from somebody who's known her a lot longer than you," he says. "Your mother—"

"What are you doing?"

Both of our heads snap to the doorway, where my dad is striding in, looking scary like he does only when he's really, really angry at something. And his face is red. His stride is long. His fists are balled. "Why are you in here disturbing my daughter?"

"Hello, Mr. Bailey," Craig starts.

"No," he says loudly. "Get out. Who do you think you are?"

"Take it easy, Gentry," Craig says, getting defensive. "I just need to ask your daughter some questions about what happened last night. We're still trying to figure out what happened and who kidnapped her."

"You're not asking her anything without her parents being present. And not when she's lying in a hospital bed like this. Get out. Now."

He stands there for a second, his eyes looking all around the room, trying to figure out if he should continue arguing or if he should just listen to my dad. If I were him, I would listen to my dad.

"All right, all right," he says, holding up his hands in surrender. "We'll talk at a later time."

"Goodbye, Detective." My dad's voice is still very aggressive. Craig nods his head and leaves the room. My dad sighs and collapses into the recliner he had slept in all night. "Man, I really hate that guy."

This makes me giggle. "Thanks for rescuing me," I say. "I really hate that guy, too."

CHAPTER 97

WARNER

Seeing Lyla is all I want to do. I went nearly crazy in the hospital waiting room yesterday when I wasn't allowed to. But it was also understandable; Amelia and Gentry Bailey aren't exactly eager to have me around, given what's been said about me and everything going on. Yes, I know. I think that Amelia isn't worried about me having been the one to kidnap Lyla. However, I'm sure it was still too much for her to explain to Gentry last night to get him on the same page, and it was just easier for them to say Lyla couldn't have any visitors except for family.

I hardly slept last night. Even when I went home—but to the Bailey residence first to retrieve my Jeep—and felt exhausted from battling out in the flames and dealing with all the adrenaline of the night, I didn't want to go to sleep. I felt this great relief that Lyla had been found, and I was afraid that going to sleep would change it all somehow. That I'd wake up again the next morning and find out that another horrible thing had happened. Or it all had just been one big dream, and Lyla was still gone.

When I wake up, it's to the smell of bacon. It's foreign, wafting through the crack in my door. I don't wake up to the smell of any breakfast in this house. Normally. Not unless I'm the one who is cooking it.

Feeling confused and curious, I get out of bed and wander into the kitchen, throwing a T-shirt on.

Either going crazy, or I'm seeing my mom moving around in the kitchen cooking us breakfast.

"Mom?" I stand there in the arch of our small U-shaped kitchen and gape at her.

"Good morning!" she says, jumping slightly, making some eggs fly off her spatula as she stands at the stove, scrambling them. "I didn't think you'd be awake already! Breakfast will be ready soon."

"You're cooking us breakfast?"

"Yeah. I figured after last night... we definitely need it."

I walk over to our small table, sit in one of the rickety chairs, and yawn. "I suppose you got that right."

Things are weird with my mom and me right now. I'm still mad at her for never telling me about Dean Reeves my entire life. But since I've had some time to sit on it, I've had some time to give it some thought. To really try to understand why she kept it a secret from me my whole life. She didn't want me to know because Dean had abandoned me. Abandoned her. He didn't want to be in our lives. She was just protecting me. And I could tell when she was explaining it to me how heartbroken she was about it all. I could tell that she just wanted the best for me.

I can't help but think two incomes would've been better than one growing up and that whenever Dean decided he did want to get involved, he would've at least been able to help out with bills a lot more. Or that Mom could take him to court and demand he paid child support or something. Instead of this big elaborate lie claiming she didn't even know who he was. But I do have a new respect for her—she had the option to take him to court and demand financial support, but instead, she worked hard to take care of me all by herself our entire life together.

So no. I don't hate my mom.

"So..." she trails off carefully. "How are you doing?" She moves the scrambled eggs, taking them off the burner, and goes back to the bacon, carefully taking it out of the grease using some tongs and placing it on a paper towel-lined paper plate.

"I don't know," I admit. "I'm okay."

"That's good."

"Are you okay?"

"Um... yeah. I think so. I think maybe I'm still in a little bit of shock. As you know, I didn't see what Amelia apparently saw last night."

"About how she saw that Carson Price person?"

"Yeah. About that... I guess you and I have a lot to discuss."

Maybe a lot less than you think.

"I guess there's a lot I'm confused about," I agree. "Like, who is Carson Price? Why did he kidnap Lyla? Why didn't the police seem very trusting when Amelia told them? I don't know. It's all very... confusing."

There's a quick popping noise, and I watch the pieces of toast fly out of the toaster. She picks them up, practically juggling them between her hands because they're so hot, and then plates our breakfast.

"Yeah. It is confusing." She brings my plates over and sets them down. Scrambled eggs with cheese, bacon, and toast. Then she goes back into the kitchen to grab the condiments, like the hot sauce, salt and pepper, and butter.

Finally, she sits down.

My stomach growls, looking at it all. So I dig in immediately.

"I'm glad you're hungry," she says. "There's still a lot more on the stove."

I nod as I stuff my face.

"I don't know what you know already," she says after sipping her coffee. She's a lot slower to eat her breakfast. She stabs at her eggs with a fork but doesn't put any bites into her mouth. "But when Amelia Bailey and I were friends way back when she was Amelia Flynn, her younger sister, Nora, was dating Carson."

"Okay."

"Um... and then Carson... Carson hit Nora. He hit Nora on prom night, and then he fled."

"Dang. So he's a piece of crap."

"Warner."

"What? He kidnapped Lyla. Of course, he is."

She smirks. "Yeah. A piece of crap." She finally takes a bite of food. She's slow chewing it like she wants to savor every little taste of it before it slithers down her throat. Then she speaks again. "But anyway. I... I've never told anybody this. Not a soul. You'll be the first one to know. So if you can, I would really appreciate it if you could just keep this to yourself. But I think it's good to be getting things out in the open between us. I don't want there to be any more secrets, Warn."

It feels good to hear her say it. It feels believable, almost. "Me neither."

"Okay."

So after Carson hit Nora—and I mean he really hit her—she was bleeding everywhere. Amelia and I—even though we had gotten into this huge fight, and I was pretty sure we weren't gonna be friends anymore after that—were furious. I loved Nor like a little sister. So it mattered to me what happened to her, too."

"What do you do?"

"I'm only telling you this because I asked Amelia already, and she said it was fine if I did."

"Telling me what? Are you two friends again?"

"It's... complicated," she says.

"Huh. Well... what did you do then?"

"He dipped from the prom, so we followed him. And we followed him all the way to the Boldosa Redwoods. All the way... to that house."

"Where the police claim Nora found his body all those years ago?"

She nods. She's still only taken one bite of her food, and my plate is almost gone. "Exactly. But this is where it doesn't really start to make a lot of sense." She sips her coffee some more. I think she's just trying to prolong spitting the words out. I already know what it is she's going to tell me. But I am surprised that she's going to do it. That she and Amelia agreed to do it.

"Just tell me," I say.

"We confronted him inside that house. And things got ugly. The railing on the balcony ended up breaking, and Carson fell through it. He fell into the pool and cracked his head open. We pulled him out, and we tried to save him, but... all of these years, Warner? Amelia and I thought we killed him. Especially after Nora found him not long after and claimed to have seen his dead body. All this time... we've been trying to keep it a secret. Because killing him was an accident, but we didn't think anybody would believe us if we tried to tell someone."

At the revelation, even I have started slowing on my eating. It's so weird to hear her say it out loud.

"But according to Amelia, Carson never really died. So... I guess we never killed anybody."

"Good thing," I decide to say. She lets out a weak laugh.

"Yeah. Good thing."

"Maybe Nora saw what you guys saw. Maybe she saw Carson dead. And then, somehow, he just came to shortly after. And for some reason, he decided to stay hidden."

"Just hiding out in the woods all of these years?"

I shrug. "I don't know."

"I just... I don't think Lyla was the only one he's been messing with."

I swallow. I've been thinking about it too, but I've been trying my hardest to think about anything else. Anything except for what's been going on. "You mean like with your car bomb?"

"Exactly. I think he's messing with you, too. And Audrey. And me. And Amelia."

"Why would he wait twenty years to do it?"

"That, Warner, is something I would give my left leg to find out."

"Me, too."

"I'm glad you're okay," she says, finally digging back into her food. I think we've tabled this discussion for now. It's a good thing. Because I don't know if my head can take anymore.

"Yeah, Ma," I say, thinking about how she almost died last night as that balcony collapsed under her feet. "I'm glad you're okay, too."

And even though things are still tense between us, even though I don't trust her and don't know if I'll ever trust her again, I really do mean it.

CHAPTER 98

AUDREY

When Lyla finally gets back home sometime in the afternoon, it's crazy outside our house. Not only are there news reporters and journalists outside, but it seems like half of Toxey has arrived to welcome her home. Lyla maybe let them see half of her face as she got out of the car in the garage and was quickly ushered inside by our dad, but still, the town went nuts over it. Even as we all sit in the living room now, there are still people outside. People who are just excited that she's safe, and people who are just nosy.

"Lyla!" Joey leaps off the sectional and practically slams into my sister before she can even make herself comfortable. Tears are streaming down his cheeks, and they're streaming down Lyla's, too. I think Joey is glad she's safe for more reasons than just the fact that she's safe. Her being safe means he's probably safe from being removed from our family by the foster care agency. For now, at least.

"Hey, Butthead," Lyla says in a tender voice as they hug.

"What happened?" he asks as he pulls away. "Where were you?"

None of us have really given Joey any details about what went down. He's too young to know it all. I wish I could just keep him in the dark forever. I wish I could just eliminate this whole week from his life so that he never has to remember any of this.

"Just some jerk wad decided to keep me in the shed for a few days. That's all," Lyla says. "I'm totally okay."

"Who?" he asks immediately.

"Joey, why don't you come sit down by me?" Gentry says. "Give your sister a little time to breathe. She just got back."

"He's happy to see his sister," Mom says, sounding annoyed.

"He's smothering her," Dad snaps.

"It's fine," Lyla says. But still, Joey goes back over and sits down by him.

"So," Dad starts, addressing Mom. "We think Carson Price, that guy who dated your sister all these years ago, is the one who kidnapped Lyla?" He's acting like she's responsible for all this. He has this look in his eyes. Something I haven't ever seen in them before. Not when he looks at Mom, anyway. It's like there's hatred in them.

"I don't have an explanation for how or why," Mom says, flinging her hands in the air desperately. "I just know what I saw, okay? And I know it's been twenty years. But it was Carson. I saw his face."

"Yeah. It's been twenty years, and he now wants to hurt our children," Gentry says. "You honestly can't tell me why?"

"No," she snaps. "I can't. The last time I saw him was twenty years ago. Last time I talked to him was twenty years ago. I don't know why this is happening, Gentry."

"Well, you had to have done something," he says. "This didn't just happen for no reason, Mia."

"What are you trying to say?"

"Guys, stop," I say.

"What are you trying to say, Gentry," Mom repeats, ignoring me.

"I just want to know why this happened. I want an explanation. And Carson Price isn't here, is he? So who else am I going to get that explanation from?"

"I don't know!" she snaps, getting even louder now. "As I said, I don't know why this is happening, Gentry!"

"I sort of think you do, though!"

All they do is fight.

And Mom has an online dating profile.

And Dad talks to secret women on the phone.

They don't even like each other anymore.

Why are they putting themselves—and us—through this?

I don't want to hear it anymore. I've had a long, long week.

I stand up while they continue to argue with each other.

This is going to be huge, but I'm going to say it. I'm not keeping anybody's secrets. Keeping my own is already too much.

I have no idea what it's going to do once it's out there, but I need to just get it out there.

Everything out in the open.

No more secrets.

I prepare myself as Mom nags at Dad. "I can't believe you're sitting there, in my home, telling me that you think—"

I take a deep breath, use a loud voice, and let it out. "Just STOP! I know you guys are cheating on each other!"

CHAPTER 99

AMELIA

*W*hat. *Did.*

She.
Just.
Say?

I have no words. All I can do is just sit there and stare at Audrey. Just at her. Not Gentry. Not Joey. Not Lyla. Just Audrey.

How is this even possible?

"Audrey," Gentry says in a slow voice. "I don't know where you got that idea, but your mother and I—"

"Don't even try to deny it," she interrupts.

"Audrey," I say in exasperation.

"What? It's true. Do you want me to explain to you how I know?"

"You're cheating on each other?" Joey asks. He has scooted away from Gentry like suddenly he's gotten some contagious disease that Joey doesn't want to catch. He has horror in his eyes. Sheer horror.

"No," I blurt out without thinking.

"Yes, you are!" Audrey looks at Joey. "They're cheating on each other. It sucks to hear it. But it sucked when I found out, too. Remember that one time I had you make sure Mom didn't catch me on her laptop?"

"Yeah," Joey answers.

"Guess what I found on there. I found her online dating profile."

"What?" I stammer. "I don't have a dating profile!" I did start making one, but I never finished it. I didn't have the courage. I didn't want people around town to see that I was back in the dating pool. Gentry and I have just been together so long. It's scary to be seen as something other than Gentry's wife.

"I don't know why you're lying," Audrey says, scoffing. "And Dad, I heard you on the phone talking to some woman! Telling her all about how you want to see her again."

Sitting on the couch, staring at her feet, Lyla is being very, very quiet.

Gentry slowly turns to look at me.

The kids are looking at me, too. They're waiting for my reaction. For me to scream. For me to cry. For me to say something like, "How could you?" to their father.

But the truth of the matter is... I already knew this.

Gentry does have a girlfriend.

I did start making an online dating profile.

And maybe Audrey doesn't know this yet, but I did kiss Dean Reeves last night, too.

I give Gentry that look. That look that says we've been caught and that we don't need to keep up the act any longer. And then a tear falls from my eye.

He sighs and looks down at his lap.

"We didn't mean for you guys to find out like this," he says.

"So it's true?" Joey asks. "You guys are cheating on each other?"

Dad reaches out and takes his hand. Joey tries to pull out of it, but his grip is too strong.

"It's true," he says.

"But we're not exactly cheating," I correct. "You see, your father and I already know the other one is dating. Your father has been dating. And... he found a girlfriend rather quickly. He hasn't been going out of town for work trips as much as he's been going to see her. I have tried to get myself back out there as well, but I haven't been as open to doing it. Not because I still want to be with your father. I am just not ready to start dating yet; I don't think."

Audrey puts both her hands on her head. "Whoa, whoa, whoa, wait," she says. "Let me just wrap my head around this.

So you guys are, what? In an open marriage?"

She looks absolutely disgusted.

"No," Gentry says. "It's not like that."

"I know it may hurt to hear," I say, reaching over and taking Lyla's hand. She lets me hold it. But she's still not looking at anyone or anything. "But, your father and I haven't been in love for a long time now."

"A long time?" Audrey is still standing with her hands on her head. "What does that mean?"

"For over a year now," Gentry says. "We agreed to start seeing other people a while ago. But it took us a while to get to that point. And we were just going to wait until ... I don't know. However long it took to make sure we didn't hurt you guys. And to make sure that nothing happened with our situation with Joey."

"We've basically been having a sham of a marriage because we wanted to stay together for Joey's sake," I say. I give him a loving, tear-filled smile. Gentry is crying. Joey is crying, too. Audrey looks confused and flabbergasted. Lyla looks blank.

That's what terrifies me the most.

CHAPTER 100

Audrey

I spend most of the rest of the afternoon in my room in tears. I should want to spend the day with Lyla. I should want to keep her in my sight. But after everything that just happened in the living room—after my parents told us they don't love each other anymore and that they only wanted to stay together for us —all I want to do is be alone.

I wipe my eyes and grab my phone when I see it light up with a text. It's from Warner.

Warner: *Any chance you wanna meet up at our spot?*

Maybe what I need is not to be alone. Maybe what I need is to get the heck out of this house. Away from all of this toxicity.

Me: *How soon can you get there?*
Warner: *15?*
Me: *Perfect.*

Again, I have to sneak out of the house without telling my parents. But I think I'm the least of their worries at the moment. After our family talk, they retreated into the bedroom to talk some things over with each other alone. Lyla went with Joey into his bedroom, and I went into mine. So when I left, nobody even saw me go.

I'm surprised that Warner didn't ask Lyla to come to meet up with us, too, but I also figure he assumes she isn't going to be up for it. If I were Lyla, I don't know if I'd want to leave my house ever again after all of that.

When we meet in the parking lot, I see that he's driven his Jeep for a change, and we hug.

"How's Lyla?" he asks. But then he sees my face. "How are you?" I think he can tell I've been crying.

I sniff. "I've had better days," I admit. "Lyla has, too. Things are kind of crazy with our family right now. But... we're fine."

We walk over to an old crumbling cement bench and sit down. It doesn't creep me out to be here anymore, even though it starting to get dark again. It feels more familiar, and I sort of like it. I like that it was Warner's spot. Now it seems to be our spot.

"This whole thing..." he says as he takes a deep breath. "It's... crazy."

I nod next to him and stare at the train tracks. "So crazy."

"I'm really glad that we're friends."

I look at him and try to gauge his expression. He seems genuine. Grateful, even.

I smile. It's tight on my face after all the crying that came with today. "Me, too," I say.

"I kind of feel like we've been through a lot together."

"Yeah. No kidding."

"With all that's happening, we're kind of in this together."

"I guess so."

I can see him gnawing on the inside of his cheek. Feeling the same amount of stress that he is—if not more—I rest my head on his shoulder.

"If it is Carson Price who kidnapped Lyla—if that's who your mom really saw in the woods. He got away."

I nod, rubbing my ear against his shoulder and saying nothing. So he takes another deep breath and falls silent, too.

It's nice to be here with him like this. I can't picture it being the same with Ryan. If I brought him to this place, he would think it was weird. He would want to do something like graffiti one of the walls in the ticket booth. He'd want to mess around and drive his car on the train tracks. Then he'd say he was creeped out and that we should do something else like hang out with some of his friends at Delilah's.

Not that I don't like Ryan. Not that I wouldn't like to hang out with all of his senior friends—and maybe make some new ones on my own—at the old ice cream shop. That's the life that I want to have. Or wanted to have, anyway.

But I also think I could like this life. The one where I sit quietly on a deserted train station's bench with my head on Warner's shoulder.

I think I could like being with him, too.

After everything we've been through, I think it's pointless to keep in how I feel. It's pointless to be scared. Besides, I'm not really scared. Not anymore. I can't go through what I went through last night and still be too scared to say my feelings out loud.

So I'm going to do it.

I'm going to tell Warner Carpenter that I have feelings for him.

Part of my heart still lingers toward Ryan. But the bigger part knows that I like being with Warner so much more.

I just wonder if he will want to be with me, too.

CHAPTER 101

LYLA

B esides taking a very, very, very long shower, I haven't exactly known what to do with myself since I got back.

I didn't exactly get the warmest welcome. I came back from five days of pure torture to find that my family is falling apart. To find that Carson Price might still be alive and might be the person who is terrorizing me, Warner, and my family.

I'm trying to be grateful. I'm glad I'm even home at all. I'm glad that my mom and Audrey were able to find me.

But why had it been them and not the cops? Why hadn't they done a good enough job in their search for me? Why didn't anyone suspect that the house near where Carson's body was found all those years ago by Aunt Nora would be a place that maybe they should check? I feel restless and unsatisfied. I feel stressed out. Like I've been given a stack of homework higher than my head.

Thinking about the homework that I'm sure I'm going to get once I get back to school also overwhelms me. I remember what it was like trying to play catch-up after I had my car accident. Completely miserable. At this rate, I'm wondering if I'm even going to graduate high school.

I told my family I was going to get some rest hours ago, but that's not the case. It's hard for me to even close my eyes because I'm worried about what is lurking in the shadows. I worry about what will be hovering over my bed once I open them again. I keep seeing the masked man. I keep seeing his return. I keep picturing him in this very house, back to finish what he started. I don't think I'll be able to sleep until they catch this guy.

So when it's late enough, and I know everybody else in the house is asleep or at least in their rooms, I tip-toe out of my bedroom and go out into the backyard. I don't want to disappear on my parents and make them worry again. I just want to get some air.

I take a deep breath, sit on one of the pool loungers, and stare at the still water. I know it's a bit cold now, but part of me wants to jump into it. Wants to immerse myself in the water and hear the noise of it filling my ears and making it impossible for me to hear anything else.

I don't know the first thing about what I'm supposed to do next. How am I supposed to move forward from everything that happened to me? But I know the promises I made to myself when I was locked in that shed. The promises that I would be the perfect daughter. That I will get the perfect grades and that I will turn back into my old self.

Can I really do that?

My phone buzzes, and I pull it out. Wrigley has sent me a text.

Wrigley: Hey. I'm sort of out in front of your house right now. Is there any way we could talk?

I wasn't allowed to have visitors at the hospital. So I haven't seen Wrigley yet.

But I thought about him a lot while I had been in that shed.

Me: Meet me around the gate on the side of my house.

I get up and walk over to it. I hear the footsteps moving through the rocks in my front yard.

"Lyla?" Wrigley's voice whispers. I open the gate and let him through. I barely even get to look at him before his arms are around me. "I'm so glad you're okay."

"Hi, Wrigley," I say casually. I feel a lump in my throat, but I don't want to act upset in front of him. I'm braver than that.

"God, it's good to see you," he says when he steps away. He has a giant smile on his face and relief in his eyes. His curly hair is getting long. I like it like this, though.

"We have to be quiet," I say. I get the feeling that if my parents came out here and find him in the backyard, they're going to make him leave.

"No problem," he whispers. "Do you wanna sit down?"

I go back to the loungers in front of the pool with him. We each sit at the end of one, and the whole while, Wrigley doesn't take his eyes off me.

"What are you doing here, crazy?" I ask, trying to be playful in my mood. That's the way the old Lyla would've acted.

He sheepishly grins again. "I've just been going crazy wanting to see you. I went crazy the last six days wanting to see you."

"That's...... oh," is all I can think to say. I feel myself blushing.

"I tried to help the police. I tried to get answers on my own. I guess I'm not going to ever try to become a detective when I'm older. Clearly, I am kind of cruddy at it."

I laugh. "I appreciate knowing that you tried."

"Are you okay?" His expression changes into something more serious. I don't like it. I don't want people to be serious around me.

"Yeah," I say, waving it off like it's really no big deal. "I'm totally fine. I wasn't, like, beaten or tortured or anything." As if that makes it any better.

"You were just... kept in the shed?"

"Exactly."

"Just the thought of it makes me sick."

"Well... I'm out now."

"And look," he says, continuing like he's had this train of thought going and doesn't want to stop. "This whole thing with Trinity. I get it now; why you stopped texting me. Why we stopped being friends. I had no idea that I was the reason you had gotten into that accident. I... I feel terrible. And I just want you to know that you shouldn't blame yourself. That driver was drunk, and he was probably not paying any attention, and he was probably speeding, and he made that accident way worse than it could've been if it had been a sober man driving while you had rolled that stop sign."

Great. Now I really am going to cry. He's the only person that's tried to make me feel better about it all. The first person to say something other than, "It's not your fault," when it clearly is.

"Everybody at school hates me." I will my eyes not to leak tears and sniff up the snot threatening to drip out of my nose.

"No. You're wrong about that," he says. "Everybody's been looking for you, Lyla. It's all anyone's been able to talk about. Everyone just wanted you back. I didn't hear a single person tell me otherwise."

"If you say so."

"Fine. Even if I am wrong—which I don't think I am—who cares what everyone thinks? Forget about them, Lyla. You've been through so much. You can't be worrying about all this. Just focus on what you can control."

"Maybe you should be a psychiatrist," I suggest.

"Huh. I've never thought about that." He looks as if he's genuinely thinking about it for a moment; then, he shakes the thought away. "Ly, there's another reason why I came tonight."

"What's... up?"

"I don't really know how to do this because it's not something I've ever done before, but all I know is that I like you, Lyla. And I nearly missed my chance to get to show you how much. So I don't want to let the moment pass me by again.... I was wondering if maybe you'd let me take you out on a date."

My eyebrows raise.

"It doesn't have to be right now," he continues. "Whenever you're ready. There's no rush. I know you probably need some time to... rest and recover. When you're ready, I just want to at least be first in line."

Wrigley Hall.

Asking me on a date.

I don't think he's ever had a girlfriend. He's always had this mysterious air about him. He throws his parties and keeps to himself. I feel special because I think I'm the only one who sees this side of him.

I grin. "Wrigley. I really am fine. I don't need time. I already wasted some of it being trapped in that shed. So yes. I'd love to go on a date with you."

He looks away from me and smiles bashfully, the happiness plain on his face. "Oh. Cool, then. That's... really cool."

I playfully reach over and nudge his knee with my fist. "You're right," I say, catching his eye again. "It is really cool."

It's like they say.

Life is too short.

CHAPTER 102

MADDY

While things might be headed in the opposite direction with Steven now, they're at least headed in the right direction with Warner. Or I hope they are, anyway. He has at least seemed to tolerate being around me again, and that's not something I've gotten to see for quite some time now. I think opening up to him made him feel like he can trust me again. So if continuing to be honest with him is what I need to do, then I will try harder to do it. After all, he's hardly a kid anymore. He's going to be eighteen before I know it. Eighteen and moved out and on to bigger and better things, leaving little old me behind.

It's late, and I know Warner should be in bed, but he's outside working on his Jeep. I don't know what that kid does to it to keep it in such great shape, but I know that he has learned a lot about cars online by watching videos and reading blogs.

I am on the sofa, checking my phone every three minutes, hoping Steven is going to text me and tell me that everything is okay. That I'm forgiven and that he still wants to see me. I hate that I'm thinking about it so much. That I can't just get over it easily like I'm usually able to do with other failed relationships in my past. I really like Steven. And I really like that I can picture our future together. That's not something I've been able to say about many other men I've dated. I think that's what makes it all so hard.

When my phone rings, my heart flies into my throat at the anticipation of it finally being Steven.

But it's not.

It's an ex-boyfriend of mine.

Detective Craig Fritz.

"What?" I say in a sharp tone when I answer.

"Hey. Warner can have his computer and phone back. They'll be up at the front desk at the station whenever either of you can swing by." He sounds like telling me this is the last thing he wants to do. Like he hates that he's failed.

"Perfect. Were you able to find anything incriminating on it?" I ask, already knowing the answer. If he had, he would've arrested Warner. If he had, he wouldn't be calling to tell me this.

"No. There was nothing on his phone and nothing on his computer. But I'm not letting it stop me, Maddy. Let me be clear: we're going to find something that ties Warner into what happened to Sydney Hutton. We're going to find it soon."

I no longer worry that Warner did something to Sydney. Yeah, things don't exactly look good in terms of his involvement with her death, but Warner is my son. And if I want him to trust me, I have to trust him in return. I remember the way I felt when he accused me of being the one to kidnap Lyla. I didn't like it one bit.

"You're not going to find anything," I say to Craig. "Because Warner didn't do anything. Think about it. If all of this is connected somehow, then maybe it's Carson Price who did something to Sydney Hutton." I don't know how it would tie together, but maybe in some way, it does. And if so, it's the police's job to figure out how. Not mine. My job is just to keep Warner safe.

"Even if Carson Price is still alive, and even if Mia really did see him in the woods, that doesn't necessarily mean that he's the one who kidnapped Lyla. He could've just been in the wrong place at the wrong time. He could've been there because he followed you guys. He could've been there to rescue her. We don't know anything. There's no proof."

"Are you kidding? He was staying in that house. He started the fire."

"We have no way to prove that," he says. "No fingerprints on the gas canisters. No cameras on the property. And everything is burnt to a crisp over there. All we have is your word, and it doesn't mean much."

"It was him."

"Carson is dead, Maddy," he snaps. His voice sounds a little slow. Like he's tired. Or something else. "The only murderers in this town are you and Mia and your son. And I'm going to prove it."

Amelia

Gentry decided to sleep in the guest room since we don't have to keep up this act anymore. I hung out in my bedroom alone for a long portion of the afternoon and evening, but I eventually decide to sneak out with my shoes on and my car keys in my hand. I want to sneak off to see someone, just as I had done last night after leaving the hospital.

I freeze when I look out the glass panes of the back door and see my daughter sitting on a pool lounger. Next to her, there's another person.

I recognize him to be Wrigley Hall.

I almost open the door and demand to know what the heck he's doing on my property this late at night and to scold Lyla for not telling him to leave, but then I see the expression on Lyla's face. I see her smiling.

And that's very, very rare.

I watch her for a little while as Wrigley says something that makes her giggle and keeps the smile on her face. Just relieved to see that she's happy, I keep my mouth shut and sneak into the garage.

The drive over to Dean's is quick. And when I pull up to the sidewalk, he's already standing in his open doorway. He's been expecting me.

My stomach dips. I had to have a somewhat serious talk with him, and I am not exactly sure how it's going to go. But I'm hopeful that it's going to go well.

I get out of my car, feeling more put together than I have in weeks. I smooth my skirt, tuck back some flyway hairs behind my ear, and walk up the pathway to meet him.

"You look nice," Dean says to me as a way of greeting.

"Thank you." I feel myself blushing.

"Come in." He steps aside and lets me in, and closes the door behind me.

"Thank you for letting me come so late," I say as he takes my coat off.

"I'm always happy to see you," he replies, sending shivers down my spine when his breath is on my neck. "Any time, day or night."

So far, so good.

I turn and smile at him. He leads the way into his living room. Already, he has a tray of what looks too light of a color to be coffee and a small bag of marshmallows.

"Did you make us hot chocolate?" I ask as we take a seat.

"I figured it was a little late for coffee. And I'm not really a tea guy."

How adorable is this?

"Is that okay?" he asks when I don't say anything.

"It's perfect," I reply. I pick up one of the mugs—one that has the Blackfell High School logo on it, and then I take a sip of the hot, creamy sweetness that is the chocolate mixture he used.

"You forgot your marshmallows," he says.

I giggle and take some from the bag as he holds it open. Then I drop them in.

"Now it's perfect."

He puts some in his own mug, one that I think he might've stolen from Delilah's at one point, and we clink them together and quietly drink.

"So, I sort of had a really big night tonight," I say after. I set the mug down because I don't want to start trembling and then spill it everywhere.

"What do you mean?"

Dean is all ears. There's no music around. No sound coming from the TV to distract him. He's facing me on the couch; his knees turned toward mine.

I swallow.

"Is everything okay?" he asks.

"Yeah. Or—I think so."

"Talk to me."

I briefly smile. "Tonight, Gentry and I sort of told the kids, and we're getting a divorce."

There.

It's out.

The words are out of my mouth and hanging in the air between us. The worst part is over. Now all I can do is wait.

"Wait... You and Gentry are divorcing? Not because of what happened last night, right?"

"Oh! No. Definitely not," I say. "I... I probably should've just told you this yesterday. But, Gentry and I have sort of been living separate lives for a while now. We've been living in the same house, yeah, but we agreed forever ago to start seeing other people. He's had a girlfriend for around four months now. She lives a couple of hours out of town."

Dean sits there and says nothing. I've rendered him speechless.

"But I'm okay with it," I say. "It has been hard with the kids. With Joey. We wanted to seem like one happy family. But the truth is far from that."

"You... you've known for a while now that you're getting divorced?"

"Yes. I suppose so."

"Wow."

"Yeah. I know it's crazy."

"It would be nice to have a little heads up, you know?"

Oh no.

Something is off about Dean's tone. He sounds upset.

"I just didn't know how to tell you. I didn't want it getting around that things weren't going well between Gentry and me, and—"

"And what, you thought I would tell somebody?"

Now I've offended him.

"No! I just... I don't know. Look, this hasn't been easy for me—"

"And you think it's been easy for me? Come on, Mia. I've been beating myself up for weeks now over how I feel about you. Over how horrible of a man I am for being so attracted to a married woman. And then last night when we kissed? I couldn't even sleep. I just... if you've had feelings for me, and if you've known how I feel about you—and I'm pretty sure you've known for a while—then you should've said something. Instead, you just led me on like that."

"I... I am so sorry," I say. "I didn't realize that—I guess I wasn't thinking..."

I'm not even quite sure how he wants me to fix this. Sure, I could've told him sooner. But I'm telling him now, aren't I?

Dean clears his throat. "You know what? I completely spaced until just now. I have a giant stack of essays I have to get graded before Monday."

I know he's lying. I know this is his way of telling me he wants me to get out of his house. And now.

I nod and look away from him. I pictured this night going much differently. I pictured myself confessing to him that I was basically single and that we had nothing to feel guilty about. Then I thought we'd stay up all night talking to each other, wrapped in each other's arms.

But this couldn't be any more opposite than that.

"I get it," I say, standing up. "Thank you for the hot cocoa, Dean. I'll... I'll see myself out."

I walk into the foyer, put my coat on, and then rest my hand on the doorknob. I want him to tell me not to go. To tell me he knows he's overreacting and that he's sorry. But when I glance at him over in his living room, his back is to me on the couch.

And I know I'm not going to get what I want.

So I leave.

CHAPTER 104

MADDY

When I get another phone call even later in the evening, I wonder if maybe my clocks are broken. Either that or nobody seems to have any respect for what time is decent to be calling somebody.

When I look at my phone again and see that it's Nora who is calling, I'm immediately worried.

"Nor?" I answer.

You helped find my niece," she says to me. There's almost a disbelief in her voice.

"Oh. It was really Warner and Audrey who found her," I say. I don't feel like taking credit for it. I hadn't even found Lyla. I had nearly died inside that A-framed cabin on that balcony.

"Still. You were there. Thank you so much. I can't believe it took them so long to find her. All these stupid search parties for nothing. Who kidnapped her?"

"Oh..." My stomach dips violently. She hasn't heard? Amelia or her mom hasn't told her?

"What?" she asks.

"Um... we don't know," I say. If they haven't released it to the public, and if Mia and her mom haven't told her, then maybe there's a reason for it. I don't want to send her spiraling. I don't want her to get mad and tell us we don't know what Mia saw and that Mia is full of it. Because for as long as I've known Nora over these years, ever since Carson disappeared, Nora has been thoroughly convinced he died.

"We don't know," I say. "We got her out of that shed, and then all of a sudden, everything was on fire. We didn't see anybody. They were pretty good at staying hidden. And Lyla says they were in a mask the entire time she was in that shed. Any time she saw him, anyway."

"So whoever did this is still out there?"

"Unfortunately."

"I'm going to call Craig. I'm going to tell him what a sucky job he's doing. This is my niece's safety we're talking about. We can't just let this monster roam the streets!"

"Yeah," I agree.

"Sorry. I'm just a little worked up."

"I would be, too," I say. "I am, actually. It is stupid that they haven't caught him. Why do we even have police, you know?"

"Exactly."

"But at least she's safe now. That's all that we really need to focus on."

"Yeah. How was it having to be around my sister?"

"Oh…" I trail off, not sure how to explain myself. "It wasn't that bad. We were more focused on just figuring out where Audrey and Warner were going. They figured out where Lyla was, and we just followed them. We had nothing to talk about other than our kids. It was weird. But fine."

"Ugh. I'm sorry you had to do that. My sister is not easy to be around."

"It really wasn't that bad," I say. "I think she's changed."

"Ha. I'm surprised she wasn't ripping into you."

"Why?"

"Because… I sort of might've accidentally let it slip that you and I have been friends all these years."

Do I tell her I already know? That Amelia came clean to me about it? For some reason, it makes me uneasy, too.

"Oh… you did?"

"Sorry."

I think back to that night. The very first time I visited Nora after she was sent away.

I suppose I was expecting some rundown haunted-looking old building when I pulled outside of the Serenity Heights Psychiatric Institution. Like I had seen in movies. But it didn't look anything like that. It looked like any old average hospital. Built sometime in the late twentieth century. But it also had an air about it that made it feel... like a prison.

"Here we go." I got out of my trusty old Jeep and walked inside. It smelled like a hospital, too. Anti-septic. Slightly bitter. Artificial soap.

The lights were bright.

I walked to the receptionist's desk, which was behind bulletproof glass windows. I told them who I was here to see, and they had me sign in. Then they had me sit in the waiting room. Pastel blue metal armchairs were lined in neat rows along the wall. I didn't look at anybody when I sat down. I was too uncomfortable to do so. Too worried about the kind of people I would see in there.

When my name was called, I had to go through a metal detector. Then I was led down a plain hall. When I went into one of the rooms, I was surprised and a little scared to see that we were in some sort of community room. That it wasn't just Nora and I getting to have exclusive one-on-one with each other.

Nora was sitting at a small round table. She was the only one at it. Around her, it was slightly chaotic. There were some screaming noises. Some people talking loudly. Some incoherent babbling.

I sat across from her. She didn't smile when she saw me. She looked absolutely miserable. But it was understandable. There were far crazier people in this place than her.

"Hi, Nora," I said when I sat down.

"Oh. They told me I had a visitor. But they didn't tell me who it was."

"Surprise," I said with feigned excitement.

"Besides my mom, you're the only one," she said. "Mia hasn't even seen me."

"I'm sorry," I said. "I'm sure she'll come around."

"I am her sister."

"It's hard for her, too. I'm sure. I don't really know; we don't talk, but..."

"Don't make excuses for her, Maddy."

I snap my jaw shut. "I won't. I'm sorry."

"It's good that you decided to stop being friends with her."

"Yeah. I think you're right."

"She's selfish. Self-absorbed."

"I know. I was totally over it. Done. I ended it."

"Good."

"So... how is it here?"

"Horrible. Scary. Uncomfortable. I have this secret admirer who keeps leaving me his fingernails outside my bedroom door."

A shudder rippled through me. "That's disgusting."

"Yeah. And that's not even the worst thing I've seen."

"What else?"

She shook her head. "I won't say anything while the person is in the room."

I carefully looked around but didn't see anyone staring at us as if they were waiting for Nora to spill their secret. When I looked back at Nora, she had tears in her eyes.

"I just want you to know, Maddy, that I know what I saw."

"Are we still talking about what you saw around here?"

"No. I'm talking about Carson's body."

And there it was. The nausea was back. Of course, she knew what she saw. Because I saw it, too.

I caused it.

"I believe you," I say. "You would have no reason to lie about something like that. They haven't found him. So why shouldn't everyone else?"

"I don't know. Why am I in here?"

"I don't know, Nor. But I'm so, so sorry."

And I was sorry.

I had never been sorrier in my entire life.

"Mads? Are you there?"

I snap back to the present. I have no idea what it was, Nora just said to me.

"What?" I ask.

"I asked if you're mad at me. For telling Amelia about our friendship."

"Oh. No. She... can't hate me more than she already does, right?"

"When it comes to my sister... I guess we'll just have to see."

"I guess so."

My phone buzzes in my ear, so I pull it away and see a text on the screen.

Dean: *Maddy. I really think we should talk. Not just me and you. But Warner, too. Can we at least give it a try?*

Then he texts me again.

Dean: *I want us to get together and talk about trying to become the family we were always supposed to be.*

CHAPTER 105

AUDREY

I get home late from hanging out with Warner.

I had the opportunity to tell Warner how I felt right then and there when I made up my mind that I was going to do it, and I chickened out.

But I'm still going to do it. I'm determined.

I open the garage with the click of a button and pull into it with my Mini Cooper. I notice a strange truck parked in front of our house. It's old, navy blue, and doesn't look like it's been taken through the wash in multiple years.

I'm curious if whoever owns it is inside our house and what it is they're doing in there, so I'm a little hasty when I get out of my car. A little apprehensive.

What if belongs to the man in the mask? And what if that man in the mask is Carson Price?

"Excuse me," a voice says behind me as I head toward the door into the mudroom. I spin on my heel, my blood running cold, and see that an unfamiliar man is walking up the driveway toward me.

I slowly step back. Instinctively, I'm terrified of him. What is a stranger doing on our property?

He holds up his hands as if he's trying to calm a frightened animal. "I'm sorry, I don't mean to scare you," he says in an even voice. He's tall and muscular. Like overly muscular. Like the type of guy who goes to bodybuilding competitions or fights in those wrestling rings. He has a bald head and a scraggly blond beard. He looks to be older, maybe in his mid-to-late fifties. He's got the wrinkles on his face that give away his age, despite the great shape that he's in.

"Who are you?" I ask in a shaky voice. I'm still slowly backing away toward the mudroom door.

He pauses outside the garage and doesn't attempt to come in.

"I'm sorry," he says. "I was just hoping to talk to you or someone in your family."

"Who are you?" I repeat. I don't like this one bit.

"Sorry. I've—my name is Eric. I... I heard about what happened to Lyla Bailey and her kidnapping. You're not Lyla, are you?"

"I am her sister. Her twin."

"Right. I heard she had a twin. Anyway. I received some information about the person who took her. About what you guys said to the police. That you think Carson Price kidnapped her?"

"We know he's been missing for over twenty years and that a lot of people think he's dead," I say. Is he going to start yelling at me about how idiotic I am?

"No, no, no," the man named Eric says quickly, waving his arms in the air. "I'm not here to tell you I don't believe you. I'm here for the opposite reason, actually. You see... I'm sort of... well, I'm Carson Price's father. And I think he's alive, too."

CHAPTER 106

LYLA

"Only eleven days until Halloween!" Joey says to me as soon as I enter the kitchen. He's on a tablet, and I can tell from where I'm standing that he's scrolling through a Halloween costume catalog off some website. "Do you know what you're going to be?"

He seems to be in high spirits, which is surprising with everything that happened yesterday. But Joey's already been through a lot with his real family. Maybe he's more capable of dealing with things than I thought.

"I haven't even thought about it," I say. Is it really already the twentieth of October?

Time flies when you're trapped in a shed.

I don't say it to Joey, but I'm dreading Halloween. I'll probably stay inside and not do anything. It's been out there, on the news, what my kidnapper wore. First, when Audrey was attacked by him in our house. Then when I had to talk to the police after my kidnapping. I know that people are going to go out like crazy to buy masks exactly the same or similar to the one he wears. And I hate the idea of wandering around Toxey seeing twenty different versions of the man I'm most scared of.

"I think I want to be an Avenger," Joey says. "But I just don't know which one."

"You'd make a cool Hulk," I offer.

He makes a face like he hates the idea. I shrug and sit at the counter.

"Your sister awake yet?" Mom asks, giving me a friendly smile.

"No. Where's Dad?" I ask.

"Probably with his girlfriend," Joey says in a mocking voice.

Mom shoots him a look, then turns to me. "He is... out for most of the day. Let's just leave it at that."

So Joey is right. My dad is actually with some random woman. Someone who's not my mom.

This can't be real life.

Mom finishes unloading the dishwasher and closes it; she dries her hand on a rag. "I was actually going to talk to you and Audrey at the same time, but since you're up now, I'll just talk to you. Can we go into the front room?"

Something is up.

"The front room?"

We're never allowed to go in there.

"Yeah," she says with a harmless smile.

"Why can't I come?" Joey asks.

"Because it doesn't have anything to do with you, sweetie," Mom says.

"This family and their secrets..." he mumbles, staring down at his iPad with a scowl on his face.

Mom and I go into the front room and sit across from each other.

"What's this about?" I ask.

"I've just... I'm starting—sort of—trying to work through some things regarding... what happened to you. What's happening around the rest of Toxey."

"What's happening around Toxey?"

"Well, mainly the unresolved murder of Sydney Hutton."

"Oh."

"I know you two were friends. So I wanted to tell you about something I've learned. Maybe it will make more sense to you than it does to me—or to the police, evidently."

"What is it?" I don't think I like being in here. It doesn't feel like I'm at home. I feel like I'm being formally questioned in a psychiatrist's office or something.

"Recently, I learned that Sydney Hutton isn't who she said she was. Her name is actually Megan Young. Have you heard that name before? Has she ever told you that before?"

"How did you...?"

She shows me a picture on her phone. It's a missing-person flyer. It has a younger-looking Sydney on it. But the name underneath the photo is indeed Megan Young.

"You look surprised," Mom comments.

"Because I am," I say. "She had a fake identity. I... I never knew."

"She never told you anything about who she really was?"

"No. What did you find?"

Mom sighs and falls back into the couch, clicking her phone off. "I was hoping you knew something. Because I haven't been able to find anything."

"I... I didn't know. I had no idea."

Who was Sydney Hutton? And what was she doing in Toxey in the first place? Right now, I'm beginning to think everything she ever told me was a lie.

CHAPTER 107

WARNER

I'm stoked that Lyla is finally able to meet up with me. I haven't even really gotten to talk to her since we stood outside of that burning cabin in the middle of the woods. So when she texts me and says she's allowed to see me if I go pick her up, I take the quickest shower of my life, brush my teeth extra good, and use mouthwash, and then I jump in my Jeep—which is now dent free—and retrieve her.

When she walks out of her front door, she's smiling. It's a good sign. It makes me happy to see her smile.

"No, Audrey?" I ask when she opens the passenger door.

"She is at some weekend cheer practice thing," Lyla says. I reach over and give her an awkward hug. Secretly, I'm sort of glad it's just us.

"Is it cool if we just go back to your house?" she asks me, looking a little embarrassed. "I promised my mom we'd stay out of the public. For now."

"Yeah. No biggie."

"And I would've just biked to you, but my mom and dad, they don't want me out alone like that. They think it's too risky."

"It's okay. You don't have to explain anything to me. I'm happy to be your chauffeur."

I start driving, and I'm thinking of where to start the conversation I want to have with her, but instead, she moves her hand toward my dash. "Can we listen to some music?"

"Sure." I turn on the radio, and a rap station is playing. It's a popular hits one, so I just leave it on that. She doesn't seem too upset about it, and she turns the volume up enough to where I can't really make conversation with her. So I guess it's just going to have to wait until we get back to my house.

I pull up to my Jeep's spot outside my house, then we both hop out of the car.

"It's sort of perfect outside," she says. "Mind if we stay out here?"

"Yeah. I mean... no, I don't mind."

She giggles, then we walk over to the porch and sit on the steps. It's weird because just days ago, Audrey and I were sitting in this exact spot. And I think... I don't know.

I think we sort of had a moment.

"So I learned something today," she says, gripping her knees with her hands.

"What?"

"I learned that Sydney Hutton is actually a nineteen-year-old named Megan Young who went missing years ago."

My brain can hardly even comprehend it. "What?"

"Yeah. That's pretty much how I reacted. My mom is the one who apparently found out about it."

"But I don't—how does that even—what would she—?"

What was a nineteen-year-old doing coming to Toxey and pretending to be a junior in high school? Especially a missing person?

"Yeah. I don't know. My brain feels like it's on fire. Like it's a computer that overheated. It's been fed too much misinformation, and now there's a Chernobyl-style meltdown happening."

"I... wow. Don't get me wrong; I think it's important that we learned that. But with everything you've just gone through, to come and talk to you about it now..."

"I'm fine, Warner," she says in a strong voice. Almost as if she's appalled; I would think otherwise.

"Well, yeah," I say, then clear my throat. "I know. It's just..."

"I don't need to be treated all fragilely. Okay?"

"Yeah." I give her a thumbs-up with both hands. Then I feel stupid for doing so. "I hear you."

"He just kept me in a shed. It's not that dramatic."

I think the opposite, but I don't want to argue with her. The last thing I want to do is upset Lyla right now. Not when I finally got her back.

"No. Yeah. Uh... for sure." I'm babbling like an idiot. I have no idea what to say to her.

Apparently, my babbling makes her laugh. "Are you okay?" She grabs my knee and shakes it slightly.

I stare at her hand.

Her hand. On my knee.

"Warner?"

I look back at her. Her hand doesn't move from my knee. Her lips are pulled into a small smirk, and she has a glimmer in her eyes. Her head is tilted slightly.

I find myself looking at her mouth.

I don't say anything, and neither does she.

Then I find that I'm moving in slightly toward her.

And her head is moving slightly toward mine.

I think the moment I've been waiting for has finally come.

I am going to kiss Lyla Bailey.

We get close. So close. I can smell her honeydew-scented body wash. The cherry-flavored Chapstick on her lips.

"Hey!"

Lyla and I break apart, both startled, but her more than I. She practically jumps to her feet as we look up to see who had just yelled at us.

Jackson is marching toward us, his face red and his stride angry. "What do you two think you're doing?!"

I can only think one thing as I get to my feet as well and try to mentally prepare myself for what's about to go down. All I can think is one word.

Crap.

CHAPTER 108

AMELIA

"Where is she?"

My sister is standing on my doorstep, wearing a faded floral maxi dress with her hair down in loose waves over her shoulders.

"Hi, Nora," I say, surprised to see her here, showing up unannounced like this. "Are you looking for Lyla?"

"Where is she?" She nudges her way past me and into the house.

"I'm sorry, you just missed her. Her friend came to pick her up."

"She's not home? You just let her leave? After what just happened to her?" She instantly looks livid. I think she's mad at me.

But when is Nora not mad at me?

"I can't keep her home forever," I say calmly, shutting the door. "You're welcome to wait. I just don't know how long she'll be gone."

"Oh, I'll wait," she says snippily. She strides right into my front room—with her shoes on—and flops down on the sofa. "I wanna know what happened, anyway." She pats beside her, signaling that she wants me to join her.

I had been just about to see if I could take Joey to a movie or to get some ice cream—or anything to cheer him up—but now I feel as if I have no choice.

Nora wants to know what happened.

Slowly, I sit down on the sofa next to her. I know she doesn't know who I saw in those woods yet. She would have said something immediately if she had.

"So?" She takes her large bohemian bag off her shoulder and sets it on the ground by her feet. The bag looks like it hasn't been washed or wiped down in quite some time, and I fear for my white rug. But I'm not about to say anything to her about it.

What I have to say is already going to be hard enough.

"I'm glad you came over," I say. "Because it's definitely better for me to tell you this in person."

"Tell me what?" she asks. "What happened to her that night?"

I don't even know where to begin. But I know I just have to do it.

"Nora, do you know where Lyla was found?"

"Some cabin in the woods?" she asks like she doesn't care about the location. "I saw it on the news, but it was all burned down."

She doesn't know which cabin.

"Right. Lyla was locked in a shed at the house near where... where you saw Carson's body."

Her lips part slightly. She says nothing. She just sits there and stares at me.

"Did you hear me?"

"What are you saying?" she finally asks. "Why that house?"

I swallow to give myself a second. "I believe what you saw, Nora. I know you think Carson died... but after he lit the shed and the house on fire, I—"

"No."

It makes me pause. The no was so resounding. So firm. She wants me to stop explaining? Or is she just saying it in disbelief?

Unsure, I continue. "I... I saw his face, Nora. It... it was Carson who kidnapped her."

Quickly, she jumps to her feet.

"Carson is dead," she tells me, looking around the room like she's searching for something to hit me with. It makes me get to my feet, too, my heart beating a little quicker.

"But he's not, Nor," I say. "I know what I saw."

"No, you don't!"

Her voice is loud enough that I know Joey can hear it upstairs.

"Nora, come on."

"He's dead, Mia! Why are you even saying this to me right now? What are you trying to do?"

She picks her bag up and throws it over her shoulder. I don't even care to look down at the rug now to see the mess her shoes and purse left behind.

"Where are you going?" I ask, stepping toward her.

"Get away from me!"

Her face is red. Her hair is all over the place as she turns wildly about herself. "You're crazy. You don't know what you're saying! You're just trying to upset me. I don't know why you do this!"

"Why are you so certain that he's dead?" I try.

Suddenly, she spins on her heel and slaps me across the face. "How could you even ask me that?!"

Then we just stand there. My face is stinging.

But I'm too afraid to move.

Tears are streaming down her red cheeks. She looks like if I say one wrong thing again, she's not afraid to hit me twice.

"I was there that night," she spits out. "I saw blood. I don't know who killed him. I don't know if he somehow did it to himself. I have no idea what happened that night. But I know that he died. So don't try to tell me anything different."

"I'm just trying to be honest," I whisper.

When she speaks again, her voice cracks with her sobs. "You're not being honest! You've never been honest, Mia! I don't know what you're trying to pull, but I'm done with it. I'm done with you. Just... don't ever speak to me again."

"Mom?" Joey's voice calls from the top of the stairs. I can tell he's making his way down. I don't say anything. I don't even move as Nora turns around and storms out the front door, not even saying anything to Joey, who has appeared in front of her. She leaves the door open behind her. Joey stands there staring through it with his eyebrows furrowed.

"What just happened?" he asks.

I don't answer him.

Because I have no idea.

CHAPTER 109

MADDY

The banging on my screen door is so loud and fast that it makes me leap off my sofa.

I open the front door and see a frazzled-looking, crying Nora standing on my porch.

"Did you hear what Mia is saying?!" she asks, her voice shrill.

"Nora!" I gasp. I can't believe she's here. I can't believe she's standing on my porch.

"Did you?!" she continues, looking like she's gone insane. She's not even bothering to ask to come in.

"What is going on?" I ask. I don't move to open the screen door because I'm honestly a little afraid of how she's acting.

"She's saying that it was Carson! Carson Price!"

"Wh—what about him? Are you okay?"

"She's saying that he is alive! Can you believe that?! After all this time, she still doesn't believe me!" That's when her dam breaks, and she bursts into sobs. "All this time, I've just been waiting for her to change. For her to be a good sister. To be truly on my side. But it's never going to happen!"

Nora is such a wreck right now that I don't know what it will do to her if I tell her that I believe Mia. Or if I tell her that Mia and I started becoming friends again. So, making up my mind quickly, I decide to fake ignorance.

I brace myself and open the screen door, but instead of asking her to come in, I step out there with her and wrap my arms around her to comfort her.

"Nora, I'm so sorry." I'm quick to think of the lie. "To be honest, Mia did tell me that she saw Carson. That she thinks he's the one who did this. But I don't believe her! And that's why I didn't tell you!

Because I didn't want to upset you because I know there's no way that it's true!"

She lets me hug her but doesn't hug me back.

"Why doesn't she believe me?! Why doesn't anyone?"

I stroke her hair gently with my fingers and make shushing noises. "It's gonna be okay, Nora," I tell her. "I believe you."

She sniffs and looks at me. "You swear?"

"Yes. I'm with you, Nora. I don't think Carson was ever out there. Mia just saw what she wanted to see. She had a lot of smoke inhalation. I think she was just hallucinating."

"Yeah. Definitely hallucinating. I'm not the crazy one. She is."

"I know."

Mia, wherever you are, I'm sorry.

I continue. "She's crazy, Nora. That's why we're not friends."

I stand out there on the porch with her for another ten minutes, then once she calms down, I invite her inside—even though I really don't want her to say yes—and thankfully, she tells me that she doesn't want to intrude and that she has somewhere to be anyway.

When I'm finally able to go inside and close the front door, I jump yet again because of the figure standing in the hallway with a questioning, accusatory glare on his face.

"Warner!" I gasp out, putting my hand to my chest.

"What was that?" he demands. And there's no point in trying to even cover it up. Because I can tell based on the look on his face that he had seen and heard my and Nora's entire exchange.

"Um, I can explain," I begin slowly.

He shakes his head. I can tell he doesn't want to hear another word out of my mouth.

"Great. I knew it," he says, stepping backward and preparing to retreat into his room. "Once a liar, always a liar."

CHAPTER 110

CARSON

April 25th, 1998

I wake up to someone shaking me violently. And their wailing is loud in my ears, causing the pain I'm feeling in the back of my head to hurt even worse than it would in total silence.

When my eyes flutter open, it's Nora who is practically on top of me, sobbing and jerking me around.

"No!" she bellows.

"Nora," I try to grumble, but the word doesn't fully form. Still, it does the job because Nora gasps and looks down at my face.

"C-Carson?"

For a second, I have no idea why this is happening. Why I am in pain, why we seem to be in the middle of the woods, and why Nora is sobbing all over me.

But then I remember.

I remember everything.

"Oh my God!" she cries out. Realizing I am not dead, I guess, she falls on top of me again and continues to sob. "I thought you were dead!" Then she looks at me again. "Don't move. I'm going to call an ambulance. You're gonna be okay."

She tries to stand up, but I reach out my hand and firmly grip it around her wrist. "Wait," I say. I notice the dried blood on the corners of her nostrils. "No."

She looks horrified. "What do you mean, no?" She looks down at the hand that's gripping her wrist instead of meeting my eyes.

"Help me up," I demand.

"Carson, I don't know if it's a good idea for you to move—"

"Help. Me. Up."

She does as she's told this time. Her entire body is trembling. I look behind us to see if anyone is around.

To see if they are still around.

My head hurts so badly I can barely even concentrate. But I know exactly what I have to do. I know exactly how this is going to work.

"Can you walk?" she asks me. "Can you get in the car?"

When I'm satisfied and certain we're alone; I look at her again. Then I grip her shoulders with both my hands. I make sure my grasp is firm. One, so that she can't get away. And two, so that she pays careful attention to what I'm about to say.

"As far as you're concerned, I stayed dead. I am dead," I tell her.

Her watery eyes look back at mine and grow wider. "What are you talking about?"

"Nora, listen to me."

"I don't understand—"

"I'm dead! Okay?!"

She's not getting it. But she has to get it. I have to make her understand.

"You do whatever you can, Nora. But you have to convince the police—everyone—that you found me dead here. Okay?"

She doesn't say anything. She just stands there staring at me.

"Do you hear me?!" I shake her a little.

"I—yes!" she squeaks out. "But Carson..."

"No buts! You can't ask me any questions! You found my body in these woods. I died, and you believe it more than you believe that the sky is blue. Got it?"

She continues to cry. So I shake her again.

"Got it?!"

She's terrified.

Good.

Sniffling, she finally nods her head yes. She finally understands.

Carson Price is dead.

TO BE CONTINUED

Up Next

I really hope you enjoyed the latest thrill-ride in the "Moms Who Lie" series.

Yeah, Carson is alive and Nora has been lying about it all these years.

What's up with that?

Join McKenna and me for the next twisted tale, "Lies That Stalk Us: Moms Who Lie Psychological Thriller Series Book #4"

Amelia is obsessed with finding the killer... assuming he actually exists.

Amelia Bailey feels like she's losing her mind.

Her marriage and business are in shambles and her thoughts and feelings are out of control. That makes it hard for her to prove that the person behind all the deaths, attacks, and sadistic threats to her family is the person she saw kidnap her daughter.

Someone she thought she and her best friend Maddy had killed twenty years ago.

When the police refuse to even investigate her claims, Amelia decides to track down the murderer herself. But she's starting to experience blackouts and having a hard time concentrating.

How can she stop the killer if nobody trusts her... even Amelia herself?

"Lies That Stalk Us" is the fourth novel in the gripping 5-book *"Moms Who Lie"* domestic psychological thriller series by Brett Monk and McKenna Langford.

If you like **twisty psychological thrillers** with **relatable teen and adult characters** and a **drop-the-mic cliffhanger** at the end of each book, then you'll love *the* *"Moms Who Lie"* series!

Buy *"Lies That Stalk Us"* to help Amelia track down the stalker today!

Author's Notes by Brett Monk

Can we keep in touch?

Seriously. Especially if you've now read three or more of my books.

I'm an independent author and my loyal readers are really important to me. I'd like to know what you like and what you'd like to see more of.

I've gone to a lot of work to create an email newsletter, a private Facebook community, and other ways that I can interact with my fans, and that my fans can interact with each other.

You might want to become an ARC READER. (Someone who gets free e-book copies of my books before they're published in return for feedback to me and reviews on Amazon and other places.

You might even want to become part of my "STREET TEAM." That's for folks who would like to help me share news about my books and movies on their blogs and social media platforms. I provide memes and fun graphics for people to use, and I've been known to send gifts of appreciation to my highly active Street Team Members.

I correspond personally to my emails and to comments in my social media, especially with my ARC readers and Street Team Members.

Also, If you want to learn **all the details about what happened back when Maddy and Mia were in high school, the night Carson disappeared**, you can download the free bonus novella, *"The Lying Begins"* at the link below.

More details are available at this link: **https://www.brettmonk.com**

www.BrettMonk.com

About the Authors

Brett Monk

B rett Monk is an author, movie director, and voiceover artist.

He holds degrees in Communications and Psychology and spent over 30 years writing and directing films for businesses and government agencies in the Washington, DC area before turning his focus to creating books and audiobooks.

He also directed and co-wrote two feature-length murder mystery movies which are in worldwide distribution.

Originally from the Shenandoah Valley area, he now lives in Northern Virginia with his family and a rambunctious Bernedoodle named Merlin.

McKenna Langford

McKenna lives in Arizona with her husband and two goofy Boxador brothers.

Before she dove into the world of ghostwriting and co-writing, she got her bachelor's degree in interior design and published her first five novels. She worked in a boutique interior design firm in the valley for two years, moved to Seattle with her husband to explore for another two years, then moved back to Arizona and made writing her full-time career in 2021.